Cody released his hold on Viktoria. What kind of jerk would steal a kiss when her son had just been kidnapped?

But without a word, Viktoria closed the distance between them. She pressed her lips onto his cheek. "For luck," she whispered.

Without another thought about right or wrong, Cody slid his arm around her waist and pulled Viktoria closer. Her breasts pressed into his chest, warm and inviting.

He placed his mouth on hers. Viktoria wrapped her arms around his neck and parted her lips. He moved his tongue into her mouth and she greeted him in return. Cody's hands traveled down, memorizing her form. Their kiss became his world. His universe. His everything...

* * *

Rocky Mountain Justice: These Colorado mercenaries fight for duty and honor

Dear Reader,

Confession time: I've been a lifelong Harlequin romance reader, so I'm especially thrilled to introduce Rocky Mountain Justice, my first series for Harlequin Romantic Suspense. More even, is that this is a holiday romance, which are my favorite kind of books to read! Nothing says the holidays to me like a book that brings together family, traditions—and, of course, love.

Although I've been known to scour the shelves at my local bookstore in October looking for the latest holiday romances, I also love a great romantic suspense. Because what's better than two people trying to save the world while at the same time losing themselves in each other?

For you, dear reader, I wish you all the joys and wonder of the season. May your days be filled with laughter and your nights filled with love. I also hope you enjoy reading *Her Rocky Mountain Hero* as much as I did writing it!

Happy holidays,

Jennifer D. Bokal

PS: Please visit me on Facebook at Facebook.com/ Jennifer-D-Bokal-1527295950883205 or follow me on Twitter, @jenbokal. Looking forward to chatting with you!

HER ROCKY MOUNTAIN HERO

___

Jennifer D. Bokal

HARLEQUIN® ROMANTIC SUSPENSE

Recycling programs
for this product may
not exist in your area.

ISBN-13: 978-0-373-40236-6

Her Rocky Mountain Hero

Copyright © 2017 by Jennifer D. Bokal

www.Harlequin.com

Printed in U.S.A.

Jennifer D. Bokal is the author of the bestselling ancient-world historical romance *The Gladiator's Mistress*, and the second book in the Champions of Rome series, *The Gladiator's Temptation*. Happily married to her own alpha male for twenty years, she enjoys writing stories that explore the wonders of love in many genres. Jen and her husband live in upstate New York with their three beautiful daughters, two aloof cats and two very spoiled dogs.

In memory of my father, Jim "Mac" McDarmont.
A girl couldn't have asked for a better dad.
Thank you for always believing in me and
teaching me to believe in myself.

And to my husband, John. Without you,
I wouldn't be me.

Prologue

December 23
4:00 p.m.
Telluride, Colorado

The sun hung above the horizon; the final rays of the day cast long shadows over the mountains and into the valley below. Cody Samuels shouldered open the door of his house and propped his skis against the wall. Balancing his poles next to them, he then worked his feet out of his hard, formfitting down-hill boots.

He was glad he'd had a chance to go skiing. It looked like he might be forced to stay inside for the next few days. The weather was about to turn nasty and bring what the local meteorologists were calling "The Blizzard of the Century." Actually, being snowed in for a few days didn't seem so bad. It would help take away the sting of being alone over a holiday.

Closing the door, he carried his gear to the storage room next to the kitchen. His tablet sat on the counter, and he gave it a glance as he passed. A message icon glowed. When he finished putting his gear away, he returned and tapped it to open the email.

To: Samuels, Cody
From: Rocky Mountain Justice
Re: Mateev, Viktoria

Mateev, Viktoria. Cody's shoulders tightened and his pulse spiked. The name Mateev was one he hoped to never see again and at the same time he looked for everywhere.

23 December
This message is an alert. One or more people hired to be found by RMJ have been located via facial recognition software. Please access the case file and make all necessary contacts.

Sir Ian Wallace
Founder and CEO, Rocky Mountain Justice

Scrolling down, he found a heavily pixelated photo of a blonde woman behind a steering wheel, along with an inset photo of the car's Colorado license plate. A link took him to the case file. It contained half a dozen separate documents. Most originated from New York State's Child Protective Services and contained reports of severe neglect by Viktoria Mateev of her son Gregory, aged four.

Damn the Mateevs. They'd haunted him since his days with the DEA. Clearly, he wasn't through with them yet.

The Mateev family had been embroiled in crime from their very beginnings. They were infamous, not just in their native Russia but throughout the world. In the 1990s the Mateevs had strong ties in Brooklyn, New York. After being brought up on racketeering charges, the Mateevs left the country, but continued to practice their brand of lawlessness in Russia.

Cody discovered they'd returned to the US when a confidential informant had come forward with information that linked several Denver drug dealers to a cartel. Cody's superiors were unimpressed with the CI, low-hanging fruit as far as the criminal underworld was concerned, and they never opened an investigation.

But Cody's gut told him otherwise.

He began developing a case on his own time and met with the CI on several occasions. It was in one of those meetings that the name Nikolai Mateev was brought up.

Cody already knew of Mateev by his family's very nefarious reputation. He again approached his superiors, this time with a signed affidavit. Cody's supervisor promised to send the information up the chain of command.

To this day, Cody had no idea if the promise was ever kept. The next Saturday afternoon, he met the CI at a crowded Denver park. The man said only a few words before pulling out a gun and aiming it at Cody. Cody had no choice but to fire his own weapon in self-defense. A perfect shot to the head killed the man instantly. But the CI's gun, which Cody clearly recalled him drawing, was never found, and too many witnesses saw nothing more than an armed federal officer shooting what they believed to be an innocent man. That moment ended not only a life, but Cody's career with the Drug Enforcement Administration, as well.

He stared at the screen, seeing only the CI's lifeless body and a gun that at one time had been real, but had apparently disappeared into thin air. An ache began between his shoulder blades and shot up his neck, enveloping his whole head. It ended with a stabbing pain between his eyes. Cody took in a long breath and held it to the count of ten and then twenty. He exhaled, still feeling that old fury rising within him, but then forced himself to read on.

The next document was an intake from RMJ and gave the case's history. Viktoria Mateev was last seen in August as she left a hearing to determine her parental rights. When court reconvened the next day, she never showed. Calls and visits to her apartment were fruitless. Fearing for the safety of her son, the Department of Justice issued an AMBER Alert.

There were no leads.

A month later a car was sold for cash in Grand Junction, Colorado. The VIN was entered by the dealership into the DMV's database and brought up Viktoria Mateev's name. Searches of Grand Junction and the surrounding communities turned up nothing. Then New York State hired Rocky Mountain Justice.

Cody found that fact odd. RMJ was expensive, exclusive and not usually involved in simple custody cases. It raised questions for which he had no answers. Unless this wasn't a simple custody case.

As was protocol, if Viktoria or Gregory Mateev were found, he'd been instructed to report to local law enforcement and offer all information obtained and any assistance required.

The final document contained a known picture of Viktoria along with basic personal information. In it, a smiling Viktoria wore a tailored red blazer and gray silk blouse. A double strand of pearls hung around her neck. She had large brown eyes and perfectly straight chin-length blond hair. She was attractive in a very cosmopolitan kind of way—beautiful, really. And certainly, the woman in the picture bore a striking resemblance to the one in the traffic photo. Still, it was Cody's job to be certain.

Alongside was a picture of Gregory Mateev, a family snapshot of a kid with a mop of dark hair, sitting on a beach with a bucket in his hand.

A short bio followed: Viktoria Mateev, age twenty-nine, was the wife and now widow of one Lucas Mateev. Viktoria was the custodial parent of the missing Gregory Mateev, age four. Residents of New York City—Manhattan, specifically—Viktoria was a stay-at-home mom and Lucas was listed as a medical sales representative. Or he had been until his death in July, the victim of a hit-and-run accident while crossing a New York City street.

Neither the driver nor the car that struck and killed Lucas was ever found. Alarm bells began clanging in Cody's brain.

Cody returned to the original traffic picture, expanding it until it filled the screen. The woman's hair was longer and now fell around her shoulders, but that was to be expected if she no longer had it cut regularly. The nose and lips were the same, but there were also differences. He studied her face, complexion—pallid, with dark smudges under her eyes and a tightened jaw. In a word, she looked haunted.

Or maybe hunted.

Without question, that was Viktoria Mateev in the photograph. Like the best Christmas present in the world, Cody had been gifted with a Mateev needing to be brought to justice. And this time would be different—*this* Mateev wouldn't get away.

But to find out where she was now, he had to figure out where she'd been. The bottom of the photo had a small location and time stamp—Telluride: West Colorado Avenue/South First Street. 23 December, 1:32 p.m.

Cursing, he ripped his fleece cap from his head and threw it on the counter. More than two hours gone. If Viktoria Mateev was just passing through, she could very well be in New Mexico by now. Then in Mexico by tomorrow. He compressed the picture, examining the whole. The car was a late-model sedan, from an American manufacturer, gray and covered with dust.

The car was completely unremarkable, maybe even intentionally so. He examined the photo further. Strapped securely to the roof was a small pine tree. In the back seat, Cody could see the outline of a child.

No, Viktoria Mateev was not simply passing through Telluride. She was local, planning to celebrate Christmas with her son—and who knew who else. Maybe someone from the Mateev family?

Using her license plate number, Cody searched satellite images from earlier in the day and traced a route that led to a cabin tucked away in the foothills of the Rockies. The same car was parked in the drive. Another search gave him an address and the property's owner. The cabin had been rented for the winter, and the current tenant's name was not listed. Bingo.

Cody slipped his phone out of his pocket, then paused. For a moment, he thought about the significance of the date—December 23.

Casting his gaze at his refrigerator, he quickly glanced at the card his sister, Sarah, had sent—a family picture taken at Thanksgiving was attached with a magnet. On the bottom, next to the printed holiday greeting, was a note in Sarah's loopy script inviting him to visit.

Memories of other holidays—some happy, some

bittersweet—came to Cody. He blocked them all. He'd never been much for celebrating, but this year might be different. Would anything bring him more joy than bringing down a Mateev?

Chapter 1

December 23
9:00 p.m.
Outside of Telluride, Colorado

The timer's insistent beep filled the small cabin. A slender pine tree stood in the corner. Red, green and white lights twinkled from each branch. The sharp scent of pine mingled with the sweetness of baking sugar cookies to create an aroma that was wholly Christmas. Viktoria Mateev set the bowl of green frosting aside and rose from the table. Before walking to the oven, she leaned over and placed a kiss on the top of her son Gregory's head.

He held up a cookie—Kris Kringle's profile

dripped with thick red frosting. "Do you think Santa will like this one?" Gregory asked.

"It will be his favorite," she said. She opened the oven door and heat rushed upward, immediately fogging the windowpane nearby. The darkened outline of full evergreens and the frail branches of white aspens that surrounded her cabin were suddenly invisible.

It was almost as if the rest of the world could not see her, or Gregory, either. She exhaled and her chest contracted as if embracing the emptiness of a holiday spent alone. It was her first Christmas since her husband, Lucas, had died. She couldn't even call her parents, fearing that their phones were being monitored. Standing taller, Viktoria reminded herself that she wasn't alone. She was with her son and they were safe.

After pulling out the last two trays of cookies, Viktoria set them on the back burners of the stove to cool. "What else are you going to make for Santa?"

Gregory held up a reindeer-shaped cookie covered in green frosting and bright red sprinkles. "This one is for you." He spoke around a spoon that had once sat in one of the frosting bowls. Pulling it from his mouth, Gregory smiled. His teeth and lips were stained green. Her son's enthusiasm for the season was infectious and Viktoria couldn't help but smile in return.

It was the simplicity and love in this moment that she sought. To give Gregory some Christmas joy, she had risked everything by slipping down the mountain and into town. The streets of Telluride had been teeming with people, an interesting combination of locals and wealthy tourists who came for a holiday on the slopes. At first the crowd had left her terrified of being seen and recognized. Yet as she turned off the oven, Viktoria convinced herself that the crowd had been a blessing. Certainly, she and Gregory had blended in—just two more faces out of many.

As Gregory iced another cookie, Viktoria knew the risk had been worth it. Even if the state of New York considered her to be an unfit parent, even if all the evidence against her had been lies, even if she knew that her deceased husband's family had unparalleled wealth to orchestrate it all—Viktoria couldn't deny her son the joy of the season. Maybe she even needed some holiday tidings herself.

Gregory yawned and leaned into the side of his arm. The clock on the back of the stove read 9:05.

"It's bedtime, Captain Kiddo," Viktoria said as she tousled his hair.

"But we still have more cookies to decorate," he complained.

"How about this," she suggested. "You get ready for bed and I'll put everything away. Tomorrow is Christmas Eve, and Santa won't come until midnight, so there's plenty of time to finish decorating cookies in the morning."

"This is the best Christmas ever," Gregory said with a mock salute as he scooted off one of the mismatched chairs. "I'm going to get ready for bed,

Agent Mommy." The soles of his footed pajamas pitter-pattered as he crossed the room.

They had to find something else to watch beyond the DVDs of *Phineas and Ferb* that had been left in the cabin. "That's Secret Agent Mommy," she called after him, "and do a good job brushing your teeth."

With a wistful smile, Viktoria rose and walked to the stove. Using a spatula, she lifted cookies from the tray and placed them on a plate. In the stillness, she suddenly heard an engine revving as it climbed the steep road several hundred yards away. She froze, not daring to breathe. She listened for the telltale sounds of a car approaching. The crunch of wheels on the cabin's gravel driveway. The muffled music of a far-off radio or the near-silent shushing of windshield wipers as they cleared away a few stray snowflakes. A second passed and then another. There was nothing and yet she still held her breath.

She moved to the window and wiped the steam away. Outside she saw only the vast blackness of the winter night. As she exhaled, her breath collected on the glass, creating a barrier between her and the night once more.

They couldn't have found her. No one in Colorado, much less Telluride, knew who she was. "They couldn't have," she said aloud.

"Who couldn't have what?" Gregory asked.

Viktoria whirled around.

Face scrubbed, with a dab of toothpaste at the corner of his mouth, Viktoria's son stood right behind her. She'd been so absorbed that she hadn't heard him approach. The past several months had taken their toll on Viktoria and she was so weary that she imagined she could sleep for days.

On the eve of her final hearing, Viktoria had been desperate, convinced that Gregory could be taken from her. She'd packed up their things and left their Manhattan apartment in the middle of the night, driving almost nonstop across country. During the intervening four months her son had asked few questions. He had no idea why they'd been living in relative seclusion. Nor would he. Their situation was her burden, not Gregory's.

"I thought I heard reindeer hooves on the roof," she said. If Viktoria was going to tell a lie two days before Christmas she might as well make it a big, fat, juicy one. "Then I thought, *They couldn't have come early.*"

"Or one of Santa's elves might be checking on us right now," he said.

With mock sternness, Viktoria nodded slowly. "I bet you're right."

Gregory's eyes grew big and his mouth hung open. With a deliberate snap of his jaw, he gave her a salute. "Good night, Secret Agent Mommy."

He scampered up the stairs to the loft, where they both had beds. "I'll be up in a minute for prayers," she called after him. Viktoria knew what she would pray for. It was the same thing every night. She needed a miracle that would clear her name and allow her to return to the life she had abandoned to protect and keep Gregory.

* * *

Cody Samuels lay on his stomach, a thermal blanket between his body and the snow-covered ground. He looked through a set of binoculars and peered at the cabin set deep in the woods. Not for the first time, he cursed his bad fortune that the affable Sheriff Raymond Benjamin had assured Cody that his guys had the Mateev arrest covered and didn't need the extra help. The weather, the sheriff claimed, was about to change and he didn't want anyone caught in the storm. Cody's interest in the case was far more compelling than his worry over a little snow. Their tactics had ruined more lives than Cody's and moreover, he refused to lose a chance to question Viktoria Mateev.

The call Cody placed had been hours ago. Since then, he'd seen neither the promised storm nor a deputy. Yet here he remained, perched on the side of the hill—like a wayward Christmas tree.

The temperature plummeted after the sun sank behind the mountains and Cody was thankful that he'd thought to dress in layers of fleece and Gore-Tex. Yet all the time he waited gave Cody a sense of Viktoria Mateev.

Tall and lithe, she looked more attractive in person than she had in her photos. She wore blue jeans along with a red plaid shirt over a light-colored Henley. More than her beauty, she was clearly a loving and attentive mother, spending time teaching her son how to measure, stir and bake. Laughing with him. Talking with him.

In fact, Cody couldn't quite find any sign of the unhinged parent the paperwork described. Or one hint of any of the other ruthless people he knew her family to be. Meaning…she had to be here alone.

The kitchen light went out, leaving the cabin dark. Viktoria and Gregory had gone to bed for the night. Why the hell hadn't local law enforcement or social workers shown up yet? Slipping his phone from his breast pocket, Cody hit the home button. This far into the mountains there was no cell service, but the time was still accurate—9:15 p.m.

On his last trip to RMJ headquarters in Denver, Cody had returned his satellite phone because of a promise for an upgraded model with tighter security software in the New Year. At the time, Cody had doubted he'd need much over the holiday weekend.

He'd never been more wrong in his life.

With a sat phone, he could call Sheriff Benjamin and find out what was amiss. Because there was one thing Cody knew for sure—something was wrong about this case.

Turning his field glasses to the east, Cody followed the road. In the moonless night, the asphalt coiled in and around the snowy terrain, like a large black snake. Nothing. No headlights. No taillights. It was as if the report he had filed with the sheriff's office had been forgotten.

And then the black road undulated. Rummaging in the pack at his side, he withdrew a pair of binoculars with night vision capabilities. Looking through the ocular, the world turned an eerie and unworldly green. Glancing back to the road, he saw two black SUVs traveling without lights. They turned up the long drive to the cabin, their engines running whisper quiet. Clouds of exhaust billowed and rose in the cold mountain air. At the front door of the cabin, three men dressed all in black exited the two SUVs. They adjusted balaclavas over their faces and checked their sidearms.

These definitely weren't the local sheriff's guys.

Instantly, Cody was on his feet, slinging the pack over his back as he ran toward the cabin. He dodged trees and jumped over fallen logs. Frigid air burned Cody's nose and lungs, as his cold, stiff muscles protested from the sudden exertion. His pulse thrummed and sweat covered his skin.

With less than one hundred yards to go, Cody watched as the lock on the cabin's front door was picked and two men rushed inside. The third man ran to the back of the property. Mere seconds later, one man exited the cabin and made his way to one of the idling SUVs. When he opened its back door, the interior light clicked on. Cody could make out someone seated in the rear who reached for a bundle the other man had carried from the cabin.

Not a bundle. The kid.

Mateev, Gregory. Cody saw the case's paperwork in his mind's eye. Age 4.

During Cody's time with the DEA he'd borne witness to heinous acts committed by lawless people. But still, he believed everyone deserved justice and protection by the law. At the same time, most of the victims he'd encountered were involved in the illegal drug trade, as well. In short, there was no denying that if you played with fire, you'd eventually get burned. As far as Cody was concerned, it was easy to assume that Viktoria Mateev was complicit in bringing these men to her door. Even so, he was morally obligated to help—regardless of his own investment in her capture.

But the kid? He was too young to be tangled up in any criminal enterprise and Cody pushed his legs faster, refusing to let someone so innocent become collateral damage.

The man in the back seat pulled the door shut while the other one slid into the driver's seat. The car's tires kicked up snow and gravel as they searched for purchase. Once the tread gripped, the SUV sped backward down the drive. It turned on the street and disappeared, blending in to the black road in the black night.

Never one to believe in coincidences, Cody knew it wasn't an accident that Viktoria Mateev's son was kidnapped on the same day he'd verified her whereabouts. He hated to think that somehow Sheriff Benjamin was involved. Because that meant something even worse—Cody had inadvertently led these men right to her door.

The man came from the darkness just as the heavy feeling of sleep pulled Viktoria under. Yet, as his hand encircled her throat, she knew this was no nightmare and he was no apparition. He was blood and bone. When his fingers dug into her flesh, she cried out in pain but her voice wouldn't come. Her throat burned. Her eyes watered.

The man pushed her down into the mattress as his grip tightened. With both hands, she pulled his wrist with a strength she hadn't known she possessed and his hold broke free. Viktoria drew in a single gasping breath. She tried to rush from the bed, but the blankets tethered her and she fell to the floor.

Her pulse raced, echoing inside her skull. Her breath was shallow and she gasped. "Gregory," she screamed.

There was no answer.

She scrambled forward, reaching for her son's bed.

It was empty.

Her assailant, dressed in all black, face obscured, gripped her arm and yanked her to her feet. Pulling backward, Viktoria kicked out at the same instant, aiming for the man's knee. Her socked foot connected, snapping cartilage and ligaments as the kneecap slid. For once, she was thankful for the self-defense classes she'd taken as a high school student. The man swore and fell over, releasing his grip on her as he went down. Viktoria stumbled back and turned, racing to the wooden stairs that connected the loft to the single room that made up the ground floor.

Suddenly her hair was grabbed from behind and her head snapped back. Viktoria clawed at the hand that held her, and finding the thumb she pulled back until she felt a pop. The man let go and Viktoria pitched forward, tumbling down the stairs. The floor rushed up and the air rushed just as quickly from Viktoria's lungs in a single gust. Pinpricks of light danced in front of her and the coppery taste of blood filled her mouth. The inside of her lip throbbed.

Still, she managed to pick herself up from the floor and run to the phone. Lifting the handset, she dialed 9.

The shadow of another man, a faceless silhouette against the darkness of the night, filled the space at the open front door.

She stifled a scream and fumbled for the next number—1.

That man ripped the phone from Viktoria's grip. He slammed the handset onto the counter, leaving only plastic-and-metal rubble. He then jerked the base from the counter, pulling out the cord and chunks of plaster with it.

Viktoria dove for the door, but the man blocked her exit. Just as she drew back her fist to strike him, the attacker from upstairs came up from behind and grabbed her wrist. He wrenched her arm down and around, pinning it behind her back. Pain shot through her shoulder, forcing her to double over. No matter how desperate she was, she knew she couldn't fight them both. Terror gripped her throat as she tried to think of a way to escape and found none.

"Gregory?" she said hoarsely. Her son was all that mattered to her.

"He's safe," said the man, who still held her wrist.

"Go to the car," he said to the other man. "This will take only a minute."

"What have you done with my son!"

The man twisted her arm and forced Viktoria to drop to her knees. He spoke with a slight Russian accent. "You should have taken the offer. You were foolish to fight the *vory v zakone*."

The offer. One million dollars to relinquish custody of Gregory.

"All of this is so my dead husband's father can take Gregory back to Russia? You can't steal my son." Yet, tonight they were doing just that.

"In Russia, a man is the head of his family. This boy belongs to his grandfather."

"This is America," spat Viktoria. She struggled to rise to her feet. "And Gregory is my son. Nikolai Mateev cannot hope to raise my son as well as his own mother can. Take me to him!"

"Your son will be treated as a prince and will grow up wanting for nothing. You should have taken the money. But, you are a proud American and now your stubbornness will kill you." He pushed her toward the floor. "Kneel."

"No," said Viktoria. She braced her feet and tried to pull away. The man held her wrist even tighter. Despite the pain searing through her shoulder, she twisted her body to try to break the man's grip.

"Always the fighter," said the man. "I admire your bravery, but you lost this battle before it even began."

Something cold and hard pressed into her skull. Viktoria had never held a real gun, but it was not hard to imagine the barrel of a pistol shoved into the back of her head.

She saw only the wooden floor and the man's shoes behind her own socks. Feet? Was this to be the last thing she saw in the world? She lifted her gaze and saw the Christmas tree sitting in the corner. At its very top stood the angel, her wings outstretched. It gave her a measure of solace and courage. Certain she was about to die, Viktoria closed her eyes and fixed her mind on her son.

Cody pressed his back into the worn wood of the cabin's outside wall. He slipped the Glock 22 from the holster on his hip. One round in the chamber, thirteen in the magazine. It was the same sidearm he'd carried when he worked with the DEA. The weight and balance of the gun felt right, like shaking the hand of an old friend.

Crouching low, he cast a quick glance around the corner. The front door of the cabin still stood open. He had originally seen three men storm the cabin. One had left in the other SUV with a fourth guy holding Gregory Mateev. That meant two remained. A man now sat in the driver's seat of the waiting SUV. Where was the other man? And more importantly, where was Viktoria Mateev?

He recognized an older-model sedan parked under a nearby canopy as the one Viktoria had been driving when caught by the traffic camera. The stench of gasoline rolled off the car and burned Cody's eyes. Fuel trickled down from the rear bumper, where its gas line had been severed. Cody could see that the two rear tires had been slit. He imagined that the front ones had been cut, as well.

What had begun as an ordinary custody case had spiraled quickly out of control. These men were true specialists, sent on a professional hit. No matter what Viktoria Mateev might have done, Cody was duty bound to make sure that she wasn't murdered.

Staying low and quiet, Cody raced to the other side of the cabin, coming up behind the SUV. As Cody crawled forward on his stomach, auto exhaust rolled over him in a putrid gray cloud. Looking up into the side mirror, he could clearly see the man in the driver's seat keeping his eyes trained on the cabin's front door.

The cabin remained dark and silent. Cody didn't want to catalogue everything that might be happening inside. Before he could deal with that, he had to get past the driver.

With a whir, the driver's side window lowered and acrid cigarette smoke cut through the stench of the exhaust. Reholstering his Glock, Cody marshaled the strength in his legs as he launched himself from the ground. Midstride, he redirected his body's energy to his fist, which he aimed at six inches behind the man's jaw.

The punch connected and the man's head snapped back. For a moment, only the whites of his eyes were visible, then he fell sideways, his seat belt holding him upright. The cigarette dropped to the ground and Cody crushed it underfoot. After turning off the

SUV's ignition, he pocketed the keys. Reaching for his sidearm again, Cody turned to the cabin.

In the hours that Cody had spent watching Viktoria Mateev and her son, he had learned the cabin's layout. The first floor contained one open living area with a sofa, chair and table against the far wall. The kitchen table stood in front of a fireplace that bisected an exterior wall. A small bathroom sat under stairs that ascended to a loft. All of it was accessed via a single door at the end of the kitchen counter.

The cabin's interior was even darker than the outside and it took a minute for his eyes to adjust. When they did, what he saw was horrifying. A man, clad completely in black, had Viktoria's arm pinned behind her back and a gun pressed to the back of her head. She struggled against the assailant, but had nowhere to go.

"Do you pray?" the man asked her. "Because now's the time for it."

"Gregory," Viktoria whispered. Cody could barely hear that she had spoken.

"He is safe." With a soft click, the man released the safety on his weapon. "You, however, will see him in the next life."

Chapter 2

Viktoria tensed. Like the hammer of God had fallen, a gun's report boomed in the small cabin. The noise pressed in on her chest, squeezing her heart and lungs. The stench of burning sulfur wafted over her. She waited for the agony, the heat, the nothingness.

The man's hold on her arm lessened, then released altogether. Free of his grip, Viktoria fell hard to her knees. She flipped over, ready to fight again. The assailant stared at her blankly and then tumbled to the side. In the meager moonlight seeping through the windows, she saw the shadow of another man. A tendril of smoke rose from the barrel of the pistol he still pointed toward her.

Scuttling on hands and feet, Viktoria pressed her back into the wall. A branch from the Christmas tree scraped her face but she paid it no mind. Her attention was trained on the man with the gun.

Dressed in black from head to foot, he was nothing more than a shadowy figure, his features lost in the darkness. Yet, she saw his eyes. They were light blue—the same crystalline blue of the sky over the Rocky Mountains on a crisp winter's day.

He approached the man on the floor and placed two fingers under his chin. With a sigh and a shake of the head, he stood. Even without someone checking for a pulse, she knew her assailant was dead. A pool—black as tar—surrounded him and grew. The coppery scent of blood filled the cabin. It mingled with the tang of the pine tree and sweet scent of the cookies. She pressed a hand to her mouth and fought the urge to retch.

The man with the gun approached, trapping her against the wall and at the same time allowing her to see his features. He wore a black fleece cap. It was pulled down low, but not so low that it covered his face. The fringes of his dark brown hair were also visible. A dark sprinkling of stubble covered his cheeks and chin. At another time, in another life, she would have seen him as handsome. But now, he still held his gun. He was dangerous, deadly, and Viktoria was wholly at his mercy.

Panic and adrenaline made Viktoria's breathing short and ragged. Her tongue was leaden, her mouth dry. Somehow, she managed to ask the only question that mattered. "Gregory? What have you done with Gregory?"

The man shook his head and took another step toward Viktoria. She shrank back, as if the cabin's wall could absorb her.

"I don't have your son," he said. "I'm here to help."

"Who are you?" Her voice was nothing more than a whisper.

"I'm Cody Samuels," he said. He slid his gun into a holster on his hip. "If you want to live, come with me."

Viktoria pressed her hand to her mouth, unsure whether she should laugh or cry. Cody Samuels's line sounded like something out of a bad movie. Yet this was real life, not a B-rated thriller. Her son was gone. Gregory was the only reason she had strength to get out of bed in the morning. How would she ever get him back?

More than the grief—that awful, sickening hollowness in her chest—was the despair at knowing she had been made powerless. Her only hope now was a stranger with a gun. Much like the man who had tried to kill Viktoria, Cody Samuels had materialized from the darkness, bringing with him death and destruction.

Indecision weighed her down. She knew nothing about Cody Samuels, less than nothing. Was he any better than the men who had stolen her son? In fact, Gregory might be *his* real target.

Perhaps he'd only spared her life to use her to meet his own wicked goals.

"We have to go," Cody said. He lifted his hand a bit, reaching out to her.

Viktoria ignored his outstretched palm and rose on shaking legs. "They took my son," she said. Somehow the words made this nightmare real. Fear took over and gripped her middle. Its intensity bent Viktoria double, escaping in a sob.

Cody stepped toward her.

"Are you hurt?"

The unexpected kindness of his question surprised her and she stood upright. Viktoria had a hard time imagining a possible assassin inquiring about her health. She catalogued her injuries—lip, shoulder, knee—and decided they were all manageable. She realized, though, that she was freezing. Her whole body trembled. Her teeth chattered. The room grew dim; the outline of furniture became indistinct. "I'm cold," she said. The words she spoke didn't seem to come from her.

"You're in shock," said Cody. He slipped off his parka and draped it over Viktoria's shoulders. He gripped her biceps, and with his hands on her arms, he steered her past the body on the floor.

Something about the calm command of his voice, along with the warmth of his touch and scent of his coat—pine and earth and sweat—snapped Viktoria's mind back into her body.

"I'm okay," she said, her voice was weak and her throat tight. "I'm okay," she repeated, more to convince herself, and she stood up taller.

"Good," he said. "We have to get you out of here. Now."

She looked around the tiny cabin that had been her

place of refuge for the past two months. All her meager possessions were here. She was wearing one of her two sets of pajamas—fleece bottoms and a long-sleeved thermal tee. For a moment, she wondered what she should take with her and how quickly she could pack. Once she and Gregory were together he would want some of his toys and books. She needed her money. Cody already stood by the door, looking into the night. His pistol was once again out of the holster and in hand, angled slightly down. Viktoria cast one more glance at the dead man on the floor, a vapor cloud rising from the pool of blood surrounding him. The sight left her light-headed and uneasy on her feet. She held on to the wall for support and moved to Cody's side. Her boots sat nearby and she slipped them on over her thick wool socks.

Viktoria began to tremble again. "There were other men," she said, "the ones who took my son." How many had remained to make sure that her fight to keep Gregory was over, permanently?

Cody nodded toward a black SUV that sat silently in the driveway. "As far as I can tell, only three men invaded your cabin. One took your boy and left. Then, there's the one back there." He hitched his chin toward the dead man. "And the last guy is in the SUV."

"How do you know all that?" she asked. Cody may have saved her, but who *was* he? His stare pinned her where she stood.

"I just do," he said, before casting his light blue gaze out the door. A few fat snowflakes drifted lazily from the sky, silvery white against the darkness of the mountains.

A spark of anger flickered to life inside her chest.

"What's that supposed to mean? I just do?" she asked. Someone had taken her son and tried to kill her. She deserved some answers.

He didn't bother to turn around, much less give her a response. Cody edged toward the door. The small spark of anger licked to life and became a flame. Fury warmed her and gave her something to cling to while dangling over the gaping pit of despair.

"Hey!"

She reached for his shoulder. The solid muscle was unmistakable under his polar fleece jacket. How long had it been since she had touched a man? Months—well before her husband, Lucas, had died. Cody turned and looked at her hand on his shoulder then raised his eyes to meet hers. Viktoria's skin suddenly felt too tight. She pulled her hand away and pressed it to her chest.

Her son was missing. As handsome as Cody Samuels was, Viktoria was crazy to see him as anything other than a necessary—and risky—means to an end.

They stared at each other, not speaking, not moving. Viktoria didn't even breathe.

She finally broke the silence. "Those men took my son. I need to know what you know." After a moment, she thought to add, "Please."

"I was keeping watch on your cabin," he said, "I

saw the men arrive, but was too far away to stop the kidnapping."

At least he'd been close enough to save her life.

"Why were you watching me?"

"It's a long story that's going to get longer before this night is over. For now, you need to trust me. Can you do that?"

"I really don't have any choice, do I?"

Cody ignored her question. "We need to neutralize the driver," he said and then added, "These guys were sent here to do a job. I don't think they wanted to kill your son. If they did they would have done that right away."

Small blessing that it was, Viktoria felt better knowing that Cody also believed that Gregory was safe, although she imagined he was terrified.

Cody continued, "If we're going to get your son back, I don't want the driver to warn anyone."

Viktoria took in a sharp breath and her chest swelled with joy. Cody was going to help her get Gregory back. Before she could ask how, she had an awful thought. He clearly was prepared to kill the driver next. What if Cody's ultimate plan ended with her son as his final target?

She was wholly unprepared to deal with kidnappers and murderers on her own. Cody, at least, was ready to help. All she could do was stay vigilant. For now, Cody was her only hope.

"Stay here," he said, then slipped into the night. She started to go after him. With the moonlight seeping through the overhead cloud cover, Viktoria got her first clear view of Cody Samuels. Even in the darkened cabin, she had seen that he was handsome, but now she understood he was truly a magnificent male specimen. His chin and jaw were strong, as if part of a sculpture. Those arrestingly light blue eyes were a strong contrast to his darker hair and complexion.

Gun lifted, he pointed the barrel into the SUV's open window. Cody retreated a pace and waved Viktoria back to the cabin. "The driver's not here," he whispered.

A shot, like a clap of thunder, rang out. A single stream of hot wind rushed toward Viktoria. At the same instant, pain erupted in her head and she tumbled forward.

Chapter 3

A bullet flew past Cody's ear. Instinctively he dropped to the ground and immediately looked for Viktoria. She lay facedown in the snow, a jagged hole visible in the door directly behind where she'd been standing. Cody's mouth went dry. He hadn't meant for her to become a casualty, no matter her associates.

The voice in Cody's head was strong and without remorse. *Stupid. Stupid. Stupid.* He never should have allowed her to follow him from the cabin.

He looked back at her still body, her fingers splayed, as if in surprise. A volcanic rage rose inside Cody for having unwittingly played a role in the death of Viktoria Mateev. He'd never forgive himself, and yet the game was not over.

The gunman had gone silent, but Cody was far from safe. The other man was out there, somewhere, lying in wait for his chance to strike again. He stared at Viktoria, still angry at himself and full of disbelief. The tips of her fingers twitched, a movement so slight he was almost convinced that it was his imagination.

Then she lifted her eyes and sought out his.

A great wave of relief washed over Cody and for a moment, he thought that he might melt into the snow.

Cody pressed his palms down to the ground, in the universal sign for *stay put*. She gave a nod, just a quick lifting of the chin.

With Viktoria prone on the ground, Cody rose to one knee. He peered through the SUV's window and scanned what he could see of the horizon. The cabin sat in a bowl with peaks on all sides. The surrounding woods were thick, shadows turning every tree into a possible perpetrator. Or vice versa.

A quick estimation of the bullet's trajectory told Cody that the shooter was on the hill, in approximately the same place from which he'd been observing Viktoria and Gregory earlier. It was a prime location, with a view of the cabin's front door, the driveway and the road beyond. The SUV was parked between the hill and the door, momentarily providing cover for Cody, but not Viktoria.

Another shot boomed, this one lower and only slightly to the right of where Viktoria lay on the ground. The next bullet shattered the doorjamb and the one after hit the ground in front of Viktoria, sending snow, gravel and dirt flying.

As unsafe as she was by the cabin, she would become an even easier target by running the five yards to the SUV. The only way it could be done was for him to provide her with cover. He hoped that she would continue to read his hand gestures.

Two fingers to his chest, then two to his gun and then the hill. Cody pointed from Viktoria to where he was, made a fist and extended three fingers, one at a time. He repeated the sequence for good measure. Her gaze was trained on him, her jaw tight. Cody held up one finger. He lifted a bit, ready to take aim and fire. A bullet punched a neat hole in the windshield. A spider's web of cracks spread outward from the point of impact.

"Now," he called out fast. She ran, low to the ground, and dove out, sliding in next to him. She took refuge behind the SUV's quarter panel, so close to Cody that her rapid breath washed over his neck. A thin red line ran across her cheek as blood seeped from a wound.

"You're bleeding," he said. He placed a gloved hand to the cut. His pulse sped at the touch, fueled from adrenaline, no doubt—and this night that had suddenly gone awry.

"It's splinters from the door," she said. "I'll be picking bits of wood out of my hair for weeks, if we survive."

"We'll survive." Cody's hand still rested on Viktoria's cheek. He dropped it quickly, leaving a smudge of crimson on her milky skin.

Two more bullets rained down, striking the ground mere feet from where they sat. Ice and gravel flew upward and Cody shielded Viktoria with his body.

She was warm and soft. Her breath was sweet and minty. Her hair held the slight scent of the floral shampoo she used. He inhaled deeply and reminded himself that Viktoria was part of a case. More than that, he'd be damned before he allowed her beauty to distract him from what was truly important—justice.

Cody turned his attention back to the shooter on the hill, assessing the challenge he presented. "He's a good shot."

"So the men who kidnapped my son are armed and dangerous and good at what they do." The panic in her voice was palpable. "They'll take him to Moscow unless they're stopped."

Viktoria's knowledge of the kidnapper's plans confirmed Cody's suspicion that she was intimately involved with Russian criminals. Even though he'd suspected it all along, having the evidence felt like a betrayal. Another cut to his heart. Well, scar tissue was the strongest and his scars made him tough enough to do his job without question or remorse. A lesser man might feel sorry for Viktoria Mateev.

"We need to know this guy's location." Slipping the pack from his back, he retrieved his night vision binoculars and powered them up. To find the shooter, he was going to have to make himself a target. He pulled the keys to the SUV from his pocket and pressed them into her hand. At least he could ensure that she had a way to save herself if he were shot or killed. "If I get hit, take this car and get out of here. Go." He paused. He wanted to tell her to go to the sheriff's office in Telluride. But since Cody feared that Sheriff Benjamin was somehow involved in the kidnapping, he let it be. He continued, "Contact Rocky Mountain Justice in Denver. Ask for Sir Ian Wallace. Tell him what happened. Got it?"

"Cody." Viktoria placed her palms on the front of his chest. Even through the fleece, his skin instantly warmed at her touch. "Don't get shot."

"I'll try not to."

"Thank you," she said earnestly, "whoever you are, for saving me."

With a nod, Cody fixed his mind on where he thought the shooter would be located. He rose, just enough, and brought the night vision binoculars to his eyes. The crack of a pistol echoed off the hills and Cody ducked down. But, he had seen all he needed to see.

"Our shooter is just above the tree line. More than his location, the guy has a set of night-vision goggles, so he can see in the dark and fire at the same time. No question, we're at a complete disadvantage."

"If we shine a bright light in his face he'll be blinded, right?"

Cody wanted to groan. Hollywood had ruined the public's perception of law enforcement tactics.

"Let me guess," he said, "you saw that in a movie."

Viktoria shrugged. "Several."

"It doesn't work that way." Then again... Sometimes the simplest solutions were the most effective. "We'll try it. Get into the driver's seat, Viktoria, but stay low. Turn the SUV about forty-five degrees and when I tell you, turn on the high beams."

She drew her brows together. "How do you know my name?"

Cody had never intended to lie to Viktoria. He had been hired to do a perfectly legitimate job. Sure, spying on her wasn't part of his assignment, but his presence had saved her life. Why, then, did he hesitate in telling her the truth? He didn't have time to question his motivations.

Instead of answering her question, he said, "This guy is going to keep shooting at you. But, I'm going to be firing back, which should hinder his aim. Just be ready when I tell you to turn on the lights. Got it?"

Thankfully Viktoria didn't press him again about his knowing her name, although he doubted she'd forgotten. Then again, if his plan didn't work, she might not have another chance to ask.

Viktoria opened the driver's side door as two more bullets rained down. She dove into the car and huddled on the floorboard, frozen with terror.

Then she thought of her son and her fear no longer mattered. She quickly pulled the door shut. Her heart racing, she gripped the key fob with such ferocity that it dug into her flesh.

Another crack of a gun. Another echo on the hills.

Another puff of gun powder filling the air. She eased into the seat and glanced into the rearview mirror. The long driveway stretched out like a black ribbon, pulled taut. Viktoria could do this now—run, escape, live. But then, where would she go? How would she even find her son? Even though Viktoria had come to rely on only herself and trust no one, she needed Cody—at least for now.

One more shot fired, this one by Cody.

Viktoria fumbled with the key fob, setting it in the console between the seats, then hit the ignition button while pressing her foot on the brake. The engine rumbled to life and she gripped the steering wheel, careful to remain below the dashboard. With a deep breath, she turned the steering wheel and threw the gearshift into Reverse.

The SUV spun in one fluid motion as Cody fired at the hill—once, twice, three times. The shooter didn't return fire.

"Now!" Cody yelled.

Viktoria flipped the switch for the lights. The hillside glowed, flooded instantly with bright white light. A few stray snowflakes fell, dancing lazily in the beams. Midway up the rise, a man lay on his stomach. A set of goggles encircled his head. He ripped them off, tossing them aside.

Cody advanced. Bullets blazed from the barrel in rapid succession as he moved toward the tree line. "Stay where you are," he called back to her. With a soft click, his gun's empty magazine fell to the ground and he quickly reloaded.

Viktoria lost the shooter's exact location. She sat up taller in her seat and peered at the hill.

Just then a bullet broke through the driver's side window and pebbles of safety glass exploded into the car. She felt the heat and the wind as the round passed her ear. It tore through the leather headrest and lodged deep within the back seat.

Cody raced to the SUV and jumped in through the shot-out window. "Go," he shouted, as he climbed over her and into the passenger seat.

Viktoria didn't need directions. Spinning the steering wheel, she pointed the SUV down the driveway and stomped on the accelerator. The powerful engine roared and catapulted them toward the road. Another bullet flew after them, shattering a side mirror.

"Left, left, left," said Cody, as the end of the drive loomed close.

Viktoria turned the wheel and the SUV skidded as the tires connected with the cold, wet pavement. Viktoria pulled the steering wheel hard to the right and slammed on the brakes. The SUV began to spin. Mountainside. Cliff. Mountainside. Cliff.

Viktoria was determined to control the mechanical beast and bend it to her will. She let off the brakes and held tight to the steering wheel, forcing the tires to remain straight. The SUV swerved, but ceased spinning. They were aimed directly at a snow-covered steel guardrail. Another step on the brake, and the car slid sideways. Metal scraped against metal and sparks shot into the night. Snow flew in through the broken window. With a shudder, the vehicle came to a stop.

Cody held tight to the dashboard. His jaw was slackened and his tanned face had gone pale. "Where'd you learn how to drive like that?" he asked. She couldn't decide if it was awe or terror that fueled his breathlessness.

"Manhattan," said Viktoria with a shrug.

Cody leaned back in the seat and exhaled. "I should have killed him," he said.

Viktoria began to shiver and it wasn't just from the cold wind that blew at her from all sides.

"I don't like that he's still out there," Cody said. "He's not the man in charge, but he'll tell his boss you're still alive. He's probably using the phone in your cabin right now."

"He could be, but he's not."

"How do you know?"

"When those men broke in, I tried to get to the phone. One man took it from me and smashed it against the wall."

Dimitri sidestepped down the hill and stood in the middle of the driveway, the taillights of the speeding SUV just two demonic eyes of red. He heard the screech of tires on pavement and the roar of the engine. Both faded until there was nothing. No lights. No sounds. Just the frosty scent of incoming snow on the air.

He recognized the smell—knew it well. The weather in Russia was much harsher than any in the

United States, and he'd been in more blizzards than he cared to recall. If he was right—and he was— then one hell of a storm was about to hit Telluride.

His smart use of time was essential.

He returned to the cabin and, as he'd feared, his comrade was dead on the floor. Shot by the other man who never should have been there. Dimitri kicked the door closed and flipped on the light. There were bullet holes in the wall and casings on the floor. He knew there'd be several more of both outside. Concealing those would take time, never mind dealing with the corpse and all the blood.

He turned to the stove. It used gas as the heating element. Perfect. On the table sat a plate of iced cookies. Picking one off the plate, he took a bite and chewed it slowly. The Christmas tree in the corner was covered with a cheap set of lights, also useful. In a drawer he found a set of matches. In the bathroom cabinet stood a large bottle of rubbing alcohol alongside a bag of cotton balls.

Using a knife from the kitchen, he cut through the wires of the Christmas tree lights and plugged them back in. The live end sparked and hissed. He then returned to the stove and turned on all the gas, leaving the burners unlit. After pocketing half a dozen cookies, he went to the door and opened it. He placed the cotton balls in a pile and soaked them with the alcohol, then made a trail to the lights. Once across the threshold, he lit the match and tossed it into the puddle of alcohol on the floor. He closed the door and began to walk down the driveway.

As he ate another cookie, he regretted not taking time to say some words over his fallen comrade. They'd served together in Ukraine during the summer a few years ago, and the man deserved more than to be incinerated in a lonely little cabin. Well, that could hardly be helped now.

Dimitri needed to get in touch with the others and let them know what had happened. He had neither car nor phone. By now, the boss would be wondering why there'd been no contact.

A whoosh erupted behind Dimitri and heat warmed his back. His best chance at survival lay before him and he didn't bother to turn around. As his pace quickened to a run, he decided that fire was the best way to erase any sins.

"Try again," Peter Belkin barked at his driver. His second team had yet to make contact, even though they should have left the Mateev cabin twenty minutes ago.

The man lifted his walkie-talkie. "Beta, this is Alpha. Do you read?"

The faint crackle of static could barely be heard over the wailing child, who sat next to Belkin.

Gregory Mateev had been inconsolable since leaving the cabin, not that Belkin had expected anything less. Even though the boy was being taken for his own good, he was too young and too upset to understand.

"The mountains could be causing interference," said the driver, raising his voice to be heard over

Gregory. "We still don't have mobile phone service, but should be okay when we reach the house."

Gregory quieted. Belkin turned to the kid, trying to smile. Fist cocked back, Gregory threw a punch that caught Belkin under the chin. The attorney's teeth cracked together and his jaw throbbed.

"That's it," said Belkin, "I've had enough of you."

"Well, I've had enough of *you*." Gregory threw out a wild kick that struck Belkin in the arm.

Belkin gripped his biceps. He would have a bruise by the morning. From his breast pocket, he removed a syringe already filled with a sedative. He drove the tip into the child's upper arm and pressed down on the plunger. The child began to scream, but as soon as the mild tranquillizer entered Gregory Mateev's bloodstream, he quieted. With a few drowsy blinks, his head lolled to the side and he slept.

Acquiring Gregory Mateev and returning him to his grandfather was Belkin's main objective, and now at least, the boy was safe—and quiet.

The job should have been simple. Nikolai Mateev, the godfather of the Russian mafia, wanted his grandson to be raised in Russia. After the death of Nikolai's son, Lucas, Belkin had been hired to convince the mother to give up her child. But Belkin had pushed too hard in New York City, spooking Gregory's mother and forcing her into hiding with the boy for months. When Belkin had gotten word that she might be in western Colorado, he'd flown in to the area with his team to be there when she surfaced. Since then, there had been no contact. No use of a credit card. No bank withdrawals. No internet searches. It was as if she had simply disappeared and until this afternoon, Belkin feared that she actually had. Now he just wanted to complete his task and get paid.

Gregory slumped over in his seat, snoring softly as the SUV rounded a bend and pulled through a circular drive. The driver parked in front of a two-story house built in the alpine A-frame style, complete with wooden scrollwork on the eaves and a balcony to make up the A's crossbar. Light shone from an exterior sconce, illuminating the snow as it fell.

"Try to contact Team Bravo again," said Belkin, "and after you've spoken, put Gregory to bed in one of the upstairs rooms." Belkin stepped into the night. Fat, downy snowflakes floated down, coating the road and settling on Belkin's shoulders and well-trimmed dark hair.

The extreme cold and falling snow reminded him of how fickle the weather could be in Russia. Taking the phone from his pocket, he glanced at the home screen. A blizzard warning scrolled across the bottom of the display. He opened the weather application, where a digitized radar reading of pink and white, signifying heavy snow and winds, filled the entire northern part of Colorado. Future radar predicted that the blizzard was expected to hit Telluride in the early morning and last for the next twenty-four hours.

Belkin glanced at the local time—10:15. In four hours they would be airborne and on their way to

Moscow. But could they leave earlier if necessary? No. The call regarding Viktoria Mateev's where-abouts had come in only a few hours before and the private plane from New Jersey to transport Gregory back to Russia wouldn't be in Colorado yet. Now, with the storm, it was better that they wait.

Belkin added, "And tell them our departure is delayed by a day to day and a half." He had enough sedatives to keep the kid quiet until they arrived in Moscow, even with the postponement.

The driver's words drifted out of the SUV's open door. "Bravo, this is Alpha, do you read?"

Belkin paused. Waited.

"Bravo," said the driver again. "This is Alpha. Do you read?"

Belkin still thought that his plan to capture the child and kill the mother was flawless. Bribery and threats had been very effective in gaining the support of the smaller law enforcement agencies in the area. It was through one of those "strategic partners" he'd learned today that a private security firm hired by New York State authorities—under the impression that they were seeking a runaway abusive mother—had found Viktoria and Gregory hiding in a cabin less than an hour's drive from Belkin's rented house.

Cooperation. It was a beautiful thing.

Belkin had waited impatiently until dark before executing his plan. Team Alpha had grabbed the boy, and by now Team Bravo should have killed the mother.

Cold wind cut through his cashmere coat as he

waited for a response. More than the money, or even Peter Belkin's reputation, was on the line. Nikolai Mateev did not take disappointment well and if Belkin didn't deliver Gregory to his grandfather by Christmas, then Belkin wouldn't live to see the New Year.

Chapter 4

"Bravo. This is Alpha. Do you read?"

The disembodied, static-filled voice resonated inside the SUV's quiet interior.

Cody looked at Viktoria. Her eyes were wide, her gaze trained on a walkie-talkie they hadn't even noticed, nestled between the SUV's front seats.

"That's got to be the guys who took your son," Cody said, while reaching for the walkie-talkie.

She folded her hands together and pressed the sides of her thumbs into her lips. "So, what do we do now?"

Just because they'd escaped together didn't mean they were on the same side. No matter what, she was a Mateev. The name alone brought back painful memories that lodged in his chest—a leaden ball full of spikes. All the same, Cody was determined to get the kid back, which meant he had to work with the mother. Besides, he reasoned, once they'd rescued her son, Cody could still finish the job—turn the kid over to CPS and question Viktoria before she was taken away by the police.

"Bravo." The single word rang out like a shot. Viktoria started.

"What do they want?" she asked.

It was a good question with a horrific answer. "My guess is that they're checking to make sure that you're dead."

A gust of cold wind blew through the shattered window. Viktoria folded her arms across her chest and looked away. Cody turned the SUV's thermostat to ninety degrees, its upper limit. The hot air hit him and he started to sweat. Small price to pay if it would make her more comfortable.

What was it with his reactions to this woman?

"We can't ignore them," she said and turned to him. "This could be our chance to try to negotiate my son's release."

Cody understood her desperation and admired her bravery. "It won't work. First, there's nothing we have that they want," he said. Then he hesitated. "Unless there is. Do you have any idea why this happened?"

Her gaze never left his. "They want my son," she said, "and for me to be…neutralized."

Cody wasn't sure if Viktoria was purposely not revealing the real story behind the kidnapping, but at this point he needed to view this situation tactically. What he needed was a plan and intel.

"Let's start with what you know," Cody said.

"I know my son is safe," Viktoria said. "The man in the cabin, the one who held me at gunpoint…" Her voice trailed off and Cody gave her a moment to reconcile with the nightmare she'd survived. "He told me that Gregory belonged to his grandfather Nikolai."

Like a piece from a puzzle, the latest bit of information clicked into place. Once again it came down to Nikolai Mateev—the head of the Moscow-based Mateev crime family.

Now Cody knew Viktoria's relationship with the Mateevs. Yet in getting that one answer, it brought up hundreds of questions. He swallowed them all, practically choking on his desire to ask about the drug trafficking ring.

"These men are desperate and if we try to negotiate, they'll know they failed." He paused. His next words would be hard, no, devastating, for a mother to hear.

"And?" she insisted.

"Failure to have killed you might force these men to abandon their plans to take your son from the country."

She leaned forward, her eyes bright. "That's good. They'll release Gregory."

"Unless they don't." Cody couldn't bring himself to verbalize Gregory's possible fate.

Viktoria understood, though. Like she'd been

sucker punched in the gut, Viktoria sucked in a deep breath and sat back hard in her seat. In a way, Cody supposed she *had* been hit, and he'd been the one to deliver the blow.

"Bravo?" A voice, barely audible, rose from the static. "Update?"

"What if you answered them," she proposed, "and pretended to be one of them. They can't see who's speaking and the connection is full of static on our end. It has to be the same on theirs."

Cody sat taller. It was a crazy idea. "That can go wrong in a million different ways. If they figure out that I'm lying, Gregory's the one who could suffer the most."

"Please!" she said. Her fingers rested on the back of Cody's hand. Those old internal scars, the ones he'd developed and nurtured into his own personal armor long ago, began to ache. "This could be my only hope of finding my son. I'd do it myself, but obviously even with the bad connection I'm not a man."

Viktoria was right about that—she was all woman.

"Bravo. Copy."

Cody didn't like playing games with people's lives, and especially the lives of children. But Viktoria was the mother and it was her call. Without another moment's thought, he depressed the talk button. "This is Bravo," he said. "Copy." He hoped they continued to use English. His ability to speak Russian was nonexistent.

"Where the hell have you been?" the voice barked. This was something else Cody feared. Before he had to think of a reason for their delay, the voice rang out again.

"Status update."

Cody's gaze met Viktoria's. He refused to think about what would have happened if he hadn't shown up when he did. Yet, that's exactly what the man on the walkie-talkie needed to believe. Cody flicked his eyes to the windshield. He watched the snow dance in the beams of the headlights.

He depressed the talk button. "Neutralized."

"Come again?"

Like he'd just sprinted the last three hundred yards of a marathon, Cody's pulse hammered and his chest constricted. If these guys knew each other well, they could very easily recognize voices, even with the bad connection.

Cody silently cursed. He was committed now. "Neutralized," he said again. This time he was slower. Louder.

A second passed. Then another. It seemed like hours.

"Copy that," the kidnapper said. "Extraction is delayed twenty-four to thirty-six hours. Plane can't land due to the incoming blizzard. Return to your safe house and wait for my call. Belkin's orders."

Cody's head dropped back against the headrest and he let out a long sigh. He had to keep the smile from his voice. "Copy," he said.

He tossed the walkie-talkie onto the console between the seats and scrubbed his face with both hands. He turned to Viktoria. "We might not know everything, but at least we know that your son is in the area and likely to remain here for the next day to day and a half. That's good. Most important," he added, "is that we have a name."

He turned to look at Viktoria. Even in the SUV's darkened interior he could see that she'd gone pale. She licked her lips and exhaled. "I know who Belkin is."

Gregory's face flashed in Viktoria's mind. She pictured what he must have gone through tonight. Gregory's dark eyes, so much like her own, would have sought her out, wild with terror. Then, her throat closed at the memory of the very real hand that had squeezed her neck.

She had failed her son. Would she ever be able to forgive herself?

"Can you drive?" Cody asked Viktoria. "We need to get off the road."

Viktoria's head snapped over. She had almost forgotten about Cody, her handsome savior.

"Drive?" It took effort to say the word, as if her tongue were heavy. A sheer cliff rose upward on one side and the road fell sharply away on the other. Snowflakes, fat and thick, fell from the sky and dusted the roadway. They blew in through the shattered window. Balls of safety glass coated the car's interior and twinkled with reflected light from the dashboard.

"Let's get out of the middle of the road," he said. "We aren't safe here. If you can't drive, I can."

Drive? Yes, she could drive. Shifting the SUV into Reverse, Viktoria eased away from the guard-rail. The simple task unleashed a burst of adrenaline within her. "We should go to the sheriff," she said, thankful that she finally made a decision.

Although that plan wasn't perfect, either. Was she still wanted by the authorities in New York State? If she was, then the local sheriff would be interested in her case. At the same time, legalities from home didn't matter, not where Gregory was concerned. Without question, she had to stop Peter Belkin from delivering her son to her father-in-law. She could deal with the legal consequences later.

Up ahead was a turnaround. Viktoria drove the short distance and pulled in. With a little maneuvering, she turned the SUV so it faced the road. "Which way to the sheriff's office?" she asked.

"Wait just a minute, will you?" Cody said. "I don't want to go to the sheriff."

"What? Why not?"

Cody hit the ignition button and the engine fell silent.

"Before we go anywhere," he said, "tell me everything you know about Nikolai Mateev."

She hadn't expected Cody to ask about her father-in-law. "I've only met him once. He traveled to New York from Russia for Lucas's—my husband's—funeral. My husband and his father had a falling out years ago, before Lucas and I met."

"Anything else?"

"Nikolai is wealthy, I know that." She didn't

bother to add that she now knew her father-in-law to be corrupt as hell.

Cody regarded her with eyes narrowed. "So you claim to know nothing?"

His challenge hit her like a slap in the face. "The sheriff," she said, "can help sort all of this out."

"One more thing before we go. Tell me what you know about Peter Belkin."

Viktoria opened her mouth, ready to insist that he stop grilling her and just point her toward Telluride, then her jaw clamped shut.

Peter Belkin.

The man on the walkie-talkie had said they were following Belkin's orders. Viktoria had told Cody that she knew Belkin. But she'd never said Belkin's first name. And yet, Cody had known. He had known her name, too.

This night had gone wrong at a terrifying rate. Viktoria hadn't questioned Cody much—or really at all. He had saved her life twice and to her that proved some kind of trustworthiness. Or did it? Cody could be even more dangerous than Belkin, with his own deadly intentions for Gregory—and for her.

It was her turn to insist on answers.

"Who are you?" she asked.

"I told you. My name is…"

"I know your name," she interrupted. She turned to watch him, gauge his reaction. "But there's a lot about you I don't know. For starters, how did you show up at exactly the right time to save my life?"

Cody drew the black cap from his head and raked

his fingers through this thick, dark hair. "I investigated your family, the Mateevs, when I was with the Drug Enforcement Administration."

"Was?"

"Look, I owe you an explanation. I know I do. For now, can you just trust me?"

"Actually, no. I'm done trusting you for no reason."

"No reason? I saved your life," he said. "Twice. Isn't that reason enough?"

"If you really were with the DEA, why won't you go to the sheriff? Aren't you both on the same side?"

Cody let out a long exhale. He hit the ignition button and the car rumbled to life. "I have reason to believe that the sheriff was involved in the raid on your cabin tonight. That he passed on information to Belkin about your whereabouts."

Viktoria went cold. Was there no one she could trust? No place to go for help?

"Let's get out of this SUV. We can use my truck. I left it up the road from your cabin. Go to the right." Cody pointed to the road. "I'll explain while you drive."

"Everything?" Viktoria asked.

"I'll tell you what I can."

Peter Belkin unlocked the rented ski house and held the door ajar for the head of his personal security detail, who carried a sleeping Gregory Mateev. Belkin watched as the kid was maneuvered through the doorway and then followed, locking up behind them.

He was very happy to be back in comfortable surroundings. If he had to bide his time during a job,
this wasn't a bad place to do it. The house belonged
to an American footballer from San Francisco, a tax
shelter no doubt, and one of the nicest homes available in Telluride. Situated halfway up the mountain,
a mudroom, complete with heated floors and cubby-
holes for skis and snowboards, served as the entry-
way. A set of stairs descended to a well-appointed
basement that featured a sauna and a home theater
with leather recliners for two dozen along with a
popcorn machine. Floor-to-ceiling picture windows
in the great room looked out to the nearby woods,
with a private trail heading to the white stretch of
ski slopes visible between the spindly tree branches.
Beyond a fireplace large enough for a grown man to
stand in was the kitchen, which held a five-hundred-
bottle wine cooler and multiple pantries along with
what seemed like acres of granite countertops and
shiny appliances.

Even the most opulent homes in Russia were not
as luxurious as this playhouse for wealthy Americans. Standing at the window, Peter Belkin stared
at the snow accumulating on the adjoining deck. It
had already piled up around the base of the hot tub.
He had been right to postpone their escape and let
Mother Nature have her fun.

Ah, knowing that he would be back in Russia for
Christmas also warmed him. Upon his arrival in
Moscow he would go to Ugolëk and order borscht,
hot black tea and good vodka. While Russia was

always Belkin's home, he knew that he could return to the United States and a residence such as this whenever he chose—for he had also become a wealthy American.

"Belkin?"

Instead of turning to the man who now stood behind him, he used the glass as a mirror reflecting off the black night and made eye contact that way. *"Da."*

"The kid's in bed and sleeping off the sedative. What do you want me to do?"

"Leave now," he said. His team didn't know all the details of the Gregory Mateev abduction, nor did they need to. "We'll meet at the airstrip—four o'clock tomorrow afternoon. Get in touch with the other two in the morning and let them know."

"Anything you say."

"One last thing." He pinned the man with his reflected stare. "Leave the syringes." Belkin didn't want to deal with Gregory should he still be belligerent when he woke up.

Belkin waited while the other man moved through the house, quietly gathering his gear. The front door opened, sending a blast of frigid air swirling through the room, then the door closed with a soft thump.

Letting out a long breath, Belkin returned to the kitchen. He drew a chair from the large kitchen table and slid it inside one of the pantries. Perched atop the chair, Belkin stretched, reaching for the uppermost shelf. His fingertips connected with the slim, cold metallic edge of his personal laptop. He pulled it out then gingerly stepped down from the chair. Having dragged the chair back, he set the laptop carefully on the table.

Before sitting down, Belkin walked to the front door. A quick glance through the peephole showed that Alpha had taken the spare car, leaving Belkin with the SUV. He clicked the lock into place and returned to the table. True, he relied upon his security team. True, there were reasons to keep them all together. True, Belkin might still need them, even though the operation was nearly complete. Still, he didn't trust them, or anyone else, completely.

The fee for retrieving the Mateev brat had been a healthy quarter of a billion US dollars. His men were being well compensated, but they didn't know the exact take. Over the years, Belkin had learned that people were greedy. And greedy people couldn't be trusted.

Certain he was right to remain alone, Belkin powered up the computer and opened the FaceTime app. A small screen with his visage in real time appeared. Seeing his face on the computer screen always surprised and faintly depressed him. He seemed tired, old. Fine lines surrounded his eyes and the hair at his temples had turned unmistakably gray. He smoothed down an unruly eyebrow before entering a number into the contact bar. With a few more clicks of the mouse Belkin's screen dropped down to the corner and Nikolai Mateev's face popped up.

Nikolai was a large man with sparse white hair. He had small, dark eyes and a bulbous nose, made all the more noticeable by the broken capillaries that surrounded its base like angry red worms. A testament to a lifetime of drinking vodka, no doubt.

"You have good news for me, yes?" Nikolai asked.

"Very good news. You will have your grandson with you by *Rozhdestvo*. The *real* Christmas," he added quickly, meaning Russian Orthodox Christmas. "We had hoped to be in Moscow by the evening of December twenty-fourth, but a storm has delayed our plans to leave."

"And the mother?" Nikolai turned, so that his eye was level with the camera.

"She will bother you no more."

The nose filled the small inset screen again. Nikolai sniffed and a gigantic nostril appeared. "You have done well." He paused and added, "This time. I will transfer payment now."

"Thank you, *Otets*." Nikolai was no sire of Belkin's, but he did hold ultimate power over Belkin and his fate, and a little flattery by referring to the criminal overlord of Moscow as *father* always went a long way.

A meaty hand flashed across the screen, waving away Belkin's sobriquet. "There is something else I want you to handle. Once you return from Russia, that is."

"Of course," said Belkin. His pulse did a triple step.

"There is a retired MI5 agent, Sir Ian Wallace, who now lives in Denver." Nikolai leaned back, his face lost in the gloom of the ill-lit room behind him.

"I need to know all about Sir Ian and then I need him to disappear."

"Of course, *Otets*."

Nikolai's nose grew large again and then his screen went blank.

Belkin sat back and massaged his neck. It had been a long assignment that just got longer. It didn't matter. To curry favor with someone as important as Nikolai Mateev, Belkin would do anything.

He opened his computer's internet browser and spent a few minutes accessing the deep web. Give Belkin a name and there was nothing he couldn't learn about a person: from shopping habits, to favorite cable news network, to secrets, to the loved ones they would do anything to protect and the secrets of those people, as well.

It took a quarter of an hour to circumvent MI5's firewall. Once there, he had only moments to fill in a complete picture of Sir Ian's life. He had been an agent with MI5, awarded his knighthood after thwarting a terrorist attack on London's subway system. After that, Ian had been linked romantically with several famous women, and most recently with up-and-coming Denver sports agent, Petra Sloan. It explained how a Brit ended up in Colorado. He had opened a private security firm in Denver, Rocky Mountain Justice.

RMJ was a small operation; unless you knew where and how to find them, they were invisible. Yet, Belkin had pulled back the veil and now had access to all pertinent corporate information. The firm quietly found missing people and sometimes worked with a variety of agencies, such as the Colorado Bureau of Investigation and the federal big brother—the FBI—in matters such as public corruption.

Belkin stared at the computer. Certainly a firm unrestrained by laws could be bothersome to a large-scale drug dealer, but something didn't add up. Why did Nikolai want Sir Ian dead? His firm had less than two dozen employees. In fact, why did he care at all?

On a whim, he entered Nikolai Mateev's name into the RMJ search engine. An incomplete hit turned up one Mateev—Viktoria Mateev, no less. It appeared that RMJ had been hired to find her and it was their tip that had led Belkin right to her. He laughed to himself. Ironic, no?

A few more keystrokes and he found the automatically generated email and stopped. It was another name he recognized and never thought to see again: Cody Samuels.

While at the DEA, Agent Samuels came close to building a strong case against the Mateevs—one that could have crushed the family—and he had to be killed. As it turned out, Belkin's would-be assassin had become the victim. In the end, the loss of life cost Samuels' career. The case against the Mateevs was closed and Belkin considered the outcome a success.

He closed the RMJ site and placed all information gathered into an encrypted document that he then transferred to another part of his computer. From there he opened a file that he'd kept for more than a year as insurance only. As Belkin studied Cody's picture his stomach churned, filled with sour repugnance for having to deal twice with the same problem.

He moved from the file to his bank's secure website. The payment promised by Nikolai for the kidnapping had not yet been deposited. Though Belkin was weary and his jaw still ached where Gregory Mateev had struck him, he refused to go to bed before confirming payment. He was annoyed more than worried about not getting the money immediately. Even though Nikolai was a force unto himself, there were plenty of other powerful and dangerous men who would match payment for the Mateev brat—dead or alive—and the only thing keeping Gregory from that fate was Belkin's purchased loyalty.

Returning to the RMJ site, Belkin took in a deep breath and began to hum the refrain of the American Christmas song "We Three Kings." Since he had time and enough information to get started, he might as well learn what else he could about Sir Ian Wallace and the men of Rocky Mountain Justice.

Chapter 5

Viktoria drove into the relentlessly falling snow. The headlights cut a swath through the flakes, creating a tunnel of white surrounded by blackness. The tires slid on the slick roads, forcing her to steer cautiously into each turn. Inevitably, the SUV's rear fishtailed. It gave the impression that she was hurtling uncontrollably through space, and the effect left her slightly sick to her stomach.

"Turn here," Cody said, pointing to the left.

She exited the road in the direction he indicated. The SUV slowed as the tires sank into several inches of snow. They entered a makeshift parking lot, meant to accommodate only a dozen cars for cross-country skiers in the winter or hikers in the summer.

On this night, the lot was empty. Almost. A forest

green, four-door Range Rover sat alone near a cut-through in a snowbank. The pricey British vehicle gave her pause.

"I thought you said you drove a truck," she said of the Range Rover. "Every truck I've ever seen had a rear bed and was covered in rust and primer."

"Ah, spoken like a true New Yorker." Cody grinned as he reached over to hit the ignition button. The SUV's engine shuddered once and stilled. "My boss is a Brit and as far as he's concerned, this is a truck. Me, I'm a good old Colorado boy at heart, and primer is one of my favorite colors. But since Ian pays for this ride and I get to drive it for free, I call it whatever he wants me to. Although I do have a personal vehicle—a real truck, no rust or primer—back at my house."

Primer was his favorite color. Viktoria almost felt a smile pull up the corners of her mouth. Then she thought about Gregory, alone and afraid. She couldn't let anything distract her from finding her son, even Cody Samuels.

Cody opened his door and jumped down. "Let's go."

Viktoria hopped down from the SUV and her feet sank into the snow. Cold, wet flakes sifted over the tops of her boots and soaked her fleece pajama bottoms. Cody conducted himself with such confidence that Viktoria found her spirits buoyed. But she still had no idea what she would do if—no, not if, when—she was reunited with her son. How would she be able to escape the long reach of the Mateevs a second time? Would it be enough to disappear and drop off the grid as she had before?

Cody used his key fob to unlock the Range Rover's doors and start the engine. As if he were attuned to her thoughts, he broke the silence by asking, "How long have you been living in the cabin?"

"Two months. We left New York in August and moved around for six weeks before I decided we needed to find one place to stay."

"Why did you leave New York?" Cody asked, his gaze trained on her face.

Viktoria got the impression that she was being tested and that somehow Cody's knowledge of her life went beyond his having investigated her late husband's family. Still, she had nothing to lose by telling the truth.

"The state of New York had moved to terminate my parental rights. I suspect that Belkin had manipulated the system on behalf of Nikolai Mateev. They had a video of Gregory sitting in our apartment and crying—it went on for hours. In it, I was asleep on the sofa with an empty bottle of vodka cradled in my arms. The whole thing was a fake. I don't drink. I've never left my son alone for minutes…" She shook her head; the dismay and dread from being set up came back to her. "It almost worked and I ran before the courts could take Gregory from me. There was money after my husband's death, some more in savings and I knew it could last us awhile. I sold my Mercedes for cash and bought a clunker."

Cody regarded her with those intense and other-worldly eyes.

"Go on," he urged.

She continued, as if she wasn't captivated by his gaze. "I paid cash for the cabin rental, October to March. The utilities were included. When I first arrived, I hired a delivery service for our groceries and paid them in cash. I only used the cabin's landline phone that was there for emergencies," she said, covering the basics. "But there was nobody I dared to call. We never went into town. Until today, that is. I have no idea how they found me, though."

"Your image was picked up on a traffic camera," Cody said.

It made sense. "Is that how the sheriff knew to call Belkin?"

"Probably."

"Probably is hardly an answer."

Cody exhaled, his breath a frozen cloud. "Let's get out of here. We aren't being productive just standing in the snow."

He opened the passenger door of his Range Rover. Bright light spilled over the snow and bathed Cody in its glow. He was breathtakingly handsome. Was she a bad mother for noticing the dimple on his cheek or his broad shoulders? He was hot—it was more fact than opinion. Like the fact that it was snowing, or that the date was December the twenty-third or that her son had just been kidnapped.

The last thought brought her down to reality and

left her weak and light-headed. She clung to the side of the Range Rover.

"Are you okay?" Cody scooped his hand under her elbow, lifting with just enough pressure to keep her from crumpling into the snow.

Viktoria had to get a hold of herself. She'd never do Gregory any good if she continued to be so weak. "Yes," she said. Standing straight, Viktoria rolled back her shoulders. "I'll be fine."

"Okay," said Cody hesitantly. "If you're sure, jump in."

"Where are we going?"

"To see the sheriff."

"I thought you said that he helped Belkin find me. Why would we go to him for help now?"

"Because we need something he has."

Viktoria couldn't imagine a crooked sheriff having anything she wanted, much less needed. "And what's that?"

"Information about the people who took your son."

This time, Cody took the wheel. He should have been problem solving—analyzing the attack on the cabin, the kidnapping and exactly how to save Gregory. Instead he was thinking about Viktoria. She'd been honest with him about the court case against her in New York. In truth, her version of the story had shone a new light on the few facts he'd been given.

Dark shadows ringed her eyes and cords of muscle stood out on her neck. As if her body spoke to him,

he imagined that he heard stories of her strength—
both physical and emotional—and her weariness
from the fight. Cody admired her spirit. He might
even like her personally.

It brought him back to their ultimate destination,
the sheriff's office, and more important, the reason behind their visit there. Cody had worked with
Ray Benjamin in the past and found him to be a
competent and trustworthy guy. How could he have
been taken in by a dirty scheme? He tried to think
of another possible way Belkin could have located
Viktoria. He couldn't come up with anything else
that was even remotely plausible, especially when
he considered that the deputies had been a no-show
this evening.

The county office complex came into view and
Cody eased the Range Rover off the road and into the
snow-filled parking lot. Industrial lights on tall poles
illuminated the campus of five buildings. The Sheriff's office, squat and made of red brick, sat at the
back of the property. Four black-and-white cruisers
waited in a line near the front door, but Cody knew
that at this hour the office would be empty—only a
few deputies were out on patrol with the rest on call
in case they were needed. The county's emergency
services were handled at a call center on the opposite side of town.

Near the rear entrance to the building sat a silver pickup, which he recognized as belonging to the
sheriff. Several inches of white powder covered the
roof, the hood and filled the rear bed. Ray Benjamin

staying at the office late and alone only fanned the flames of Cody's suspicions. He steered into what might have been a parking place, but was too covered with snow for him to tell, and cut the ignition.

"Before tonight, I would have said that Sheriff Benjamin was a good guy," said Cody, ending the interminable silence.

"But you're convinced he had something to do with Peter Belkin finding me and taking Gregory."

"There's no other explanation," he said. The words tasted sour on his tongue. It brought back all the times he had trusted people only to be betrayed. The DEA. His former fiancée. His parents. His sister.

"Then he's not a good guy," said Viktoria.

"Like I said, I'm surprised."

"You mean you're wrong."

Cody shook his head. "I'm never wrong."

"I don't think this is a good idea," said Viktoria. She folded her arms over her chest, her chin jutting out just a bit.

"We know your son hasn't been taken from the area yet. But Colorado is a big state and if we're going to find him we have to know where to look." More than the risk, Cody wanted to ask Benjamin why he'd done it.

As a child, Cody had been too young to demand better from his alcoholic parents. In the intervening years, he'd grown beyond the hurt that came with betrayal. Or so he thought. But when the DEA—an agency to whom he had dedicated his life—cut him loose, Cody was again filled with rage so vile it poisoned his life. Even now, sitting in the silent truck, Cody knew that facing Sheriff Benjamin was far from an actual cure for his lack of trust. And yet, he could do nothing else.

"It's a calculated risk," said Cody at length.

Viktoria exhaled, her shoulders sagged. "Everything is a gamble, I guess. Do you really think that he'll simply tell us where Gregory's being held?"

"Nothing about this case is simple, and finding your son will be no exception. But we need the truth, and I won't let Ray Benjamin lie to me a second time."

He slammed the Range Rover door shut and Viktoria exited from the passenger side. As they approached the rear entrance to the sheriff's office, the door swung open. Ray Benjamin stood on the threshold. He wore his khaki sheriff's uniform, but the name tag over the left breast pocket had been removed. A thin sheen of sweat coated his face. His cheeks were ruddy and his dark brown hair was mussed. He stared into the night with red-tinted eyes and the medicinal scent of whiskey rolled off him in a wave.

"I saw you in the monitor." He pointed to a black security camera bolted to the side of the building. "Thought you might show up."

"We need to talk," Cody said.

"Thought you might say that, too." Benjamin stepped back from the door. "Come on in."

Viktoria stood close to Cody, her shoulder pressed into his arm. He slipped a protective hand around her back, connecting them and making them a single unit against whatever—or whomever—waited inside. Fluorescent lights buzzed above a white-paneled corridor. Industrial carpet of basic brown padded their footfalls.

Ray Benjamin had preceded them and his office door stood open. Cody paused in the corridor, every muscle tense. He moved his hand to the holster on his hip and unfastened the safety snap. His palm rested on the Glock.

Sheriff Benjamin poked his head around the office door, a drunken gofer. "Come on in," he said, "I'm alone and you're right, we need to talk."

Cody placed his mouth next to Viktoria's ear. "I'm going in first," he whispered. "If anything goes wrong—run."

He pressed the Range Rover's key into Viktoria's hand. She twined her fingers through his. Their gazes met and held. The moment ended with the clink of ice on glass from inside the office.

"Can I pour you a drink, Cody? One for your lady friend? I assume this is the elusive Viktoria Mateev." Sheriff Benjamin continued. "We can toast the holiday season."

Cody figured that if anyone was in the building besides the sheriff, they would have attacked already. Besides, Benjamin wouldn't be drinking so carelessly if he had company. Cody stepped into the office. A single desk lamp did little to illuminate the room, its glow a spotlight on a glass filled with amber liquid and a half-empty bottle of Jack Daniels.

Cody nodded to Viktoria, who crossed the threshold into the alcohol-fumed space.

From a drawer in his desk, the sheriff produced two more glasses and set them next to the first.

"This isn't a social call, Ray," said Cody.

The sheriff looked up from his desk, his eyes wide. "I refused them at first," he said without prompting.

"*Them* who?"

"You know who they are or you wouldn't be here."

"What does Belkin have on you, Ray?" Cody asked. "Or is it the Mateevs?"

Sheriff Benjamin downed his drink in one swallow then sank back in his chair. "Belkin. He threatened my family."

"Bull," said Cody. "You've got access to resources that the locals don't. You've got training and knowledge that can keep your family safe."

"They *did* threaten my family. You don't understand. This Belkin guy shows up about two weeks ago with pictures of my house, the kids, my wife, even my dog," said Ray with a shake of his head. He refilled his drink and leaned back into his chair, the glass balanced on his stomach. "I might have had some debt, too."

"What's your price, Ray?" Cody asked.

Sheriff Benjamin shook his head and caught a belch in his closed fist. "It doesn't matter."

"Doesn't matter?" Cody lunged over the desk and pulled Benjamin out of his seat. His drink sloshed onto the floor. "A kid was just kidnapped."

"I didn't know," Benjamin bleated.

The sheriff's breath was stale. The drunken whimpering mixed with the stench of whiskey and brought back Cody's memories of bleak Christmases past. His mother passed out on the sofa. His father staggering from the trailer, not to return until well past dawn. Cody and Sarah trying to celebrate with a shared TV dinner.

Cody shoved Benjamin back in his seat. "You are a sad sack of crap."

"The men who paid your debt took my son, which means that you're indebted to me," Viktoria said.

Sheriff Benjamin sat forward, his elbows propped on his desk. "You listen to me, lady," he said.

"No, you listen to me, you son of a bitch," Cody interrupted, momentarily shocked that he'd just defended a Mateev. "A child was kidnapped and his mother was almost murdered. Tell me, Sheriff, how much is your complicity worth?"

Ray Benjamin shook his head. "Belkin never shared his plans with me. I was only told that if I ever learned the whereabouts of one Viktoria Mateev, to call him. Besides, I never thought I'd have to follow through. I mean, what are the chances?" He screwed the top to the bottle of Jack. "I definitely didn't ask him about his plans."

"Ten thousand?" Viktoria asked. "Twenty? Or did Belkin pay every outstanding debt you have—house, car, your kids' college?"

"He gave me fifty thousand, but that's not why I did it."

"You've always been a good servant of the community. Why deceive them all now?" Cody asked.

Benjamin lifted the bottle and prepared to pour again. He stopped before a drop fell. "My son was caught a few years back selling pot at the middle school. He was sixteen—old enough to ruin his life, but he's still a kid, you know. I made a few promises, twisted a few arms, but mostly got my son the help he needed. He straightened himself out and is finishing his second year at the Air Force Academy. But this Belkin character found out and threatened to go public. If that happened, my son would lose his place in the academy and I'd be fired."

"You're a good father, I get that." Cody kept his voice flat, even though he wanted to punch Ray in his stupid, drunken face. "But you're a lousy sheriff. Covering up for your kid is one kind of bad— but assisting Belkin with kidnapping and murder is a whole different level of evil."

"I told you, he never said what he had planned. It's not my fault."

Cody's pulse spiked as years of frustration surged through his body like an electric current. He slammed his palms on the desk. Benjamin jolted, his eyes wide. "Cut the crap. You aided a known criminal. He might not have specifically told you his plans, but you knew they weren't legal. On top of it all, you only acted to cover up other crimes."

"Belkin will be done with me after tonight," said

Ray, "and I won't be asked to do anything else like this again."

"If you think that you'll ever get rid of Peter Belkin you're more than crooked," Cody spat. "You're also stupid. A corrupt sheriff is the perfect puppet and he's the ultimate puppet master."

"I'm not corrupt. I was only protecting my son."

"And the bribe?" Viktoria challenged. "Your second mistake was to take so little. Fifty thousand dollars is nothing to Peter Belkin."

Cody followed up with "If you want to redeem yourself, Ray, you have to let us know where Belkin is now."

With a shake of the head, the sheriff sighed. "I don't know anything. I was given a number—that's all. But if this were my case to investigate, I'd look through the files at San Miguel Rentals. If fifty thou' is chump change to Belkin, then he's staying at some swanky digs and San Miguel Rentals handles all the high-end stuff in the county."

Viktoria looked to Cody.

"I know where it is," he said, finally able to take another step in finding Gregory. "Getting into the computer system might be a problem. We'll need a way to see a list of what properties are rented and by whom."

Sheriff Benjamin began to twirl his glass between his palms. "That's the best part, for you, at least. SMR had someone hack into their system—oh, four or five years ago. Caused them all sorts of trouble and now they always keep a hard copy of each rental in their file cabinets." He set the glass down. "In fact, I recommend that all the small businesses keep hard copies of their transactions. One well-executed hack is all it takes to ruin a business. See? I do care about my people."

"Let's go, Viktoria." Armed with the crucial intel, Cody itched to get started. Then he added, speaking to Sheriff Benjamin, "Call the CBI, Ray. Confessing will make it easier for you. At least in a legal sense."

The sheriff leaned forward and sat on the edge of his seat. He picked up the bottle, taking his time to unscrew the lid. "I'm not drunk enough to turn myself in."

"If you don't call now, I will report you later—soon, in fact."

"What? Like you being here corrects *your* involvement?"

The gibe hit Cody in the gut—like it was intended to do. Hot anger rose to his throat. And Cody realized why the remark stung so hard.

He flicked a gaze in Viktoria's direction, imagining the look of hurt in her eyes. Brows drawn together, jaw set—Viktoria Mateev was far from injured and unsure. She was pissed.

"What involvement?" she asked. Heat rolled off her in waves. It paled next to his own internal fury.

Cody reminded himself that he had been, was still doing, a perfectly legal job. He cleared his throat. "I'm the one who called in your location to Ray. It was my job to turn you in."

* * *

Viktoria waited until they'd cleared the back door of the sheriff's office before she turned on Cody, her fury so great that she began to quiver.

"You," she said, pointing a shaking finger at Cody. "You told that corrupt bastard where to find me?"

"Calm down," said Cody as he gripped her elbow and tried to steer her to the Range Rover.

Mere seconds ago she'd assumed that her anger had reached its greatest intensity. But, to have Cody Samuels presume to touch her, to tell her how to feel, to try to direct where she should go—oh no. The first type of anger was a thunderstorm, but this was a hurricane.

With both hands on his chest, she shoved him away. "Don't you *ever* tell me what to do. I don't even know who you are."

"I told you already, my name is…"

"Yeah, yeah, yeah. You're Cody Samuels. You used to work for the DEA. I appreciate that you saved my life, truly I do. But, I might not have needed saving without your help." She paused to put her last word into air quotes. "I can take it from here."

"How?" asked Cody. "You don't even have a car. A blizzard is about to hit the county and you don't know where you're going."

"I'll manage. If I can make it in New York, I can handle Podunk, Colorado."

"I'm not going to let you leave. You have no choice but to let me help." He paused, copying the air quotes.

"Oh yeah? Try and stop me." She turned from Cody. He gripped her by the shoulder, spinning Viktoria to face him. This time, she didn't bother to push him away.

"So, who are you?" she asked.

"I used to be a DEA agent and now I work for a private security firm in Denver."

"Rocky Mountain Justice," she said, recalling that he'd told her to contact them if anything happened to him.

"The state of New York hired us to find you, and your picture came up on a traffic camera earlier today. We have facial recognition software and it sent me an automated email." He slipped his cap from his head and ran a hand through his hair. "It was my job to verify that the picture was of you and then contact local law enforcement with the information and offer my assistance, which I did."

That explained a lot, but not everything. "Why were you at my cabin tonight? It sounds like your job was done once you'd notified the sheriff."

"Your last name piqued my interest and I hoped that you were spending Christmas with some other Mateevs." He shook his head. "I also thought that if I was there when you were picked up that maybe you could give me more information."

"About what?"

"Your in-laws."

"Why?"

He looked away.

Suddenly Viktoria longed to sit down, or better

yet—sleep. "So Child Protective Services is still after me?" She shook her head and emptied her lungs of breath. "Nothing like being popular, I guess. All this time I've been more worried about Peter Belkin and my father-in-law."

"After what happened tonight you'll be exonerated, trust me. There will be no denying the evidence at your cabin—all those bullets, not to mention the corpse."

Could the terror of tonight turn into a blessing that freed her from the grip of the Mateev family?

"I suppose I should be grateful that it was you who got the email. If it was anyone else, they might have just done their job and not worried about me."

"Are you still mad?"

"Mad? No, I'm furious with you and at the same time, grateful." She gave a mirthless laugh. "Honestly, I'm not sure if I should give you a slap or a kiss."

"I thought I'd get a lot worse than a slap, but feel free to kiss me anytime."

Viktoria's gaze met Cody's. He regarded her with those crystalline eyes. An unbidden image of the two of them—naked, in a tangle of sheets—came to Viktoria. In her imaginings, he regarded her the same way he did now. She pushed the picture from her mind, ashamed that such a thought would come to her when she should be concentrating on locating her son. She looked away.

"Come on," said Cody. He hit the key fob and remotely started the Range Rover's engine. "Let's get out of here."

"And go where?" she asked.

"To find Belkin and rescue your son."

Chapter 6

Telluride's main street was made up of one narrow road. At this time of the night, and especially in the midst of a major storm, the lane was free of cars and pedestrians. Two-story buildings rose on each side, many dating from the late nineteenth century, when Telluride had been founded as a silver mining town.

The wall of one building abutted the next and created a solid block of businesses and residences. Most were brick, but the rare wooden buildings were painted in a variety of bright colors—azure, crimson and emerald. Snow covered the road and the few cars parked curbside. Bright red bows hung from every streetlight and wreaths decorated most every door. Viktoria might have appreciated its picturesque qualities at another time, but tonight she was too occupied with thoughts of her missing son.

She leaned back against the heated seat and closed her eyes. She'd been asleep when they'd soundlessly stolen Gregory. Viktoria took in a shaky breath as the tears she fought to control slipped over her lashes and trailed down her cheeks.

Cody reached for her, covering her hand with his. It was large, warm and strong. In that moment, Viktoria felt protected. The feeling completed her in a way she hadn't realized she'd been lacking.

She slipped her hand back to her lap. She couldn't let a few months alone—plus the year before Lucas had died and the few months of being a widow—cloud her judgment. All the same, a tingle of excitement registered in her belly.

"It'll be okay," he said. "You'll get Gregory back."

"You don't know that," she snapped, the warm-hearted feeling gone in an instant. "You don't know anything." Releasing the despair, even a little, felt good.

"I do," said Cody, "because I refuse to believe anything else."

Did *she* dare to believe, to hope, to trust? A tear slid down her cheek. With one hand remaining on the steering wheel, Cody reached for her and wiped her cheek dry. Viktoria instinctively leaned in to his touch and the strength and solace he offered.

"I should believe," she said. "It's the season of miracles, right?"

"Supposedly," said Cody, with a look she couldn't

decipher. "And speaking of miracles, here's the rental agency." He slowed the Range Rover and pulled up in front of a glass door that was identical to so many others.

Viktoria opened the car door and jumped down. This time the snow came up to the middle of her calf. Cody already stood before a storefront, his backpack slung over his shoulder and a slim case in his hand. The glass windows of the rental office were filled with pictures of available properties. Suites in large lodges. Ski-in/ski-out condominiums. Single homes with asymmetrical rooflines and floor-to-ceiling windows.

Viktoria watched as Cody opened the black leather case. Inside were several long, slim pieces of metal. He removed one from its holder and bent before the door. After a few seconds of working the piece of metal in the lock there was a click.

Cody rose to his feet and pushed the door open. He stepped through, paused and motioned for Viktoria to follow.

Next to the door, a gray plastic box emitted a series of beeps.

The alarm had been tripped. She froze; her heart stilled within her chest.

All the events of the awful evening came crashing down on her. Gregory was gone. She had barely survived an attack that had been orchestrated by her ruthless in-laws, and now she was going to be arrested for breaking and entering. She'd have no defense and the courts would happily give Gregory to the rich and powerful Mateevs. "Cody," she whispered, pointing a shaking finger at the wall.

Lights on the alarm's faceplate changed from green to yellow. From the case that Cody still held, he removed a pair of cutters and snipped two wires, silencing the noise and extinguishing the lights. "It's okay," he said. His voice was deep and soothing, like a warm cup of hot chocolate. He held her by the shoulders. "Look at me."

His scent—pine and cold—drifted over her and Viktoria gazed up at him.

He paused. Inched closer and closer still. She felt the warmth of his breath wash over her. He reached up. His hand hovered next to her cheek. Viktoria's pulse quickened. She wanted him to touch her, to feel his skin on hers. She leaned toward him, but then stopped.

Worse than giving in to a despair so deep that she'd never be able to crawl out and find her son, would be for Viktoria to succumb to her attraction to Cody. Or maybe it was just misplaced gratitude for saving her life. Yes, that was it, she decided. She wasn't truly interested in Cody, just extremely appreciative.

Viktoria took a step back. "We should get started. This is your area of expertise. What should we do first?"

Cody pointed to three metal multidrawer filing cabinets lined up against the back wall. "Here." He handed her a flashlight before tucking his fleece cap into his pocket. "Start with the one on the left.

Look for any rental agreement with Belkin's name on it," he continued. "Nikolai Mateev or someone else from the family might be listed as the renters, but I doubt it."

With a nod, Viktoria went to the first cabinet. She pulled on the handle. It was locked.

"Cody," she whispered, even though there was no one to hear her.

Using the same tool he had on the door, Cody worked on the filing cabinet and within seconds he had the drawer open. It took her a few minutes to figure out how to riffle through the green hanging files while holding her flashlight, but soon she had learned to tuck the flashlight into the crook of her neck and flip through the contracts. Each file was labeled with the name of the renter. She quickly sorted through the *A*s and moved to the *B*s, but no Belkin was listed.

With a click, she turned off her flashlight and leaned against the wall. "This is a waste of time," she said.

Cody stood before the third filing cabinet. He held his light in his mouth and was already crouched in front of the second drawer. He turned to her, the light blinding.

She shaded her face and continued, "Even if he rented a property from this realtor, he didn't use his own name. It would have to be an alias, which means it could be anything and we'd never know."

Cody took the light from his mouth and turned it off. "Belkin is smart and careful, but he's not perfect. He makes mistakes—they all do. Hopefully Belkin thinks he's so smart that no one will know where to look."

She wanted to believe Cody, but… "Our chances of finding him are pretty low."

"The only way to ensure that Belkin wins is to give up," Cody said. "And that means that your son gets taken to Russia. You'll never see him again. You're going to give up because Belkin didn't rent a house in his own name? I thought you were tougher than that."

Viktoria opened her mouth to argue—to tell Cody that she *was* a lot tougher than that. She turned on her flashlight. "My pity party break is over," she said and then added, "Sorry."

"No apologies needed," said Cody.

She turned back to the filing cabinet and looked through all the *C*s, *D*s and the few *E*s that were available. With a sigh, she turned off her light. "Finding Belkin can't be this random. We have to think of everything we know about him and look for a connection."

"Like what?" Cody asked.

"Well, his real name isn't Peter. It's Pyotr—a Russian spelling."

"What's the Russian spelling of his last name?"

"Belkin is a Russian name."

"No kidding?" asked Cody as he moved to the middle cabinet. He picked the lock and knelt before the second drawer. *"O,"* he said, flipping past hanging files, "*P*. No, no surname of Pyotr. Nor is there a Peter."

"Okay," she said. "He works for Crandall Stevenson. It's a law firm located in the Chrysler Building on Lexington Ave."

"You have the beginning of the alphabet," said Cody.

She did. Excitement shot through her and Viktoria moved back to the cabinet. She had already looked through all the *C*s, but had something important gone unnoticed? She flipped through a sea of green hanging files with neatly penned tabs. Once. And then again. Her stomach roiled. "Nothing," she said with a sigh. "You look at the *S*s."

Cody slid open a drawer. Viktoria came to stand next to him. She shone her light on the files. Seeger. Stevens. Stevenson, Crandall from New York, New York. This time she did smile and it felt good, hopeful, like there might be an end to her trouble. "We found them," she said. "Now let's go and save my son."

Cody glanced at Viktoria. The interior lights of the SUV cast her in a silver ethereal light. Her skin was pale and flawless; her hair shimmered like moonlight. She looked angelic and almost too fragile to touch.

He now knew, though, that Viktoria was far from a delicate flower. The set of her jaw, along with her narrowed eyes, spoke of a deep tenacity that he knew better than to cross.

Cody had to force himself to turn his mind from all things personal connected to Viktoria Mateev. She was part of his job. An assignment. And once they'd recovered her son and he'd had a chance to question her about the Mateevs, his job would be over and they'd never cross paths again.

Cody exhaled before entering the address they'd found into his navigation system. He turned his truck through the snow-filled roads, carefully following the first set of directions. He was fairly sure that Gregory was not harmed—after all, Belkin would want to deliver the boy to his grandfather in one piece. And he was also fairly sure that Belkin didn't know Viktoria was alive. In fact, from what Cody learned in talking to the thug on the walkie-talkie, he also was fairly sure that Belkin was alone at the address.

In his humble opinion, *fairly sure* sucked.

As a DEA agent, Cody never moved in on a target without being positive and having lots of backup. He thought about calling in the team from RMJ. Most everyone was in Denver and over three hundred miles away. The windshield wipers shoveled snow from left to right and Cody decided that the six, or more, hour wait for their help was too long and therefore unacceptable. And if he did call, more than likely Ian would tell him to stand down.

Well, Cody wasn't about to give up this opportunity to find Gregory. That meant only one thing—he would have to go in alone.

"Listen," he began. Talking had a calming effect

on him and slowed the intense pulse that he'd felt building with each mile traveled. "I'm not sure what we're up against. There's always a risk of injury or death in a raid."

"What are you saying?"

What was he saying? He didn't like the idea of putting Viktoria in harm's way. But why was the need to keep Viktoria safe akin to the need for water in the desert? "I don't live too far from here," he said. "I can take you to my house and…"

"Not a chance," Viktoria interrupted. "He's my son and I'm going with you."

Cody tried again. "What I have planned isn't exactly legal…"

"You think I care about the law? This is my son."

"What about your own safety?"

"I'm going," she said. "End of story."

Cody gritted his teeth. Stubborn woman. He inhaled slowly and exhaled. "I care about you." He quickly changed his words, adding, "I care about you because I care about doing a good job."

She whispered his name and Cody could easily imagine her breath on his neck as they moved together, making love. Her voice, moaning his name, over and over and over.

Like she didn't know the effect she had on him, Viktoria continued, "Gregory has been through so much already. I can't allow him to think that he's being kidnapped by another stranger, any more than I could sit safely in your house and wait."

Cody had been so intent on the thought of rescuing the boy that he hadn't thought about her kid's reaction to being grabbed and whisked away for a second time. "Fine," he said, taking the next turn indicated by his navigation system. The tires crunched through the deep snow. "The first thing we need is intel on the house—who's inside and where. From there we can devise a plan." The screen of the GPS showed an illuminated map. Two more turns up a winding mountain road were indicated, then the directions ended in a black-and-white-checkered flag. Cody took the first turn and before his truck eased around the second, he turned off the headlights.

A large ski house came into view and the black SUV from the kidnapping sat in the middle of a circular driveway. He drove another hundred feet before easing onto the shoulder.

Reaching up, Cody disabled the interior light. "Ready?" Cody asked.

Viktoria took in a single long breath and exhaled. "As much as I'll ever be."

The snow was deep now and falling heavily. The blizzard that was not yet fully upon them was as much an enemy as was Belkin himself. On a stormy night like this it was easy to get disoriented and lost, a deadly combination in the Colorado wilderness.

Cody hitched his chin toward the dense woods that surrounded the A-frame. "We need to stay in the trees," he said. "Stick to me. I don't want us to get separated."

She wrapped her fingers through his. Her hand was warm, despite the cold, and incredibly soft. His mind conjured the image of an intimate touch and his body responded in kind. He couldn't let her get to him—no matter how damned beautiful she was, or how long it had been since Cody had actually wanted the affections of another.

Cody stopped at the edge of the tree line; Viktoria stood at his back. An expanse of snow-covered lawn separated them from the back of the house.

Floor-to-ceiling windows gave Cody an unobstructed view into the building. A guy sat at a table, a laptop in front of him. It could be Belkin—Cody had seen photos—then again, it could be a million other guys.

"It's him," said Viktoria. "That's Belkin."

"Are you sure?" he asked.

She nodded. Downy flakes clung to her eyelashes and her long blond hair. She looked like a snow angel and his heart skipped a beat. He turned back to the house, trying like hell to not return his gaze to Viktoria's face.

Belkin. Cody focused on the back of the man's head, the exact place a bullet would enter and end his miserable life. Cody's palm moved the holster at his hip. Wind. Trajectory. Distance. Visibility. It wasn't an impossible shot, but a difficult one nonetheless. If he missed, then what? His hand slipped to his side.

Cody assumed that Belkin was alone, but he needed to know. He studied the back of the structure—a full three stories—and looked for signs of occupancy beyond Belkin. There were no stray lights in upstairs windows, or movements in the shadowy corners behind Belkin. Not even the whisper of a sound beyond the wind in the trees.

While Cody hadn't expected to see a platoon of hired gunmen stationed at every door and window, he absolutely had expected to see Gregory Mateev. In fact, the kid's absence was more puzzling than Belkin sitting alone.

Cody's worst fears churned through his mind, filling his chest with pain. Hadn't he seen the depths of Belkin's depravity firsthand? He wanted to give voice to his worries. But say what and to whom? He could hardly tell Viktoria that they might be too late to save her son's life. His hands shook with anger as the memory of the CI's life slipping away was once again more vivid than the snowy woods.

Life. Death. Love. Hate. Rage. Ardor. In the end, they were all the same.

He turned to Viktoria, all primal instinct and no civilized decorum. He reached for her, gripping her waist and pulling her to him. Viktoria's eyes were wide—doe-like—and she sucked in a little hiccup of a breath. Cody released his hold. She was a widow whose son had just been kidnapped. What kind of jerk was he to want to steal a kiss?

Then without a word, Viktoria closed the distance between them. She pressed her lips onto his cheek. "For luck," she whispered.

Without another thought about right or wrong, Cody slid his arm around her waist and pulled Viktoria closer. Her full breasts pressed into his chest, warm and inviting.

Cody placed his mouth on hers. Viktoria wrapped her arms around his neck and parted her lips. He moved his tongue into her mouth and she greeted him in return. Their kiss became his world. His universe. His everything.

Viktoria raked her fingers over his shoulders. Cody's hands traveled down, memorizing her form. Her arms. Her waist. Her tight, firm butt. And then his conscience came roaring in like a locomotive that had just jumped the track. He pulled away from the embrace.

"I'm sorry," he mumbled. "I shouldn't have taken advantage of you like that."

Viktoria took a step back and Cody faltered without her support. "You didn't take advantage," she whispered. Her words held an icy edge. "I'm an adult, not a schoolgirl who can be led astray."

Cody knew the fact that Viktoria was full grown all too well. He had felt her curves that suggested Viktoria Mateev was 100 percent woman. "That's not what I meant," Cody said. He immediately froze. His voice would carry on the thin mountain air, especially on such a quiet night.

His next words were cut short by the shushing sounds of rollers on metal as the sliding glass door opened at the house.

Damn, Cody silently cursed. He was better than that—to ruin the element of surprise by trying to make Viktoria understand. Understand what? Even Cody couldn't categorize his feelings. He mentally tucked his attraction to Viktoria away, something he'd tried and failed to do several times already, and turned his focus to the house.

Belkin stepped into the night and looked in their direction. He reached into his pocket and Cody instinctively stepped in front of Viktoria, shielding her from any stray bullets. Slowly, Belkin's hand became visible. Cody slid his hand to his gun, unsnapped the holster guard and peered through the swirling snow.

Belkin held something in his hand, but Cody couldn't tell what it was. It was small—palm-sized—and rectangular. A Taser? The walkie-talkie? It wasn't a gun. Belkin lifted his hand to his mouth and tapped a cigarette between his lips. From the other pocket came a lighter.

Cody could have laughed. Except that Belkin would have heard him, for sure.

He looked over his shoulder. Viktoria gave him a wry smile and shook her head. Leaning into Viktoria, Cody pressed his mouth to Viktoria's ear. "Let's move in closer," he said. "This might be the best chance we have."

They stood directly opposite Belkin. The scent of cigarette smoke was faint, but unmistakable. Cody flipped through his catalogue of ways to deal with Belkin. He found only one suitable course of action.

"We need a distraction that can get us in the house," Cody whispered into her ear. Her scent surrounded him. Who knew that the combined scents of sugar, mint and wood smoke would be so damned erotic?

"I know what will work," Viktoria said. "Wait here. You'll know what to do."

Before he could ask a single question, she had disappeared—becoming nothing more than a mist in the gathering storm.

Chapter 7

There were two pillars upon which Viktoria had built her life—her love for her son and her tenacity as a New Yorker. While neither had prepared her for dealing with Belkin, living in a city of millions gave her a unique perspective. One was that until she arrived in Telluride, Viktoria had never experienced complete silence. At first, the lack of noise was unsettling, but it took no time to become used to the beauty in quiet. That also led to a heightened sensitivity to noise and interruption. She hoped that, like she, Peter Belkin now appreciated a soundless night and would instinctively do anything to bring it back.

Following Cody's example, Viktoria stayed well into the trees and continued to circle the A-frame house. The twin to the SUV she and Cody had used to escape the cabin sat in the middle of the circular drive. It was all Viktoria needed.

Careful to make sure she was far down the drive, thus hiding footprints left in the snow, Viktoria crossed the driveway and approached the vehicle. She pulled up on its door handle and tensed, turned and made ready to run. The alarm she hoped to hear never came. She pulled again and again, harder each time. Exertion and irritation mixed. Sweat collected on her brow, her lip and pooled at the small of her back. In frustration, Viktoria kicked the front panel. The SUV rocked. *Ah-ha.*

Aiming carefully, Viktoria kicked her heel into the headlight. The plastic covering slipped back. A second later, the horn began blaring and the lights flashed. Viktoria didn't waste any time congratulating herself and melted back into the surrounding trees.

The sound came from the front of the house. Belkin flicked his cigarette over the rail. The glowing ember hissed as it disappeared into the rapidly gathering snow. The honking continued, screeching with urgency. Turning on his heel, Belkin entered the rented house, careful to lock the door behind him.

Dusting snow from his hair, he wondered what kind of faulty system had caused the SUV's alarm to turn on without reason.

Unless there was a reason.

As far as the kidnapping went, he'd thought of

everything. And yet it would be asinine to let his guard down now.

The blaring alarm grew louder, now a cacophonous and shrill beep that Belkin knew could be heard at the neighboring houses, even though the closest one was a full kilometer away. Still, he took a minute and paused at his laptop. After saving the information on RMJ, he quickly placed the electronic document in a password-protected file. The Cody Samuels file was still open, yet the noise from the SUV grew. Belkin simply closed the document and powered down his computer, leaving it where it sat.

Using the peephole, he spied the car and saw nothing amiss. Still, prudence kept him from opening the door. The SUV's key fob sat in a nearby cubby. Through the door, Belkin pointed the fob at the blaring and flashing automobile. He hit the alarm button. The lights and noise ceased.

He took a moment to watch the thick, downy flakes fall outside. How odd that this mountainous state would remind Belkin strongly of his homeland. He longed to feel the frozen air of Moscow bite his face, or watch the ice floes on the Moskva River from the middle of the Borodinsky Bridge.

With one last look at the sky, Belkin turned from the door. He never saw the person who rushed toward him from behind. All he knew was a searing pain in his head along with warmth on his face. And then, nothing.

Cody shook his hand out to loosen his knuckles as Belkin tumbled, unconscious, to the floor. Two knockouts in one night. Not bad, thought Cody—better than his record as a member of the University of Colorado boxing team. He pulled the Russian mobster across the foyer and opened the front door before stepping out onto the stoop. Viktoria materialized from the shadows and sprinted across the driveway. She took the stairs two at a time and entered the house. Cody closed the door behind her and engaged the lock. He whipped off Belkin's belt, using it to bind his wrists, before turning to Viktoria.

"There are levels both up and down," he whispered. Until he had a chance to search the house, he couldn't be certain that Belkin was alone. He drew his gun, his arm tense and ready to shoot. "I'll search right away, but first we need to take care of this guy." Cody nudged the prone Belkin with his foot.

"Take care of him how?"

Was he going to have to list all of Belkin's misdeeds to justify to Viktoria that Belkin might deserve to die? "Listen, Peter Belkin is a bad man. His job is to make all the Mateev family's problems go away. He might not pull a trigger or sell a gram of illegal drugs personally, but he makes it possible all the same."

"I know," said Viktoria. "It's just…"

"Mommy?"

Cody whirled around at the sound, his firearm raised. A bleary-eyed Gregory Mateev stood at the edge of the foyer. He lowered the gun as Viktoria rushed to her son, lifting him into her arms as silent tears slid down her cheeks. She nuzzled his face and he rested his head on her shoulder, mumbling about being kidnapped by bad men.

Cody's throat tightened at the sight, and, figuring that mother and son needed a moment of privacy, he checked all the rooms upstairs and downstairs. The house was as he had assumed all along—empty, save for Belkin and Gregory. Cody finished his search in the kitchen. Viktoria and her son followed only a moment later. Cody couldn't miss the striking resemblance between the two.

"That one, the one by the door, was the worst. And then," continued Gregory taking in a deep breath, "that same bad man put a needle in my arm. It hurt a lot, and I think I fell asleep because I woke up in a bed upstairs. Can we go home now?"

"They drugged you?"

Horrified, Viktoria held her son close again, as Cody's gaze skimmed the room. On the kitchen counter, next to the stove, sat three syringes filled with a clear liquid. To get her attention, Cody tapped the marble countertop next to the needles. Viktoria looked over. Her eyes narrowed.

"Who's he?" the kid asked of Cody.

"Gregory, honey, I want you to meet my new friend, Cody Samuels. He's the one who helped me find you."

Gregory nestled into his mother's arms farther, hiding half his face in his mother's shoulder. "Hi, Mr. Cody."

Beyond a niece and nephew, whom Cody hadn't

seen in over a year, he never spent time with kids. "You can just call me Cody."

"Gregory, can you sit at the table?" Viktoria asked. "Cody and I have to have a quick word before we leave."

Gregory held his mother's neck for a moment and then slid down and walked to the table. He traced his finger over the lid of Belkin's laptop.

Viktoria moved closer to Cody. "Kill the bastard," she hissed.

"I can't shoot Belkin with your son in the house," said Cody, surprised by his own quick change of mind. "That will give the kid all kinds of nightmares for the rest of his life."

She sighed and leaned against the counter. "So what do we do with Belkin now?"

That was the real question, wasn't it? "I don't like the idea of just leaving him here. He'll call for backup as soon as he comes to," said Cody. "But taking him with us is risky. Belkin's dangerous and I don't want to worry about controlling him while keeping you and Gregory safe at the same time. We obviously can't take him to the San Miguel County Sheriff's Office and I don't know if we can drive to another county in this weather."

"So, we stay here and keep an eye on him?"

"That's no good, either. What if one of the thugs shows up?"

She tilted her head and sighed. "We have another shoot-out, but this time we might not get away."

"Put him in time-out," Gregory called from the kitchen. "He definitely needs a time-out."

Cody looked at the kid. "Time-out?"

"Let me guess," said Viktoria with a smile. "You don't have any kids."

"You got me." He lifted his hands.

"Time-out is like when we were younger and grounded. But time-out is only for a few minutes, not a whole week. I usually send Gregory to his room."

"Sounds like being a kid is a whole lot easier now than it was when we were young." Then Cody groaned. "That makes me sound like an old fart, doesn't it?"

Gregory laughed. Cupping his hands, he used a stage whisper and said, "Cody said *fart*."

Cody would have to watch what he said in front of the kid. He picked up on everything and was smart, too. In fact, maybe so smart that he'd given them the best solution to their problem. "You know, Gregory. You actually might be on to something. Time-out sounds like the perfect place for Belkin." He looked at Viktoria. "If we lock Belkin in a room, we don't have to worry about him contacting his other thugs. Nor do we have to stay here, which might be dangerous."

"Or take him with us, which also would be dangerous," Viktoria said.

"Exactly," said Cody.

He moved to the open pantry and rapped his knuckles on the door. "It's solid wood, and unbreakable. The lever handle can be easily held in place by a chair back or tied together. It's a simple place to hold him. But we don't need fancy, only effective." The rest of his plan, Cody didn't share.

He grabbed the three syringes of sedative that sat on the counter, planning to fill Belkin's veins with whatever he had given the kid. And if three doses were too much for a body to handle? Well, Cody hardly cared if Belkin quietly died.

"Where are you going?"

Cody opened his palm to reveal the needles. "I think Belkin needs a long winter's nap."

Belkin's prone figure was sprawled across the floor. Blood leaked from his misshapen nose. Cody's chest filled with searing heat, his mind with images of death. A fist clamped around a throat. A hand placed over a nose and mouth. Or even an air bubble in the syringe... The list of quiet ways to dispatch Belkin was endless. Yet for him to slip away in a dream would be too easy for a monster like Belkin. He needed to be brought low—and to know that Cody had caused his downfall. He removed the plastic coverings and plunged all three needles into Belkin's arm.

The prudent thing would be for Cody to return to his truck for a set of flex-cuffs. Yet, he didn't like the idea of leaving Viktoria and Gregory alone. It was more than a real concern that she might slip away while he was gone. Cody now saw it as his responsibility to keep mother and son safe, which meant he would neither leave them alone with Belkin nor make them traipse through the growing blizzard.

It left Cody improvising with what was on hand. He returned to the kitchen and conducted a quick search of the drawers but didn't find anything useful. Maybe he'd be forced to cut the cord off a light or an appliance.

Looking around for something handy, his eye was immediately drawn to Viktoria. She sat at the kitchen table with Gregory on her lap, Belkin's laptop resting next to her elbow. He'd been using it right before they'd arrived. What kind of business had kept him awake after midnight? The desire to know what insider info Belkin might have on his computer about Mateev burned fiercely inside Cody. But they had more immediate problems. Then again, the laptop might provide just what he needed right now.

It took Cody only a few minutes to secure Belkin's hands with the cord from the laptop and drag him to the large pantry. He shut the door and placed the back of a kitchen chair under the doorknob. For good measure, he cut the cord from a lamp and tied the pantry handles to each other.

Cody found the phone line outside and jerked it from the wall, making it impossible for Belkin to call for help—even if he escaped.

Cody returned to the kitchen. Viktoria and Gregory remained at the table. "Let's get out of here."

Viktoria rose, with Gregory in her arms. The computer sat on the table. Cody stared at the laptop, fisting his hands, reminding himself the DEA followed strict protocol when seizing evidence. There was a chain of custody that maintained the integrity of the evidence for a fair trial, and hopefully a conviction.

But Cody wasn't with the DEA anymore—because of Belkin—and that meant that the rules no longer applied. He grabbed the computer and headed to the door. Viktoria followed.

"I'm so glad you found me, Mommy," Gregory said, as he held tight to his mother. "Those men were really scary."

She planted a soft kiss on the top of his head. "You're safe now, Captain Kiddo."

Gregory was returned to his mother, and Belkin would soon be arrested. It was a win for the good guys.

Then why did Cody feel so miserable?

"I'm ready to go, Mommy," Gregory said.

"I know, Captain Kiddo. I know." She sighed. "I'm not sure where we *can* go."

Damn. She was right. Cody could hardly take them back to the cabin where they'd been hiding out. Aside from the dead guy in the living room, the other thug might still be in the vicinity. A hotel was a possibility, but they'd need protection in such a public place. That left Cody with only one option—although truth be told, it was his preference—for professional reasons, as well as personal. "If you're ready," said Cody, "I know someplace real special."

Gregory lifted his head from Viktoria's shoulder. "Yeah? Where?"

Cody smiled. "You and your mom are coming to my house for Christmas Eve."

Chapter 8

Viktoria quickly reviewed her options.

She'd come to trust Cody. He had offered his home. On a practical level, staying with him made complete sense. All the same, Viktoria's insides quivered with excitement and trepidation. Now that Gregory was safe, Viktoria could no longer ignore the raw and primal draw of Cody Samuels. Her feelings were a tangle of wariness and desire. He was deadly and she was damaged.

Then again, she had no other choices.

"If you're sure," she said. "I don't want to put you out." Wow! That was weak.

Cody shook his head at her protest. "I insist," he said. He slipped out of his polar fleece jacket and draped it over Gregory's shoulders. Left only in a tight-fitting black turtleneck sweater, the muscles in his arms and shoulders were well-defined.

"We have a little bit of a walk to the truck and you need to stay warm," he said to Gregory.

Her son leaned his head on Viktoria's shoulder. She kissed his soft hair, swearing that she'd never let anything hurt her son ever again.

"Thanks, Cody," Gregory said, his voice muffled and small.

Cody's gesture was chivalrous, but the cold was a problem for everyone—Cody included. Especially as Viktoria was still wearing his coat. "Here." Viktoria began to maneuver Gregory so she could take off Cody's parka. "You need this."

"Keep it," said Cody as he opened the front door. "I'm tough. In fact, let me carry your boy."

It had been so long since she'd had anyone consider her comforts along with the needs of her son that she wanted to give in, even though she knew she shouldn't.

Cody reached for Gregory.

Her son began to wail. "No, I want Mommy."

Gregory's heartbeat raced; she felt fluttering in his chest. Viktoria smoothed back her son's hair. "I won't ever let you go," she assured him, promised herself. "He's had a rough night," she said to Cody.

"No need to explain," said Cody. "I get it."

With his arm on her elbow, he kept her steady as she maneuvered down the snow-covered steps. Again, her eyes were drawn to Cody's toned chest and arms. As she stepped into the storm, the snow swirling and the wind howling, Viktoria decided that a little admiration of his physique wasn't bad, especially if she only looked.

They followed the road to where Cody had parked the Range Rover. Viktoria did hand Gregory to Cody, and watched as her son was settled in the back seat, the large fleece jacket serving as both blanket and pillow. Viktoria snuggled into the passenger seat, resting her arm on the center console. Cody eased the Range Rover down the hill and then placed his arm next to hers. It was so close that she could feel the heat radiating off his skin. Viktoria looked down. Her fingers rested next to his, close and yet not touching.

Her lips still tingled where they had kissed. His taste was on her tongue. Her skin still remembered the feel of his hands as they traveled down her body. These past few months Viktoria had seen herself only as a mother. Yet, being this close to Cody made her remember that she was also a woman with needs that went beyond the maternal.

Perhaps it was the months of solitude that drew her to him, and not his eyes or his chiseled profile or his broad shoulders. And maybe her awakened desire had more to do with overcoming death and a need to live than Cody's sense of duty, honor, or the way every nerve ending had responded to the press of his hard body against hers. Yet as brief scenarios of seduction played out in Viktoria's mind, she knew that her simple explanation was far from true.

There was something different about Cody Samuels. His physicality, his strength of character, his determination, courage…and yes, his gorgeous eyes and nice butt added to the allure.

"My house is close," he said. "Less than a mile now."

Viktoria was so lost in her thoughts that she had hardly noticed the drive. Although once Cody spoke, she looked out the window and immediately recognized the area from her trip into town. They drove through a narrow canyon of craggy black rocks that eventually led to the town of Telluride. As the canyon opened, brown roadside signs announced directions to the various parts of the ski area. A dozen or so shops that both rented and sold skis and snowboards lined the road. White Christmas lights circled each window and illuminated the displays of jackets, hats and ski pants that were sold there, as well.

Cody took a left-hand turn and the Range Rover skidded, heading for a small pine tree. He expertly righted the vehicle and they drove another quarter of a mile before he pointed out the window. "That's it," he said, "right up there."

A blue cottage with red trim came into view. Snow stood halfway up the railing that surrounded the porch. A front light glowed golden through the ever-falling flakes. Next to the cottage sat a detached garage with the same paint scheme.

"It's perfect," Viktoria breathed. "Magical, almost."

"Well." Cody moved closer. "It's home." He eased the car into the drive.

Home. Viktoria envied Cody for having a place to which he could return, no matter how far he wandered. Would she ever again have a place to call her own?

Their hands had shifted during the drive, now resting next to each other on the console. Flesh pressed against flesh. Viktoria expected Cody to withdraw. Instead, he twined his pinky with hers and leaned toward her. His breath warmed her neck and yet gooseflesh gathered on her arms.

"You smell nice," he said. "Like the snow."

His words took her breath away. Viktoria leaned closer. She wanted him to kiss her. To grab her and pull her to him and take control.

He stroked the side of her cheek and his thumb trailed to her lip. "I think we have some business from the woods to continue."

"What business is that?" she whispered.

"Something about a kiss."

She bit her bottom lip. "I was hoping that you remembered."

Cody placed his mouth on hers and a groan of longing escaped her throat.

"Mommy?" Gregory's sleepy voice came from the back seat.

Viktoria moved away from Cody. Pressing her back into the seat, she gave a nervous laugh. "Yeah, Captain Kiddo?"

"I need to go potty."

Cody turned off the vehicle and opened his door. Pocketing the keys, he said, "I can show you where the bathroom is, Gregory." He moved to the back of the Range Rover and opened the door. "Hold my neck. The snow's pretty deep and we don't want to get your pajamas wet and cold."

Viktoria followed the duo after retrieving the laptop and closing all the Range Rover's doors. Gregory rested his head on Cody's shoulder. As Viktoria watched Cody Samuels with her son, she added *compassionate* to the growing list of qualities to admire.

Gregory lifted his head from Cody's shoulders. Her son placed his little hands on each side of Cody's face. "You saved me from those bad men, didn't you?"

"I helped a little, but your Mommy did most of the saving," said Cody.

"Yes, but she's my mommy and she always keeps me safe. Since you helped and you didn't have to it makes you a hero." Gregory pressed his forehead into Cody's so the two were eye to eye. "You are *my* hero."

"Thanks, Gregory," Cody said.

His voice was slower, deeper, too, and Viktoria swore that she heard a hitch of emotion in his words.

Cody scooted Gregory to his hip, removed his key from a pocket in his pants and opened the front door. He set Gregory on the floor and flipped a wall switch that turned on a tableside lamp. "The bathroom is that door over there," said Cody as he pointed to the left.

Gregory rushed for the room indicated and shut the door with a loud *thump.* It was then that Viktoria looked around the cottage. The bottom floor was a single room that encompassed a kitchen, dining area and living room.

Cody's taste in decorating had a definite southwestern influence. While most of the walls were covered in vertical planks of stained pine, one wall was stone, with a large fireplace in the middle. A large TV was mounted over the mantel; an image of the room was reflected in its flat screen. A wooden banister wound to the second story. The coffee table was made of a sanded and veneered tree stump. The sofa and loveseat were both upholstered with Native American–inspired fabric in tones of blue and orange. A recliner of coordinating blue leather had a cowhide draped over the back.

But it was the ceiling that caught her attention. Squares of ornately pressed tin sat above her head. The one directly above the door showed a picture of a chubby baby Cupid, complete with bow and arrow. For the first time, Viktoria wondered about Cody's love life.

In one part of her brain she had assumed that he lived in a cluttered bachelor pad with mismatched hand-me-down furniture. But to her, this house didn't reflect the sensibilities of a single guy. Instead it spoke of security. Closeness. Romantic evenings before the fire. If he was in a relationship she should be irate that he'd kissed her with such passion earlier. Although if he was taken, she'd be more disappointed than anything.

Viktoria ran her hand over the cool cinnamon-colored marble of the kitchen counter. "Your home is lovely," she said. "Who did your decorating?"

Cody gave a noncommittal shrug. "Most of the furniture was here when I bought the place."

The need to know if he had been available to kiss her in the woods—and might be again—gnawed at Viktoria. She searched the walls, looking for pictures of Cody and another woman. There were none. In fact, the only personal photo was on the refrigerator. It was a Christmas card from a family of four.

"All the furniture?"

"RMJ pays me better than the DEA. I needed a way to spend my money after landing this gig. My territory is the southern part of the state, and a ski place in Telluride sounded good. I bought the place decorated and then went to a local art dealer for some Navajo pieces."

"Oh," she said, suddenly tired. In Viktoria's estimation, men never went to art dealers unless a woman told them to go, and she should know. Before Gregory was born, Viktoria had worked at a Manhattan art gallery. A good bit of business came from society girlfriends hoping to make the house of their investment-banker boyfriends into a home for them both. "And your girlfriend," Viktoria said, trying to be professional or at least not emotional, "does she like the art you bought?"

"I don't have a girlfriend," Cody said.

Viktoria stood up straighter. "You don't?" Good god. She just gushed, hadn't she?

"If I had a girlfriend," he said as he came to stand

beside her, face-to-face. Viktoria's mouth went dry and her palms grew damp. "I wouldn't have kissed you."

Her eyes were drawn to his mouth and the words that he formed. She brushed her thumb over his bottom lip. "Even if the kiss was just for luck?"

"Just? There was nothing as simple as a *just* in that kiss."

Cody's hand slipped around her waist. Viktoria allowed him to pull her closer. Heat collected between their bodies.

From the bathroom came the unmistakable sound of a toilet flushing.

"Gregory," said Viktoria, taking a step back.

"Gregory," said Cody. His hands dropped from her waist. "He's quite a kid. You ought to be proud of yourself. You're a heck of a mom and good moms are hard to find."

Heat crept up Viktoria's face as pride swelled in her chest. The bathroom door opened and Gregory stepped out. Yawning, he rubbed his eyes.

"Are you ready for bed, Gregory?" Cody asked. "I have a special place for you upstairs. It's right below the peaked roof, so the ceiling is slanted. Very cool."

"Very cool," said Gregory, his eyes bright. Then his tiny brow creased. "Hey, Mom, how come Cody doesn't have a Christmas tree?" Gregory asked.

"Since it's just me here I didn't much feel like decorating," said Cody, answering the question for her.

"That's sad," said Gregory.

It was. And yet there was no need to make Cody

feel worse. "Gregory," she said, as she lifted a single eyebrow and gave him the *mom look.* "Stop asking Cody private questions."

"But Mommy," he whined. "I think it's sad and I don't want Cody to be sad, especially at Christmas."

"And I think that we've had a long day and you should get ready for bed."

"You'll sleep with me, Mommy? Right? Just in case those bad men come back?"

"You're safe here," said Viktoria. "But of course I'll sleep with you." Truth to tell, Viktoria probably needed the reassurance of her son's presence more than he needed her. "You go upstairs and I'll be right behind you."

She waited while Gregory shuffled across the floor and up the stairs.

"I cannot thank you enough," she said and stopped. She searched for the right words to express her deep gratitude and found none.

Cody hitched his thumb to a phone that sat on the counter. "I'm going to check in with my boss at RMJ. He'll need to start making phone calls to the Department of Justice regarding Peter Belkin and his crew."

"Good night, then." Viktoria walked to the stairs.

"Do you need anything?" Cody asked. "Clean sweats? A T-shirt?"

Viktoria opened Cody's coat to reveal the fleece pants and long-sleeved tee she slept in. "I was in bed when we were attacked. So, I guess I'm ready."

"Then sleep well."

"Although, this is yours." Viktoria slipped off the coat and held it out as she walked to Cody.

"Thanks."

His fingers brushed hers as he took the jacket and Viktoria paused.

"You're welcome." Viktoria turned to follow Gregory. Part of her had hoped Cody would kiss her again, yet she was fearful of the emotions and desires that came with that longing. Instead, she took her mixed feelings and went up the stairs to tuck her son into bed.

There were two things that Dimitri learned during his years in the Russian army. The first had to do with prostitutes in Saint Petersburg and was hardly applicable now. The second was that food and sleep were essential and should be taken whenever available.

He woke, remembering quickly that he had fallen asleep in the driver's seat of a car, parked in a garage of a home.

After walking for more than an hour in the strengthening storm, Dimitri had stumbled upon a secluded residence. He'd broken into the attached garage and silently stolen the car key, conveniently placed on a hook by the door.

The trusting nature of Americans always shocked and amused him. Not that he minded, but a Russian would never make their car so easy to steal.

Not wanting to make too many suspicious noises

at the same time, he'd decided to wait. It was then that he fell asleep.

Dimitri scrubbed his face and then turned the ignition to power the battery. The clock on the dash glowed—3:04. *Damn.* Several hours gone. If he were going to get to Belkin, then Dimitri had to act now.

Dealing with the car would be easy, as he could put it in Neutral and push it from the garage. But first he had to get the garage door lifted with an electric opener noisy enough to wake most anyone. The village where Dimitri grew up had few amenities. In fact, he hadn't seen a color TV until joining the army. Yet, he'd learned and now knew that most garage doors had a safety release. He hoped that this one wouldn't be an exception. He exited the car and climbed onto the roof, careful to be silent. As he'd anticipated, there was a handle that if pulled, disconnected the door from the opener.

Dimitri lifted the door upward manually. The storm he left a few hours before was very different from the one that greeted him now. The predicted blizzard had hit the area full force, creating near-whiteout conditions. Still, Dimitri had information that Belkin needed. Luckily the snow was light and powdery; he'd still be able to move the car through it if he left without further delay. He returned to the auto. Sliding the gearshift to Neutral, Dimitri released the break and pushed the car straight back and into the night.

Cody listened to Viktoria's footfalls as she trod down the hallway of the second floor. He strained to take in the muted conversation that passed between mother and son, but heard nothing beyond muffled voices.

When Viktoria's voice from upstairs went quiet, Cody picked up the phone. He dialed the home number for Ian Wallace, his boss at RMJ. At the first ring, Cody checked the time. The clock on the microwave read 3:07 a.m.

The second ring came and Cody wandered to the kitchen. He filled a glass with tap water and sipped. True, it was an obscene hour to call, but if all that had happened that evening didn't count as an emergency, Cody didn't know what would. The third ring was followed by a fourth, and then his boss's sleepy voice came over the line. "A bit early for a call, Samuels? Or rather late."

Cody set aside his glass and moved to the sofa. "There have been some complications with the Mateev case."

"How so?"

For the next several minutes, Cody relayed the story. He didn't leave out a single event—including his killing the thug to save Viktoria's life. Cody knew that all his illegal activities had been justified and in the end, he would never face criminal charges. At the same time, he also knew that trying to hide any unpleasant truths was the best way to be implicated in wrongdoing.

After a moment of silence, Ian exhaled. "One point of clarification. You never actually saw Peter

Belkin at the scene of the kidnapping. You only found the boy in a home that you believe he rented?"

Cody leaned back into the sofa. Closing his eyes, he rubbed his forehead. "Both points are correct, but Sheriff Benjamin clearly stated that Peter Belkin both bribed and threatened him for information regarding Viktoria Mateev's whereabouts. And the communication we intercepted from the abductors mentioned Belkin personally, as well."

"We can only hope that Sheriff Benjamin corroborates your story."

"I think he will when pressed."

"I'm going to contact someone I trust with the Colorado Bureau of Investigation. Attempted murder is state crime, so they'll have jurisdiction. They might also retain control of the kidnapping case, since the child never left Colorado. Until this is sorted out, keep Viktoria and her son with you at all times."

"Right."

Cody gave Ian all the information on Belkin's rental house.

"Before ringing off," said Ian, "I think it best that we only communicate through landlines. We don't want to make it easy for Viktoria and her son to be found by tracking cell phone signals."

"Sure," said Cody.

"If there's nothing else, I'll be in contact later."

Cody paused, uneasy about ending the call without disclosing why he had been at the cabin in the first place. Yet, why had he been given the case?

Was it truly a random coincidence, or was Ian also keeping secrets? "There's one last thing. It's about the Mateev family."

"Yes?"

"You know the history of why I left the DEA. That I shot a CI and the gun was never found." Cody paused. He'd shared all the details of tonight with the man, but as Cody's boss, Ian was entitled to the facts. Could he also share secrets from the past? "What I didn't tell you was that the CI was helping me build a case against some major drug dealers. I was in the early stages of pulling together information when the shooting occurred, but he'd given me a crucial name." Cody hesitated. "It was the same name that made me take the extra steps tonight."

Silence followed his confession. Cody listened to the wind howl as it sped down the mountain.

"Her name is Viktoria Mateev. And the drug dealer I was after is Nikolai Mateev."

"And you think she's related to Nikolai?"

"I know she is—she's his daughter-in-law."

"Is she involved with the family business?"

"I don't know."

"Then it seems as if you need to keep her close and see what you can learn."

Ian was right. And yet… "What do you know about that family?"

More silence. More empty howls from the wind.

"I've heard of the Mateevs before," said Ian.

"Not from me," Cody said quickly. "Except for being let go after the shooting, all the information I just shared was classified and now I want full disclosure from you."

"I can't tell you everything."

"Tell me how I fit into the picture. Did you know about the Mateev connection when you hired me?"

Before he could ask another question, Ian spoke. "You were onto something while at the DEA, Cody. But this crime syndicate is huge. It's a kraken and would have swallowed you whole—it almost got you killed. But together, we can take it down."

"Taking down the Mateev family is all I want," said Cody, "But who is Nikolai to you?"

"What I'm about to tell you is top secret, password protected. I was supposed to forget all this information when I left MI5, but I can't."

"I know how to keep a secret," Cody said.

"Nikolai Mateev grows poppies for his heroin in Afghanistan. Those fields are protected by al-Qaeda."

"Let me guess—some of the drug profits have been used to fund terrorism."

"Exactly. But, Nikolai has friends in high places and my investigation was shut down."

"Sounds familiar," said Cody.

"Yes," Ian agreed. "It does.

"Find out everything you can from Viktoria."

Cody began to explain that he'd already questioned her and she knew less than he did. Her son had been taken from her. Wasn't she the victim?

Then again, she was a Mateev—a master manipulator. He couldn't let his attraction to Viktoria cloud his judgment.

"I'm on it," Cody said.

He ended the call and placed the phone in the charger before returning to the living room. Leaning back on the sofa, Cody closed his eyes. His head throbbed and his shoulder ached. His hands began to tremble as he recalled the moment when he'd pulled the trigger, ending the life of Belkin's henchman. He didn't feel remorse, exactly. He knew it was the only reason Viktoria was alive right now. All the same, taking a life was never uncomplicated.

There was a lot to regret—broken promises, destroyed relationships—but maybe this was a chance for Cody to redeem himself.

He looked around his house and for the first time, found it lacking. It was true that Cody had completely ignored the holiday. He should at least have gotten a Christmas tree. Didn't he still own a stand from several years ago? He thought it was in the storage room, right behind the bags of gifts he'd bought for his sister and her family last year—before the fight.

He walked to the kitchen and retrieved Sarah's Christmas card. For years, it had been just him and his sister against the world. He remembered all those Christmases when presents were passed around in bags from the store. Clothes that didn't fit, toys without batteries, books he had no interest in reading.

It wasn't that the holidays needed to be about gifts; it was the disappointment in knowing that their happiness had been an afterthought.

He put the card back on the fridge, determined to

make a difference for Gregory Mateev. The kid was only four, goddamn it. Someone that age shouldn't deal with danger and kidnappings and worrying whether he'd ever see his mother again. Especially at this time of the year, he should only be excited about Santa's visit.

Cody knew what needed to be done. Slipping into his coat, he inhaled deeply. Viktoria's scent still clung to the fabric. He liked it and wondered how long it would stay. He found the tree stand and a saw in the storage room. Tucking a flashlight into his pocket, he left the house. Snow already filled the grooves cut by his tires. Wind lashed around the cabin, turning the flakes into projectiles that sliced Cody's cheeks and chin. Snow collected in the collar of his coat and quickly melted into an icy rivulet that ran down his back.

He was damned uncomfortable, but he was equally undeterred.

There, at the corner of his lot, stood a lonely little pine tree. Cody knelt at the base and began to saw. The sharp tang of sap filled the air, and he wondered if there was a more noble calling for a pine than to become a Christmas tree for a child on the run.

Chapter 9

December 24
8:30 a.m.

The rich, dark aroma of coffee brewing, along with the scent of pine, pulled Viktoria from sleep. For a solitary moment, she hung in a blissful state between oblivion and wakefulness. For those few seconds, she wasn't even sure where she was—perhaps the home of her parents. Where else had she felt so safe and loved?

Stretching, Viktoria broke the spell and woke fully. Panic, icy and sharp, stabbed at her chest. Her throat tightened as memories of being attacked the previous night crashed down with the weight of an avalanche. Feeling trapped and needing to escape, she threw off the covers and struggled to her feet. A sheen of cold sweat coated her skin. Her gaze traveled around the unfamiliar space.

Then the rest of the night came to her in a rush. *Cody Samuels.* He'd been her savior, and not only had he found Gregory, but he'd gotten him back. Gratitude for the man in whose home she now knew she stood left her weak and Viktoria sank back onto the bed.

Soft light filtered through the sheer curtains of the dormer windows, casting the room in a muted halo of white. Gregory lay beside her, spread out across the entire bed—save for the small section where she had slept. His chest rose and fell steadily with each deep breath.

She sent up a prayer for her son. It was in moments like this that she realized how unfairly she'd treated her own parents, leaving New York without a word to anyone—her parents included. She imagined her mother and father panicked with worry. She also imagined that if they'd been faced with similar circumstances they would have done no different.

Eventually, they'd be reunited. Could it be soon?

She stroked her son's hair back from his forehead, needing to touch him and make sure that this moment was real. It was. She rose carefully and silently slipped from the room, heading downstairs.

Nestled into the corner of the living room sat a small Christmas tree. Viktoria stopped short, her chest suddenly tight with emotion. Cody had made a kind gesture to her son; at the same time, he was a man capable of taking a life. Since her first glimpse of Cody Samuels, she had been trying to figure him out. Now she had to admit he was more of a puzzle to her than he had been before.

She needed time to think and pivoted, ready to retreat to the bedroom. The stair underfoot creaked. She froze.

"Morning," he said. Cody sat at the kitchen table. He held a cardboard box in one hand and pair of scissors in the other. At his elbow was a box of paperclips along with several markers and a glue stick.

And now he was crafting?

"I didn't mean to interrupt. I was just…"

"Come down." He waved her over with a piece of cardboard. "Let me show you what I have planned."

Viktoria smiled, her insides as gooey as caramel. And it wasn't just the surprise Christmas tree, either. It was Cody and the way he looked. He was dressed in a navy zip sweater and jeans. The dark blue of the sweater offset the light blue of his eyes. His dark hair was slicked back and still wet from the shower. A sprinkling of stubble covered his cheeks and chin. To her, Cody looked casual, comfortable and undeniably handsome.

She ran her hand through her tangled hair. Her hands caught in the snarled ends and she worked them free. Until this very second, she hadn't worried about her appearance. Gregory was safe and she was lucky to simply be alive. That was all that mattered. But now, along with those priorities, she also found herself wanting to look good. Wanting to feel attractive again. For Cody.

"I hope I didn't wake you." Cody set aside his scissors.

"The aroma of your coffee did, thankfully," she said. Viktoria grabbed her hair and swept it over her shoulders. She hoped that most of the mess was hidden behind her back.

Cody rose from the table. "Have a seat and let me get you a cup."

Viktoria took the seat next to the one Cody had just vacated. From a cabinet above the sink, Cody fetched a blue-and-green pottery mug.

"So, I have to ask about the tree," she said. "You went out in the middle of the night and bought a tree because Gregory said you needed one?"

"This is Colorado," he said. A smile teased his lips. "We don't buy trees. We cut them down."

"I bought a tree," Viktoria challenged good-naturedly.

"Those are set aside for New Yorkers who don't know any better."

He set a mug of hot coffee in front of her. "Milk?" he offered. "Sugar?"

She gave a noncommittal shrug. "Either or neither, I'm fine."

"After all we've been through together, please don't act like a polite houseguest."

"Are you saying you'd rather I be rude?" she teased. "I am from New York City and people always think that we specialize in rudeness."

Cody smiled and Viktoria's insides tingled a little bit. "You can be whatever you want to be with me. I guess that's what I'm saying."

"Then I need both milk and sugar," she said. "A lot of both."

He set a carton of half-and-half before her, along with a sugar bowl that matched her coffee cup. Viktoria did a long pour of cream and then scooped in three spoons full of sugar. She stirred and sipped. "Ah," she sighed. "Almost human."

"Just watching you drink all that sugar makes my teeth ache, you know," Cody said with a grin.

"And now who's being rude?"

"Spoken like a true New Yorker."

"I'll take that as the highest compliment."

Viktoria liked the easy banter they slid into, maybe a little too much. "Have you heard anything about Belkin?" she asked. She wouldn't feel safe until that man was in jail.

"Not a thing. I talked to my boss last night and he's making calls. Getting arrest warrants and search warrants takes time."

"It's been hours. How long do these things take?"

"The calls were made in the middle of the night, on Christmas Eve, in the middle of a blizzard."

She sighed. "We don't have any choice but to wait, do we?"

"None," said Cody. "But since we're stuck inside today, I figured we could make ornaments for our little tree." He returned to the table with a glass coffeepot and refilled his own mug.

"No offense, but I wouldn't expect a single guy like yourself to think of that."

Cody leaned his hip into the counter and faced her. "When I was little, money was tight. Every year my sister and I would decorate our Christmas tree with stuff we made. Those are happy memories for me. Most of them, at least." He took a swig of coffee. "By the way, what do you want for breakfast? I don't mean to brag, but I make a fabulous bacon-and-cheese omelet."

Viktoria was hungry for more than food. She also wanted information, and was starving to know everything about Cody Samuels. She wanted to know all the details of his childhood, his family...and why he'd seemed so unwilling to celebrate Christmas before she and Gregory crossed his doorstep. And yet, she didn't want to pry. Instead she said, "A bacon-and-cheese omelet sounds perfect."

Cupping her hands around her mug, Viktoria rose from the table to peer out the kitchen window. The snow that had begun last night still fell, thick and heavy. When they had arrived at the cabin the drift had only been halfway up the bannister. Now the entire railing was covered and the Range Rover was little more than a snowy hill by the house. The huge mountain peaks that she knew to be close were lost in the complete whiteness of the storm.

"Kind of makes you feel like we're inside a snow globe," Viktoria said.

Cody set a bowl on the counter alongside a carton of eggs. "I've never thought about it that way, but it does."

"What can I help you with?" Viktoria asked. "Bacon?"

"You can, although I was going to let you shower while I cook."

His remark brought back to mind the feeling of last night. The terror and violence still clung to her skin. "That would be wonderful," she said.

Cody cracked an egg into a mixing bowl. "There are towels under the sink and a washcloth, too. I have a set of clean sweats in the dryer, if you want to grab those." He pointed the spatula toward a laundry room. "Shampoo and soap are in the shower. Feel free to open a new toothbrush in the drawer and if you don't think it's too weird, you can use my comb. Now go," he ordered.

Viktoria retrieved a set of sweats—University of Colorado Boxing Team was written across the chest and down the leg—and headed into the bathroom. Like the rest of the house, the space was small, but well-appointed. The same marble countertop from the kitchen had been used as the bathroom vanity. A copper bowl sink sat underneath a mirror. A water closet was hidden behind another door and a glass-paneled shower stood opposite the sink.

Viktoria took out a set of plush gray towels and undressed. Stepping into the shower, she turned the handle toward hot. As the water cascaded over her body, Viktoria let all the memories of the previous night slip away. Well, except for a few she wanted to keep—like Cody's tempting kiss.

Cody set to work on a mixture of eggs and milk, with a touch of salt and pepper. Once his griddle was preheated he placed the bacon in a row. Immediately it began to sizzle and fill the kitchen with its salty, sweet aroma.

Cody had taught himself how to cook while in college. As a kid on scholarship, he didn't have tons of extra cash to eat out and the food in the dining halls was always too unhealthy to bother with. In truth, he didn't mind cooking. It gave his mind time to wander. And today was no exception. His thoughts weren't too far from kitchen, though—they'd traveled to the shower with Viktoria.

Cody exhaled and imagined her naked—hot and wet—with foam sliding down her breasts and her thighs. Forcing himself to turn his mind back to the meal, he flipped the bacon—almost done—and retrieved a block of sharp cheddar from the fridge.

As he set about shredding the cheese, the image of kissing Viktoria came to him. But it was more than her raw sexuality that interested Cody. It was the total package of Viktoria Mateev. She was smart, funny and oh-so brave.

"Focus, damn it," he mumbled. Beyond her looks, intelligence and wit, Viktoria Mateev was still Nikolai Mateev's daughter-in-law. And the best chance Cody had to clear his name.

* * *

Viktoria rinsed her hair one last time and turned off the shower. She felt revived and renewed. It was as if the hot water and soap had somehow washed away more than just dirt, but also some of what she had endured. Now she had to face the day—hopefully one that found Peter Belkin in jail and her no longer facing criminal charges.

After drying quickly, she found the new toothbrush he had told her about and brushed her teeth. She wrapped her hair up in a messy bun at the nape of her neck and then dressed in Cody's college sweats. It seemed crazy that only last night Cody had saved her life. It felt like yesterday belonged in another lifetime.

Dressed and refreshed, Viktoria found that the kitchen table had been cleared of cardboard. There was a mug of steaming coffee, a glass of orange juice and the most delectable omelet she'd ever seen waiting for her on a plate. Cody stood at the stove sliding a second omelet onto another plate for himself.

"Sit," he said without turning around. "You don't want your food to get cold."

Viktoria took a bite of the omelet. It was perfect. "You're a very good cook," she said, washing down a bite with a swallow of tangy-sweet juice.

"Actually, this is my specialty." Cody pointed at his plate with his fork. "I like cooking but my skills are pretty basic."

Before rushing into Viktoria's cabin, Cody had had a life of his own. The chance to learn more about Cody hung like a loose thread and Viktoria was tempted to work it free. At the same time, she didn't have any right to pry into Cody Samuels's private life.

"You must really love skiing to have a house so near the slopes."

"Growing up without a lot of money is hard anywhere, I suppose. But in Colorado poor kids don't get to ski the way the rich ones do. Not having a season's pass at a resort hanging off your winter coat makes a kid feel like he's not worthy." He ate a bite of his omelet. "Once I'd saved enough money for this place, I bought it. Kind of sounds silly when I say it out loud but it's a symbol of accomplishment to me."

"I admire that you made your dream come true. Not many people can say that."

"A dream? Sure. But I do love to ski. There's nothing like being on the slopes. The powder. The speed. Being in control, but always on the edge."

"Sounds exhilarating. There's skiing in New York State and all over the Northeast, but I never took up the sport. It's not a huge deal like it is in Colorado." Viktoria glanced at the window. The falling snow now clung to the pane, obscuring the view even more.

Cody wiped his lips. "Ski and work, it seems like that's my life."

"We all need to be productive. Then we need downtime and a hobby," she said, although Viktoria had the distinct feeling that Cody was sharing more than his schedule. She waited to see if he would add more.

He did. "I've worked hard my whole life and always played by the rules. Even though the DEA let me go, I thought that the job with Rocky Mountain Justice was a reward—along with this house and my expensive skis, you know?"

"They are. Right?"

Cody sipped his coffee slowly. "Most of the time they are, but sometimes they have less value than the paper ornaments I used to make as a kid."

She reached for his arm. Cody was lonely. His pain registered as an ache and an emptiness in her chest. She wasn't sure what to do, but somehow felt that sharing the silence would be more profound than anything she might say.

Without looking up, Cody said, "I'm not a workaholic, or some guy who doesn't have any friends." He lifted his gaze. "Although I do work a lot. But." He paused. "Well, I just wanted to let you know that I'm not some odd reclusive ski bum."

Viktoria squeezed his arm. "I never would have thought that of you. It sounds like you're close to your sister. Does she live nearby?"

He shrugged. "About an hour and a half away."

"What about your parents?" Viktoria asked, even more curious about Cody's family.

He took another sip of his coffee. "My parents liked to drink. It killed my father years ago, drunk-driving accident. Although it's not exactly accidental if you get behind the wheel of a car after consuming a twelve-pack of beer. My mother died not long after. My sister thinks it was from a broken heart."

"I'm sorry," said Viktoria, thinking about her own parents again and hoping that she could contact them soon. "The holidays can be hard."

"I did have plans for Christmas," he said, toying with pieces of omelet on his plate, "but they changed."

Viktoria sat back and took a sip of her coffee. He'd spoken so openly about the deaths of his parents but now he was getting all evasive about something as unremarkable as holiday plans. Cody was proving to be quite a mystery, one that she desperately wanted to solve. But to what end? She wished she understood her own motives a little better. Was this just idle curiosity to keep from worrying about her own life? Or was she developing feelings for Cody that were more profound than simple attraction and admiration? "My plans changed, too." She gave a little laugh at her dark humor and added a shrug.

"I guess you do win the award for the most derailed Christmas."

"Ok," she said, her palms lifted in surrender. "I give up. I'm not trying to be nosy, although obviously I am. What were your plans?"

Before she could add, *You don't have to say anything if you don't want*, Cody leaned forward.

He said, "I planned to get married tonight."

"Wow." Viktoria sat back, slumping in her seat. What a fool she had been! Drawn at first to the sensual appeal of Cody's dangerous side and then completely seduced by his good-natured charm—she was only a job to him. "Thanks for the sweats, by the way." She was now keener to change the subject than she had ever been to find out the truth.

"You're welcome," Cody said, taking a sip of coffee. "They're my favorites. Does what I just told you bother you?"

"No," said Viktoria, stabbing her omelet with her fork. Molten cheese oozed from the puncture marks. "Why would it?"

"Because of the kiss," Cody said.

"Isn't there a line in a poem that says something about kisses not being contracts?"

"I prefer that my actions mean something," he said.

"Because you want to be in control."

"Because unless you're deliberate, things unravel."

Unravel? Like this morning? Maybe it *was* best if Viktoria just worried about things that mattered to her and her life. "You said you were hired by the state of New York to find me…"

"A bench warrant was issued for your failure to appear in court and for taking Gregory from the state. If Ray Benjamin had done his job, you'd have been arrested and charged with kidnapping."

A wave of nausea crashed down on her. It was that feeling of an unrelenting fight ahead that roiled in her stomach. "Kidnapping," she repeated. "It doesn't make sense. How can I kidnap my own child? Gregory hadn't been removed from my custody yet."

"I can show you the RMJ file I received." Cody tapped on the screen of a tablet computer before handing it to her. "It's all there," he said.

It took several moments for Viktoria to read the few documents that put into question her qualifications as a custodial parent. "It's all lies," she said as she handed back the computer. "I never had a breakdown."

"After meeting you, I have no doubt that you're the best mom in the world."

"Thanks," she said. Her eyes stung and watered. She used the napkin to dab the corner of each eye, feeling even more grateful for having her son so close. "Thanks for trusting me. Thanks for believing me, too. You have no idea how hard it is to be wrongly accused. It's like fighting in a dark room. It feels like everything might be against you. Or it might only be shadows."

"Trust me," he said. "I do know."

Suddenly ravenous, Viktoria took a huge bite of her omelet. She chewed and swallowed. "It sounds like you have stories of your own."

"Yeah, but they're not very interesting."

"I doubt that," she said. "What if we each get to ask the other three questions?" Now she was determined to find out more about this man and who he really was.

"No."

"We can *pass* on one question if we want." Viktoria quickly made up rules as she spoke.

Cody shook his head, but gave a sardonic smile. "You go first."

She wanted to know everything, from his favorite color, to if he actually boxed in college, but one question topped her list. "Why aren't you at your own wedding today?"

"Pass."

Viktoria feigned indignation. "You can't pass on the first question."

"I can," he said, "and I will."

He sounded serious. "Maybe we shouldn't play games. After everything that's happened, there's really no reason to be silly."

Cody leaned back in his seat. "It's a boring story," he said. "There's not much to tell."

"Really, you don't owe me an explanation."

They sat in silence. Viktoria cursed herself for trying to…what? With Cody, everything was so confused. She pushed back from the table and stood. Cody gripped her wrist and looked at her with amazing blue eyes.

"Stay with me," he said. "I'll tell you."

Viktoria dropped back into the chair and Cody let go of her wrist.

"I had been in a serious relationship for two years. I left the DEA last December and I was angry at everything and everyone. I got the job at RMJ in April and felt that after all we'd been through marriage was a good idea. When I first mentioned the idea of a Christmas Eve wedding, she loved it." Cody pushed at the sides of his omelet. "And then one day she said it was over."

"That's awful. No reason? She was just done?"

"That's your second question."

"It's okay, as long as you answer."

"Of course there was a reason. I'm an investigator, aren't I? I found her emails. She'd been seeing another guy for a whole year, but didn't want to break up with me until I was reestablished." He gave a snort—not quite a derisive laugh, not quite a total rebuke. "That was her actual word—*reestablished.*"

"Good riddance to her if she can't see what a great guy you are."

"Do you?" He pinned her with his ice-blue gaze.

The room became airless and her loose clothes too tight. She licked her lips and recalled the feel of his mouth on hers. She wanted him to kiss her again, but knew she shouldn't. Reluctant to change the subject, she asked. "Is it your turn now? I thought I had one more question."

"I guess you do," he said.

"How are you doing?"

"Can I pass?"

"Not a chance."

He shrugged. "A happy life with a wife and kids probably isn't for me. My parents set a lousy example. So, it's best that she left before I messed everyone else up…" Cody ate a big bite of omelet. "That was your last question. Now, it's my turn," he lifted one brow.

She folded a leg under her, as her nerves hummed with trepidation. "Maybe this isn't the best idea."

"Fair is fair," he said with a smile. "Besides, you can pass on one question."

She relaxed a little.

"What happened to your husband?"

"He died in a car accident."

Cody nodded as if she had explained it all, yet she had told him next to nothing. What did he know? It was more than he was letting on, that was for sure. If Viktoria was ever going to be free of the Mateevs, she needed context for Lucas and his family. Could Cody provide her with that?

She continued, "A taxi hit him. Lucas was in medical sales. He had a meeting with a doctor, or so I was later told, at a bar. His blood alcohol level was high and he stepped out in front of a taxi. They never found the driver and no charges have ever been filed."

She paused and decided that even though she was only in for a penny of her thoughts, she would give a pound. "You want to know the worst part? Even though we had been separated for over half of a year when he died, I was still his next of kin. I had to make all the final arrangements and felt like a fraud at his funeral."

"That must've sucked," Cody said.

"Pretty much, but I guess we all have heartaches." Viktoria's appetite was gone, but she took a few more bites of her breakfast to keep from wasting the food. "You have two more questions to ask if you want."

Cody held Viktoria with his gaze. "Last night I kissed you."

"That's not a question," she said.

"Did you like it?"

"Yes." The small room suddenly became warm.

Cody reached for her, his fingers twining with hers. He pulled gently and she rose from her seat. He settled Viktoria on his lap and tucked a strand of hair behind her ear. He held her chin, tilting her face down toward his. His lips hovered next to hers; his breath became one with Viktoria's. "Would you like for me to kiss you again?"

She nodded, and barely a second later, their lips met and his tongue slid inside her mouth. Viktoria's body ached, feeling an emptiness that only Cody could fill. His hard erection was right beneath her and Viktoria reveled at the fact that he wanted her as much as she wanted him.

She arched her back, pressing her breasts closer to him. Cody's chest was firm, the muscles tight. His hand trailed from her cheek to her shoulder and finally rested on her waist. His fingertips found their way under the thick fabric of the sweatshirt. Viktoria leaned in to him farther. His hand traveled up her shirt, and his touch blazed a trail on her skin. He reached her naked breast and cupped her with his palm as the pad of his thumb traced a circle around her nipple. She gasped, kissing him deeper.

His mouth moved to her jaw and down her neck.

The desire to have Cody inside her became a need, a thirst, a hunger.

He released her breast, traced his hands to her waist. This time, he fumbled with the elastic of her pants. Viktoria was suddenly aware of two things. First, she very much wanted Cody as her lover. Second, her son was upstairs.

"What time is it? Gregory is just upstairs."

"It's still early," said Cody. "He's sleeping."

"I can't make love to you now," she said. "I won't be able to relax."

"Do you want me to stop?" Cody asked. His hand rested on her middle.

"No," she said. "Yes."

His hand traveled lower. "I can help you relax and we won't do anything you don't want to. Okay?"

She raked her fingers through his hair, kissing him deeply. "Okay."

His fingers grazed her hipbones. Lower still. "You aren't wearing any panties."

"You didn't loan me a pair."

"I might have to tell Santa to put you on the naughty list." Cody lightly stroked the top of her sex.

Desire, golden and molten, filled her veins and she groaned. Every part of her began to tingle. His thumb began to move in a circle as her desire grew. Every part of Viktoria thrummed, vibrating at a higher level. It was as if she were no longer flesh and blood, but emotion—love, desire, lust—and the physicality borne of the moment. She climaxed and for an all too brief instant, Viktoria felt as if she'd flown high enough to touch the heavens. Panting, she slipped back into her physical self. Cody's arms still held her, his mouth still claimed hers and Viktoria didn't know where she ended and Cody began. She nuzzled into his shoulder.

Cody stroked her hair and gently kissed her temple. He was still hard beneath her and she moved to straddle Cody. He held her face between his hands. His eyes took her in, studying her face, as if he were trying to memorize every line and contour.

"You are so beautiful," he said.

She ran her thumb over his lip. He licked her, and groaned. She did the same to him, just to see how he tasted. He was salty but the tang from the pine tree still clung to his skin.

"I want you," he said, his voice husky. "I want you like I've never wanted anything before."

She wanted him, too. To lose herself in the passion between them. To cast aside the months of worry and doubt in a single moment of ecstasy. Before she could say anything, a scream pierced the silent cabin.

"Mommy!" It was Gregory. "Mommy! Where are you? Please, I don't want the bad men to get me."

She had sprinted across the room before realizing that she had left Cody's side. Her foot hit the first stair and Viktoria knew that letting Cody distract her was a mistake. There was room for only one priority in her life—keeping her son safe.

Chapter 10

Gregory's expression, as he came down the stairs, was beyond compare. The kid's smile lit up his tiny face, the room and a big piece of Cody's heart. For the first time ever, Cody felt like he might be a hero to someone.

"A tree!" The kid's voice was a mixture of breathless wonder and joy. "You have a tree."

"We do, Gregory." The discomfort of the biting cold was long forgotten. "Santa must have brought it last night," Cody added. He didn't need credit for getting the tree. The look of joy on the kid's face was reward enough.

Gregory moved to the corner where the little pine stood. Standing on tiptoe, his fingertips brushed the uppermost bough. "Look, I touched the top. That means I can put the star on all by myself. That's neat, huh?" Then his gaze traveled around the room. "And presents? Did Santa bring presents, too?"

Damn. Cody hadn't thought about gifts. He looked at Viktoria. Her complexion paled. She let out a long breath and wrapped an arm around Gregory's shoulder.

"The snow's coming down pretty fast out there, Gregory," she said. "Santa might not be able to make it through the storm."

"Nah," said Gregory. "You always say his magic makes him able to get through anything, Mommy, no matter how hard it seems. He'll get here. We did, didn't we?"

Gregory's belief in Santa's powers—and his explanation for how he would get presents on Christmas—was sweetly naive. Yet Cody knew better. Viktoria did, too.

"You know, Gregory…" Viktoria took in a deep breath and Cody suddenly realized that she was trying to figure out how to tell her son that there was no Santa. He'd lived through too many rotten holidays to let Gregory lose the magic of Christmas at such a young age. He watched as Viktoria bit her lip and looked out the window. Tears clung to her lashes.

For a moment, Cody had the surreal feeling that he was living in a Christmas movie. This was not fiction, though, and there was no Rocky Mountain Santa who could help create that happy ending.

Unless.

Cody had a stash of gifts, bought for his niece

and nephew last year and never given. Until now, he never quite knew what to do with them.

"You're right, Gregory. Santa's magic can help him get through anything. I'm sure he'll have something special for you, even at my house."

"He will?" asked Viktoria. There was a sharp edge of irritation in her voice.

"He will. You have to trust me," said Cody. He lifted the remote to his flat-screen TV and pushed a few buttons. An animated version of *A Christmas Carol* came to life in HD. "There you go, Gregory. You and Mommy can watch some Christmas shows while I make breakfast."

Viktoria kissed her son on top of the head. "I'm going to help Cody. It's not fair for him to do all the work."

Cody was about to protest, but Viktoria grabbed his sleeve and towed him across the room and into the kitchen area. "I trust you," she breathed, her voice a low murmur. "I've trusted you with my life and Gregory's, as well. But, I'd prefer to tell Gregory if Santa's not coming, Cody. The disappointment will be easier to face today than tomorrow."

"I have gifts."

"You just happen to have a few random toys lying around your house?" she challenged.

"Actually," said Cody. He leaned into the kitchen counter. "They aren't random." He hitched his thumb toward the card on the fridge. "That's my sister and her family. Remember how I said I was angry about being fired? Well, I alienated more than my fiancée. Sarah and I had a huge fight right after I lost my job. We haven't spoken since, but before that, I had bought gifts for her kids. I didn't know what to do with the presents, so they're still here."

"But your sister invited you to spend Christmas with her this year. It looks like she's gotten over whatever angry words passed between you two."

"Don't you see, Viktoria? I'm not a good man. I don't do emotions. I don't apologize. Sarah and the kids are better off without me."

"You ended a relationship with your fiancée and your sister in a few months? That's awful."

"It's better than marrying a woman who doesn't love me."

"What about your sister?"

"That's complicated. I really don't want to talk about it."

"Oh, Cody, I'm so sorry."

"Don't pity me," he said with the shake of his head. "That's worse. Just let me give the toys to your son, okay?"

"I…" A single tear trailed down her cheek and she wiped it away with her sleeve. "I can't ask you to give gifts to Gregory that are meant for someone else."

"You didn't ask," he said, "and besides, I insist."

Viktoria pressed her lips together. "I'm so touched. I just don't know what to say."

"Just say thank you."

"Thank you," she said, "for everything."

Cody turned away from Viktoria. He couldn't let

her care about him, especially not when he was beginning to care about her even more.

The next two hours passed in relative peace. Viktoria found all the ingredients for her favorite holiday cookies and icing. As she baked, Cody kept Gregory busy with making ornaments.

Gregory lifted an ornament from the pile. On it was a picture of a Christmas tree. "This one is for you, Cody, because Santa brought you a special tree."

"Wow, Gregory. That's the nicest gift I've ever been given," Cody said.

Her son certainly enjoyed Cody's company and seemed to look up to him, even after such a short time. She also knew that Gregory needed the attention and guidance of a good man—despite what he said—someone like Cody Samuels. Warmth filled Viktoria's heart and at the same time, it left her adrift with no place to moor. She prayed for word soon that Peter Belkin had been taken into custody. Until this nightmare was over, Viktoria couldn't truly relax.

She moved to the living room and sat on the sofa. Cody and Gregory were busy trimming the tree. Paperclips had been fashioned into hooks that held ornaments, which now hung from various branches.

"What do you think?" Gregory asked with a smile.

"That," said Viktoria, "is the most beautifully decorated tree I have ever seen."

"That's a pretty big compliment," said Cody.

"It's well deserved."

Gregory moved to Viktoria's side on the sofa. He leaned into her and she wrapped her arms around his shoulders.

"Can we decorate cookies now?" he asked with a yawn.

Even from where she sat, the clock above the stove was easily seen—11:30 a.m. "The cookies need time to cool. Let's have some lunch, get you down for a nap and then when you wake up, we can take care of the cookies."

Gregory agreed with a sleepy nod. She wondered how much of the drug Peter Belkin had given Gregory was still in her son's system. Because the Mateevs wanted Gregory so badly she doubted that he'd been given anything toxic. Still, as a mother she was worried.

The Mateevs. Like a snake eating its own tail, her thoughts returned to the real problem.

As much as Viktoria was enjoying her cozy Christmas Eve with Cody, she couldn't ignore the reason they were stranded with him in the first place. They still hadn't gotten any word about Peter Belkin. That made her extremely uneasy and until she was exonerated, she would continue to worry. Cody said he'd investigated the Mateev family. He must know so much more than she about them and what they were capable of. Once Gregory was asleep, Viktoria and Cody could compare notes about her in-laws and find a way to get Nikolai Mateev out of her life for good, or better yet—behind bars.

* * *

With Gregory settled down for his nap, Cody retrieved the second box of evidence that he'd collected from the CI, along with work he did after leaving the DEA. He set it on the table in front of Viktoria, next to the first. He swiped a hand across the top, collecting a thin layer of dirt before wiping his palm on the seat of his pants. "This is everything I have on the Mateev family."

Viktoria leaned forward, her elbows on the table. "That's quite a case file," she said. "You must know everything about them."

He did…and yet, the first thing he didn't know was what she knew. Viktoria claimed to have only met Nikolai once at her husband's funeral, and knew nothing else about the family beyond that they were rich and ruthless. At the same time, her story could also be nothing more than an act and a long list of lies. He decided on giving full disclosure, if only to gauge her reaction.

"There's a heroin-trafficking ring that encompasses much of the mountain west. I learned that it was funded by criminals from Russia, and led by Nikolai Mateev…" His statement trailed off, waiting for her to pick up the thread and give him something.

Viktoria closed her eyes, as if she didn't want to see the truth. When she opened them, she said, "My husband was raised in Brooklyn by his mother, who died of cancer during his senior year of high school."

The facts she shared made sense, but nothing was helpful. "Years ago, the Mateev family ran their

United States operation out of Brooklyn," he said, deciding only to give her a brief history, even though he could talk at length. Hell, he knew more about the Mateevs than he did about his own family. "The FBI brought the patriarch up on racketeering charges. He fled the country—taking his son, also a criminal— with him. That son was your father-in-law."

She paled and her mouth hung open for a moment. "I really had no idea." She hesitated. "And what happened with your case? Someone else must be investigating them since you left."

"The DEA wasn't interested," Cody said. "They didn't think that I had enough information."

"But you have all of this." She swept her arm out to encompass the two boxes.

"It never made sense to me, either, although I pressed. Maybe too much."

"And that's why you left?"

Her supposition wasn't the entire truth, but close enough to accurate. He shrugged. "Basically." Another thought came to Cody. Sure, he was a trained investigator, but he couldn't imagine that Viktoria was without desire to learn more about the Mateev family. "And what about you? You never tried to learn anything about them?"

She shook her head. "Lucas had a maternal aunt and uncle in Brooklyn who were like his parents, so it never felt like he was lacking a family. I did urge him to invite his dad to the wedding. He refused. Same with sending an announcement after Gregory was born."

"No internet search? Nothing?"

"Before or after they tried to frame me for being a neglectful mother?"

"Both," Cody said.

"I allowed Lucas to set the level of contact he wanted with his father. Besides, Nikolai was more than half a world away. It's not like he came up in our daily conversations. So, no, I never wondered beyond what he shared."

"And after?"

"When I ran, I wanted to drop off the grid—not open up a search engine that would lead Belkin right to me. Or is that just something used in the movies?"

She was smart and her instincts were good. More than once, the Russians had proven adept at using the internet to meet their own evil ends. Which left them with the evidence he had in the two boxes—and what Viktoria knew.

"Lucas must have said something over the years," Cody coaxed.

"I know for certain that he went to his father in Russia after high school. Things didn't go well and Lucas returned to the US after a few years."

"Any idea what happened?"

Viktoria stared off through the picture window as if trying to see beyond the blowing snow. "My former husband was right about his father. In fact, this whole episode is my fault."

Her fault? His jaw tensed. "How so?" he asked.

"I just assumed that Lucas and Nikolai's falling out had been over something minor—but then feelings were hurt and both men were too stubborn to apologize—so I called Nikolai and told him about Lucas's death." She pressed her thumb to her lips for a moment and then continued. "I did what I thought was right and in doing so invited this man back into our lives."

Cody pulled out a thick manila file and hesitated. "This is all the information I have on your father-in-law, Nikolai Mateev." He continued, "After returning to Moscow, Nikolai married again. He and his current wife have several children—all girls."

Viktoria nodded. "I'm Russian by heritage and I understand how important boys are to their fathers. Very old-school," she said. "If Nikolai wants to pass his business on to the next generation, his son would be the obvious heir. Except he can't have Lucas now. That explains the desire to have Gregory in Russia. I guess stealing my son and murdering me to accomplish that isn't a big deal to a man with his morals."

Cody opened the file. "Nikolai's a pretty cagey guy. There are only a few photos. He's never mentioned by name in any of the wiretaps the FBI has had over the years, but he's tied into the drug trade all the same."

He withdrew three black-and-white surveillance pictures of Nikolai Mateev. Two of them showed a balding middle-aged man in a rumpled trench coat next to a dark-colored sedan. The last photo was a close-up of Nikolai lifting a cigarette to his lips. The gray tendril of smoke twisted upward, and the Russian squinted against the haze. His hands were covered in tattoos, as, Cody assumed, was the rest of his body. For the *vory v zakone*, the thieves in law, each tattoo meant something, a prison where they served, an offense committed. Their body was a codex of crime.

Viktoria reached for the close-up photo. "You know—Nikolai looks nothing like Lucas. My husband had dark hair and eyes. Gregory really is a perfect mix of his father and me."

Like sludge had been poured in Cody's veins, he couldn't help but feel sick with jealousy that Lucas Mateev, the son of a criminal dirt bag, was able to get married and have a kid. Where Cody, always trying to do the right thing, was alone.

"In fact," Viktoria continued, unaware of Cody's sudden change in mood, "there's no resemblance between the two, except for that." She pointed to a tattoo on Nikolai's ring finger. Inked into the Russian's hand was an Orthodox cross with triple bars, which was surrounded by a diamond.

He immediately cast his envy aside and Cody's heart stilled for a moment. "That tattoo? Your husband had that exact same tattoo?"

Viktoria lifted the picture again. She stared at it for a long moment. "He did," she said.

Withdrawing a half a dozen other files, Cody removed a close-up picture of different thugs. They all had the same tattoo. He lined the photos up in front of Viktoria.

"Is it," she asked with a small voice, "a family thing?"

She was a smart woman. She knew better.

"Not exactly." Cody gave Viktoria a moment to come to her own conclusion.

She pressed her lips together. It was a gesture Cody had come to see as Viktoria's way of keeping her emotions inside. "This tattoo is something criminal, isn't it?"

Cody nodded. "It is."

"Tell me."

"It's the initial tattoo for the *vory v zakone*, or the thieves in law. The tat basically announces to the world that you are a professional criminal and you've done time in a Russian prison."

"One of the men last night mentioned the *vory v zakone*. At the time, I was too scared to even think about what he might have meant. But...are you saying that my husband served time in a Russian prison?"

Cody didn't have time for diplomacy. "The tattoo is a clear indication of his involvement in some kind of criminal activity at some point in his life."

"He was in medical sales," she said. Her voice caught. "Last year we attended his office Christmas party." A hint of fresh loss crept into her voice. "I thought I knew him."

Betrayal was an old friend to Cody and he knew it well—the dizziness, the cut, the burn. He reached for Viktoria's hand and willed her pain to pass to him.

"He had changed over the last year," she said, twining her fingers through his. "Moody. Angry. Out all night." She gave a snort of a laugh. "I thought he was having an affair, but he might have been romancing gangland violence."

"Or something from his past could have resurfaced and his distance was meant to keep you safe."

"Either way, it makes two things clear. First, Lucas's death was no accident."

"And?" he asked, afraid of what she might say.

"And Gregory is probably in more danger than I ever dreamed."

Viktoria sat on the sofa. She wrapped her arms around her chest as she tried to fend off a sudden chill, a coldness that came not from the blowing snow outside but from the icy landscape within her heart. Her husband's death was no accident, but rather an unsolved murder and the killer was still at large.

"In a way," she said. The room was too quiet and her words boomed. "In a weird, sick, twisted way, Nikolai Mateev was right to want to take Gregory to Russia. If my husband was a criminal, despised enough to be murdered here in the States, there could be more retributions. Gregory could be a target."

"You don't know that," said Cody.

Anger toward the world flared. She rose to her feet. She paced, as if she could somehow put distance between herself and the truth.

"Listen, we can only look at facts, Viktoria."

Cody's words stopped Viktoria's feet, but her mind still raced.

He continued, "And one fact that I know is that

if Gregory went to Russia he would be raised by a criminal and undoubtedly learn the family trade. You don't want that for your son—he's too good a kid to be a mobster."

"But I can't keep him safe," Viktoria said, finally daring to enter the deepest and coldest cave of her soul. "What kind of mother am I? I cannot even keep my child out of harm's way."

Cody approached her from behind. He placed his hands on her shoulders and rubbed her tense muscles. She pulled away, wanting to hold on to her anger. It gave her a sense of strength. He continued to massage her neck. With a sigh, Viktoria relented and leaned into Cody's solid chest.

"I will keep you safe," he said. He leaned forward, his lips grazing her hair, his breath warming her. "As long as I am able. I swear to you. Do you believe me?"

He leaned into her more, until they both supported each other. "Sure."

His mouth moved to the place where her shoulder and neck met. He kissed her, his lips traveling upward. His tongue flicked over Viktoria's earlobe and gooseflesh sprang up on her arm. Cody's hands moved from her shoulders to her breasts. Through the soft fabric of her sweatshirt he found her nipples—already hard—and rolled each of them between his thumb and finger.

She gasped. Arching her back, Viktoria pressed her breasts more fully into his hands.

"You are strong and beautiful and brave and

smart," Cody whispered into her ear. "In a word, perfect."

The exquisite pleasure he was giving her combined with his words and Viktoria became weak in the knees. Cody held her up, his hands moving to her waist. And then they moved lower.

His touch skimmed under the fabric of her sweatpants. Flesh to flesh, Viktoria's lust began a slow simmer. Lower still, as he began to explore her body. He traced a circle around the top of her sex and Viktoria moaned. Cody reached farther and slid a finger inside her. He was aroused; she could feel him through the fabric of his jeans.

"Tell me you want me," he said.

Viktoria had never desired anyone more. "I want you," she panted, as every inch of her body came alive. "I want you inside me. Now."

Cody whirled Viktoria around to face him. He placed his hands on her face and kissed her deeply. Carefully, he lowered her to the nearby couch. Viktoria gazed at Cody as he stood above.

He removed his sweater to reveal broad shoulders and tight abs, just as she'd imagined. Better, really. A light sprinkling of hair covered his pecs and surrounded his nipples. It came together at the center of his chest and dove downward to the low-hanging waist of his jeans.

He was a work of art. Yet more than that, she had begun to care for Cody. At the same time, her life was far from simple—and falling for a guy was a complication she did not need. All she did know was that she was with Cody right now and that nothing else mattered.

She gave a quick glance at the clock. Gregory was upstairs and asleep. He shouldn't wake from his nap for another hour—maybe a little more—giving Viktoria time to be something other than a mom.

He knelt before her and tugged down her pants. Viktoria slipped off her sweatshirt. She wanted his flesh warming her skin as they moved together and became one. He slipped off his pants and let them fall to a heap on the floor. He was hard and Viktoria bit her lip in anticipation of him entering her fully.

Cody slipped his finger inside her again. And then another. He knelt on the sofa, his head between her thighs. His tongue teased and explored. Viktoria's hips lifted as her pleasure mounted. Cody continued to touch and taste and savor. Her ecstasy expanded, crested and Viktoria cried out with her climax.

Sliding up between her legs, Cody hovered above her. He kissed her—the taste of her pleasure lingered on his lips. He reached for his jeans and removed his wallet from his back pocket. From one of the compartments, he withdrew a foil packet. It was a relief to see that Cody was being responsible for the two of them. When he removed the translucent condom from the packet, Viktoria reached for his hand. "Can I help you with that?"

"Sure," he said.

Viktoria stroked Cody as she slipped the condom over his length, unrolling it down his shaft.

She scooted back on the sofa and Cody moved

above her. He situated himself and slid forward, entering her just a little. He moved in deeper with his second stroke and she rose upward to meet him, taking him inside her all the way.

Cody took in a hissing breath as he filled her. "Perfect," he said. "You are absolutely perfect."

In her estimation, it was Cody who was perfection. Handsome, well built—in all ways, brave, honest and smart.

He began to move. She met him slow, languid stroke for slow, languid stroke. Yet, the more he was inside her, the more she wanted. The deeper she needed him. Viktoria wrapped her legs around Cody's waist and he entered her just a little more. His thrusts became harder, stronger. Viktoria cried out with pleasure as she met the tempo he set.

Cody reached for the top of her sex. He barely touched her, manipulating her flesh with the slightest pressure and another orgasm crashed down upon her. It was like being drowned in pleasure, every part of her submerged, unable to breathe and so very aware of her physical body and yet not entirely within herself. Yet, she was not alone in the depths, Cody was with her and taken away by the same current.

His body. Her body. One.

As she surfaced, her heart racing, her pulse resounded in the base of her skull. Cody thrust again and again. Rearing his head back, he came. He collapsed atop Viktoria, his body slick with sweat. She pushed back a wayward lock of his dark hair.

His face was so close that she could examine his

cool blue eyes. They were more than the icy crystalline that she always saw. His pupils were ringed with azure that lightened by degrees to cerulean and then to cornflower.

A slim cell phone on the mantel chirped and interrupted Viktoria's musings. Was it news about Belkin?

Cody rose and reached for the phone. He sprinted for the bathroom with his jeans in hand. Viktoria followed his cue and re-dressed in the sweats.

"Hello?" Cody said from the other room. And then, "Sure." He returned, wearing only his jeans. "Can you give me a minute, Viktoria?"

She was being banished? An ember of indignation sprang to life deep within her chest. She breathed deeply, snuffing it out. Cody had other cases, along with the rest of his life. Certainly a moment of privacy wasn't too much to ask.

"No problem. I need to check on Gregory anyway."

She rose from the sofa and headed for the stairs, turning to give one fleeting look into the living room. Cody stood by the fireplace, with the phone to his ear.

"Ian?" he said. "Sorry about that. I can talk now."

His boss. The Brit. A new chill went down Viktoria's spine. Without knowing why, she knew this call meant nothing but trouble—for all of them.

Chapter 11

"Cody," said Ian. He sounded breathless. "I'm glad to finally ring through." Without preamble, Ian Wallace continued, "This Colorado weather has wreaked havoc on so many levels, more than just your landline being down."

As Cody listened, he lifted the house phone from the receiver. No dial tone. How could he have let himself become so preoccupied that he'd failed to notice that the phone service was down? All at once he felt like an ass for spending the morning taking pleasure in Viktoria's body when he should have been solving the Belkin and Mateev problems.

Ian continued, "As bad as the weather is in the southern part of the state, it's worse in the central Rockies—up here, near Denver, has been hit worst of all. Most of the passes through the mountains have been closed for hours."

"Sounds awful," said Cody, because it was, but really—what else was there to say? And yet, there had to be a reason for Ian's call beyond a weather report.

Ian paused; the wait stretched out endlessly. While waiting, Cody shrugged into his sweater and shoved his boxers into the pocket of his jeans.

"The point I'm trying to make," Ian said at last, "is that no one is able to arrest Belkin at the moment."

Cody's insides turned as icy as the wind that whipped the snowflakes into a frenzy. "I don't understand," he said.

"I talked to my contact in the CBI. There's a great deal of interest in speaking with Belkin but for the time being, Colorado is under a state of emergency."

Cody stared at the screen before putting the phone to his ear once more. "They want to *speak* with Belkin?" The name tasted sour. "Belkin arranged the kidnapping of a young boy and the attempted murder of his mother. What is there to speak about? Other than to ask if he wants a plea bargain or not?"

"I understand your frustration, Cody," said Ian. He spoke in a soft voice meant to appease.

Cody was in no mood to be placated. He had been forced to kill a man—justifiably—but now the authorities wanted to simply speak with Belkin? "With all due respect, I doubt you do."

"Samuels," snapped Ian, suddenly all business, "control your passions, man."

Cody clenched the slim phone as his arm ached with desire to throw the mobile across the room. In his mind's eye, he saw it shattering in a spray of glass and plastic as it hit the opposite wall. Then it would be as if he and Viktoria and Gregory were truly alone and safely ensconced in a snow globe. That fantasy fix to a very real problem calmed Cody a bit and he managed to mumble, "What do you need me to do now?"

"This is a complicated situation, you understand. The Colorado Bureau of Investigation did find the cabin," said Ian. He paused. "But the entire structure was burned. It looks like faulty wiring and gas from the stove."

In an instant, Cody knew that the shooter who had been left behind was the arsonist. A true professional, he'd wiped away every trace that they had ever been in the cabin. So much for finding any evidence that would corroborate their story.

Ian continued, "When they arrived, there was nothing beyond embers and ashes."

"And no body? No bullets?"

"Just a charred shell of the cabin. It's not that the fire won't be investigated, just not now. First, it's impossible. Over a meter and a half of snow fell last night. The only thing the highway patrol is worried about is keeping the main roads clear."

"What about Sheriff Benjamin?" When confronted by the CBI, Ray would have confessed.

"There's a problem with that, too. Sheriff Benjamin is dead."

Cody gritted his teeth and quietly cursed. "What happened?"

"The official version is that he accidentally shot himself while servicing his revolver."

"And the unofficial story?"

"Sheriff Benjamin's injury was purposely self-inflicted. They have video from his office."

Cody shook his head. He could just picture Ray Benjamin—drunk, morose, guilt ridden. Maybe he thought that suicide was the only way out. "Did he leave a note?"

"None that's been found so far."

"That means there's no mention of his dealing with Belkin or the Mateevs."

"No."

Another death because of the Mateevs. Sure, Ray Benjamin had been weak, but he'd been pushed and enticed by Belkin. He grunted a reply.

"I'm not your enemy, Cody. I know that Peter Belkin is bad news, and that the Mateev family is worse. It's simply that at this moment, there is no irrefutable evidence connecting Belkin to any of these crimes."

"Gregory remembers Belkin from the car. The bastard even drugged the kid."

"A child aged, what, four? Will never testify. And if he did his testimony would easily be explained away as a child's faulty memory, especially if a sedative was administered."

"Thank you for the update." Cody managed to sound civil, although he wanted to yell. "If you hear more, you'll call?"

"Just one more thing," said Ian. "There is a problem with Mrs. Mateev."

"Viktoria?"

"As far as the authorities in Colorado are concerned she is still wanted by the state of New York for her flight from justice." Ian's words became hollow and faint. "Again, this blasted storm has made it impossible for her to be picked up by the police, but I assured them that you would be responsible for her until they arrived."

Cody's gut tightened once more. How was he supposed to tell Viktoria that it was she who was wanted by law enforcement and not Belkin? More than that, he was to be her captor, her Judas. He couldn't be that duplicitous. Hell, the taste of her still lingered on his lips.

From upstairs came the sounds of voices—Viktoria's soft and soothing along with Gregory's, high-pitched and excited. Cody could not have this conversation with them in the room.

"Anything else?" Cody barely kept the disappointment and hostility from his tone.

"You tell me," said Ian. His voice held an icy bite that cooled some of the fury burning in Cody's chest.

"I told you everything that happened last night."

"No, not last night, before then. You built a case that involved the Mateev family while at the DEA. Did you keep a case file? Perhaps Viktoria Mateev can be of some use?"

"I did keep a case file," Cody explained, "and

showed Viktoria what I had. She knew nothing of Lucas Mateev's family. Less than nothing, really."

"Pity," said Ian. "I'd love to nail those bastards to the wall. Stay where you are, Cody. The CBI will be in touch."

Cody looked out the window. Snowdrifts touched the bottom of the sill and fat flakes still fell quickly from the sky. And just like the fantasy of being in a snow globe, Viktoria, Gregory and Cody were trapped. "I'm not sure I have any choice," he said.

"I wish I had better news for you."

Viktoria's and Gregory's voices and footfalls from the stairs were unmistakable. "So do I," he said as he ended the call.

Viktoria came into view and Cody tossed the phone on the kitchen counter.

"Everything okay?" she said. Taking a seat at the kitchen table, she tilted her chin toward the phone. Gregory climbed into his mother's lap and leaned his head into her shoulder.

The Madonna and Child, Cody thought. It was a fitting image for Christmas Eve.

Cody took a deep breath. He was torn about what he would and would not tell Viktoria. She had a right to know that Belkin had not been taken into custody and moreover that she was a wanted woman. At the same time, neither fact needed to be addressed now. Besides, it was Christmas Eve. Did he really want to ruin the remnant of her holiday with devastating news?

"That was my boss. Apparently, there's a lot of

snow out there and no one is going anywhere unless it's an emergency—even the Colorado State Patrol is stretched thin. It might not be until later today or tomorrow before anyone can get to Belkin." He stopped there. Hadn't he sworn to protect Viktoria? Didn't that also mean he should try to shield her from any more unpleasant truths?

"That's disappointing," she said; her voice was small.

"Belkin?" asked Gregory, fear creeping into his tone. "Is he the bad man who took me from Mommy?"

"One of them," said Cody.

"But, Belkin was the man in charge. I remember when…" Gregory bit his bottom lip.

"You remember what?" Viktoria asked. Her voice held a breathless tinge of panic. Cody could well imagine what horrible scenarios might race through the mind of a mother whose son had been kidnapped.

Gregory looked down.

Cody knelt to eye level with the kid. "It's okay, Gregory. You can tell us. You're safe now. I'm not going to let those bad men bother you ever again."

Gregory drew in a deep breath and nodded. "I know that I am supposed to keep hands to myself and use my words if I get mad, but I hit that man— Belkin." He swung out in a wild punch. "I kicked him in the arm, too. I was real mad and real scared. I didn't know if I'd ever see my mommy again." Tears pooled in the boy's eyes.

"It's okay, Captain Kiddo." Viktoria stroked her son's head.

"Do you think," asked Gregory, "that Santa will put me on the naughty list for hitting the bad man?"

"I am sure you will stay on the nice list, Gregory." Cody mussed the kid's hair. "It's Peter Belkin who will get coal in his stocking."

Belkin—and his boss, Nikolai Mateev—had ruined enough lives and had to be stopped. All the same, Cody imagined that Belkin would weasel out of his legal troubles. If only there was some way to shine a light on all the ugly things Belkin hid.

He paused, the idea stopping him in his tracks.

"I know what we can do," said Cody as he rushed to his storage room that stood next to his kitchen.

"What we can do for *what*?" Viktoria called after him.

"We can use the laptop," Cody yelled back. He rummaged under the bags of Christmas gifts to access his rudimentary hiding place for Peter Belkin's computer. "I have it," he said as he returned holding the slim silver rectangle. "There has to be something on this," he said.

Viktoria stood. "I might not know everything, or anything, about law enforcement—but don't we need a warrant to look on someone's computer? If we go to court, won't a defense lawyer say that we planted evidence? The Mateevs are smart, and have access to lots of technology that they'll use in court. They did it to me once before, remember."

"Technically speaking, you're right. Although if

this case goes to court then a reasonable programmer will be able to tell what documents were created or changed and when."

"Beyond a reasonable doubt? Isn't that the threshold for proof under the law?"

"If Belkin wanted me to be a slave to the law, then he shouldn't have ruined my career with the DEA," Cody snapped.

Viktoria grabbed Cody by the sleeve and pulled him into the living area, away from Gregory and the kitchen table. "Is that what all this is about?" she hissed. "Retribution for your lost career?"

Her question was a slap in the face. Didn't she see how he was trying to help her? Beneath the roar of thoughts in his head came a small idea—like a whisper. Who was he trying to serve? Or worse yet, would he have become involved if Viktoria wasn't a Mateev, and therefore a way to clear his name? Cody's jaw ached.

"I want these guys as badly as you do, but I also don't want to create a legal loophole for Belkin to slither through," she said.

"You're right, but it's evidence we need."

Viktoria exhaled. "Give me a minute."

Cody gave her a nod, and grabbed the laptop before returning to the living room. After sitting on the sofa, he placed the computer on the coffee table and lifted the lid.

Viktoria set out a plate of cookies and icing for Gregory, along with a warning about eating too many sweets.

With his interest divided between the laptop's home screen and the kitchen, Cody powered up the computer.

The computer's screen was a stock image of a hardwood forest at the peak of autumnal color. Along the bottom ran the most used applications. Photos. Documents. Presentations. Text Messages. Calendar. Email. Internet Search Engine. Games. Along with several others that Cody didn't recognize.

Viktoria stood behind Cody and leaned over the back of the sofa. Her hair was loose and a tendril fell over her shoulder. Cody longed to touch the silky strands. Instead he turned his gaze back to the laptop. He wanted to shield Viktoria from the truth, but he also knew that for her to understand his desperation, she needed to know all the facts.

"The Colorado Bureau of Investigation went to the cabin," he said. "There was a fire that consumed the cabin. With all the snow, they didn't have a chance to search the site."

She sucked in a breath, looking quickly over at Gregory to make sure he was intent upon his icing and not paying attention to the discussion. Cody hoped she was okay, too, because his news was about to get worse.

"And Sheriff Benjamin committed suicide, although it's being called an accident."

"Dear God, no."

Cody turned in his seat. He looked into Viktoria's deep brown eyes and hated himself for what he was about to say next. "An attempted kidnapping is a serious crime, but neither of us saw Belkin at your cabin. Moreover, the cabin's gone. Because no evidence can be collected right now—Belkin isn't exactly wanted for anything."

Viktoria recoiled, as if slapped.

"There's more." Cody reached for her hand. It was ice-cold and he wrapped it in his own. *Just stick to the facts.* His lifelong adage felt as hollow as he feared it would at that moment. "Listen, there's a lot to be sorted out. But, New York State's Child Protective Services continues to be involved."

"After all of this and I'm still the one who's wanted?"

Viktoria's voice had risen and she immediately looked over her shoulder at her son. Gregory, kneeling on a kitchen chair, paid her no mind and continued to spread icing on his cookies.

"All of this," Viktoria whispered and rolled her hand around as if indicating Cody's entire home. "Bringing Gregory to Colorado. Shooting our way out of my cabin. Breaking into the realtor's office just to find my son. All of this could be for nothing?"

Cody tightened his grip on her hand and quelled an unreasonable fear that she might slip away.

"It is not for nothing. We're together. A team."

"You say that…" she began.

He gestured to the laptop. "I refuse to give up, although it makes me nervous that there was no password. A smart guy like Belkin wouldn't leave damning information on a computer that anyone could get into. We didn't search his house. There could very easily be another device we missed."

Viktoria rounded to the other side of the sofa and sat next to Cody. She pulled the laptop toward them. "Let's see what Belkin has on his hard drive."

Using the built-in mouse, Cody opened each application. They found nothing of importance in the documents, emails or pictures Belkin had stored. He had several presentations saved, but none would have been considered criminal—unless being boring was a crime. The only thing that Cody found interesting was that Belkin had several game icons, none of which were well played, except one.

"I don't know," said Cody, moving the computer so that Viktoria could get a better look. "The most interesting thing might be his level on Angry Birds. He's up to two hundred and two. Sounds impressive."

Viktoria leaned back and laced her fingers behind her head. "If this computer is all we have by which to judge him, Peter Belkin looks pretty ordinary. And we know, he's anything but."

Cody opened the documents again. "There has to be something here. He was working on this computer when we came to rescue Gregory. It was so special that he had to be alone to have it out. Unless he doesn't want his hired thugs to know what an Angry Birds fanatic he is. Really, who has the time to get to that level of a game?"

Viktoria scooted next to Cody. "Open up Angry Birds again."

He double-clicked the application. A big red bird

with bushy black eyebrows filled the screen. He flew through the air, Superman-style, with one arm tucked into his chest and the other extended in front of him. In the background were other varieties of cartoon birds, green pigs and castles made of gray stone blocks.

"Level two hundred and two," Cody said, pointing to the big yellow numbers. He touched the screen, just beneath the level. "Password required. Odd, don't you think?"

"Is it?"

"It is." Cody's fingers hovered over the keyboard. "What's his password then?"

"First initial, last name?"

Belkin would never have such an easily guessed password. Most likely, it was a random grouping of numbers and letters. Then again, Belkin would need to be able to remember the password, so it could be something personal. In the end, Cody didn't have a better idea.

He typed "PBelki..." The password field shimmied and cleared itself. "We know it's a five-character password." Cody typed. "Peter."

The field shimmied and cleared itself again. Then a message appeared under the field. "Three attempts remaining."

Cody cursed. He glanced quickly up at Gregory, who was concentrating on a cookie covered in thick white icing. "Sorry," he mouthed to Viktoria.

"You said you have information on the Mateev

organization. Do you have a case file on Peter Belkin? Birthday? Wife's name?"

"I do," said Cody.

"Good," said Viktoria. "We need to find out what he's hiding behind the birds."

Huddled in the corner of the kitchen pantry, Belkin cursed his luck. All the same, he knew it might have been worse. Even though his hands were bound behind him and the solid wood door was locked tight, he wouldn't starve. Getting food and water had been clumsy and messy, yet he had access to both.

What Peter Belkin did not have was a toilet and the pantry reeked of urine. If he was locked in here much longer it was going to smell a lot worse.

When Belkin had awakened several hours earlier he had made a huge commotion, one that would have drawn at least the curiosity of Gregory Mateev. Since Belkin never saw tiny pajamaed feet exploring from the crack under the door, he assumed that whoever had done this to him also had taken the boy.

Belkin had only begun to catalogue all the possibilities of who had thrown him into the pantry when the front door opened and closed with a forceful bang. He froze. One of the previous scenarios—that he'd been double-crossed by the Mateev family—came to the forefront of his mind. If that were the case, then what was left of Belkin's life would be a nightmare.

Would he be shot at short range? Tortured to death?

That was a wholly unpleasant thought.

"Belkin," a man cried out. "Belkin? Are you here?"

He recognized the man's voice—one of the two from Team Bravo. He thought his name was Dimitri.

"I'm in here," Belkin called back, giving the pantry door a savage kick.

He heard scraping and clattering, then the door swung open. The man stood aside, a kitchen chair and electrical cord in his hand. "What happened?"

Belkin rolled to his knees "I was attacked."

Dimitri hesitated and then reached out for Belkin's elbow, helping him to his feet.

"Undo these flex-cuffs." Belkin turned slowly on stiff legs and showed his back to his *nayemnik*. Mercenary.

"Those aren't flex-cuffs. It looks like you got tied up with a power cord."

Belkin was quick to assess his situation. Had the pantry door been blocked by a kitchen chair, the handles tied with a cord? And then his hands bound with whatever was easiest? If that were the case, then Belkin knew this hadn't been a professional job. Or at least, the assault hadn't been planned in advance.

The *nayemnik* cut through the cord and blood rushed into Belkin's hands, sending painful pinpricks dancing over his palms and fingers. "Go upstairs and check on Gregory Mateev," said Belkin. "Although I suspect that he's been taken."

"I have news." Belkin noted that the other man hadn't done as he was ordered. He was about to complain, when Dimitri said, "It's about Gregory Ma-teev. Or his mother, actually."

Belkin rubbed his breastbone. "Yes?"

"She survived. Escaped. A guy came from no-where. A professional."

The hired gun continued to talk—how he had tried to pin down Viktoria and the unknown man in the cabin with his gunfire, the death of his teammate and eventually setting fire to the cabin to destroy the evidence. His story ended with a stolen car and the treacherous journey to find Belkin. But Belkin was hardly listening. His mind had wandered back to what he could recall of last night. There wasn't a lot. The car alarm had gone off and then there was nothing. Except a flash of something. A memory? A face along with a name.

Cody Samuels. Rocky Mountain Justice. Had the local sheriff developed a conscience after calling Belkin, and then tipped off the RMJ operative?

Belkin had seen even more bizarre scenarios in his life. And in truth, the *why* mattered only a little.

He quickly assessed the situation—both the good and the bad. The list of bad was long. When Vik-toria had turned up in the Telluride vicinity, Belkin had seen it as fortuitous. An out-of-the-way desti-nation, far from any direct connections to Belkin and his businesses, legal or not. Now he understood how bad his luck had been. The property in which he stood had been charged to his law firm's account. All too soon he would be connected to the rental and therefore put in proximity to the crime. Gregory was gone—that was the worst of it. Belkin cast a weary glance around the kitchen. The laptop, which he had left on the table, also was missing. As far as Belkin's survival was concerned, that was almost as bad as losing Nikolai's grandson.

He had to assume that the authorities were involved.

Or were they? The easy distraction of the car alarm, along with the kitchen chair barricade and the power cord used to bind his hands spoke of people without many, or any, resources. And if the CBI or Department of Justice were involved then Belkin would have been in jail, not in a pantry and smelling of his own piss.

He leaned on the kitchen counter. Three empty syringes sat in a neat row. Belkin gripped his sore bicep. It hurt worse than it had after Gregory kicked him. In fact, it felt as if he'd received an injection or three. Drugging him with his own sedatives seemed vengeful and opportunistic.

Like something an irate mother might do.

True, the facts that Belkin had were scant. At the same time, there was only one scenario which supported them all. What if his attackers only had been Viktoria Mateev and Cody Samuels, a rogue RMJ agent?

Belkin's day had just taken a turn for the better.

He turned to the mercenary. "Do you have your gun at least?" Belkin hadn't carried a gun in years, yet if he was going to complete his mission, he needed a weapon, and fast.

"It only has two bullets. Our backup ammo and other firearms were left in our SUV."

A single gun with two bullets—one for Viktoria Mateev and the other for Cody Samuels. "That will do." He held out his hand, palm up.

Dimitri hesitated.

"That will do," Belkin repeated, his tone sharp. He grasped at the air with his upturned hand. After another pause, he added, "Now. Dimitri."

Dimitri shifted his weight from one foot to the other before drawing a Sig Sauer from the holster he wore under his arm. He placed the gun in Belkin's hand, his hold lingering on the stock a moment too long. "Sure," he said, finally relinquishing the weapon. "Anything you need."

The gun was warm from being kept so close to the other man's body. Belkin wrapped his fingers around the grip and aimed at Dimitri's head. It had been years since Belkin did any of his own killing. A current, filled with the power of life over death, surged through his arm.

Dimitri held up his hands. "You aren't going to shoot me, are you?"

Belkin exhaled and moved the sights a hairbreadth to the right, lining up perfectly with the middle of Dimitri's forehead. A bead of sweat collected at his hairline. A single trail of liquid snaked down the side of his face.

"I told you, there was another guy," Dimitri stammered. "He's a really good shot, you know. It's not my fault—besides it was me who found you. If it weren't for me, you'd still be trapped in that pantry."

Belkin grimaced. He wanted to shoot the idiot, if for no other reason than to silence anyone who had seen this shameful state. "You don't have to remind me of that." Belkin lowered his gun. "You're lucky that I need both the bullets."

Exhaling loudly, Dimitri let his hands drop.

"I'm going to get cleaned up," Belkin said, like it was any business of Dimitri's. "Look for the kid, although I don't think he's here."

A phone sat on the counter and Belkin lifted it from the cradle. It was dead. He didn't expect anything less. He finished with his orders to Dimitri.

"Then go to the safe house and alert everyone else. I don't care about the weather. We rendezvous at the airfield. I want wheels up by 10:00 p.m, local. Got that, *pridurok*?" Jerk. "And leave the SUV that's in the drive," he said as he left the kitchen.

Belkin took the stairs to the master suite. As he stripped down and stepped under the scalding-hot shower spray he didn't have a plan exactly, but a theory. And if it proved to be true, then Belkin would personally take care of Cody Samuels and Viktoria Mateev.

And if not, then he was as good as dead.

Chapter 12

Viktoria sat on the sofa next to Cody and held her breath. An open manila folder sat at his elbow. The cover page consisted of a photo of Peter Belkin, along with his personal information—birth date, address, children, former spouses. They'd tried the name of his son and the birth date for his daughter—making the month of June a 6, not an 0-6. Neither had worked and now only one attempt remained.

"His birth date won't work if we need a five-character password."

Viktoria rose from the sofa to get a glass of water. She needed distance and to move. The physical act of filling her glass at the sink, drinking it down slowly, gave her a moment to think and calmed her mind and she turned to Cody. "He's very Russian. He intersperses a lot of Russian phrases into his conversation," she said, trying to recall every detail of her single meeting with Peter Belkin. "So, the password might be in Cyrillic."

Cody leaned back on the sofa and looked at Viktoria. "I didn't know that you knew Belkin that well."

"I met him once," she continued, "or rather, he came to my apartment. It was right after Lucas's funeral. It was midafternoon and I'd just put Gregory down for a nap." Yes, she did recall that sultry August day, the heat so intense that it rose in waves off the city streets. It was quite the juxtaposition to today's heavily falling snow. "He introduced himself as an attorney with Crandall Stevenson and said that he needed to speak to me about Lucas's death. Probate in New York is ridiculous, so even though a lawyer showing up on my doorstep was odd, it wasn't wholly unreasonable."

"Did you have a doorman in your building or some type of security?"

"Doorman," said Viktoria, "He'd rung the apartment in advance. I told him to send Belkin because I assumed he had legal paperwork…" Her mind trailed off and returned to her Manhattan apartment. "We chatted for a moment. Mostly he asked if I'd ever been to Russia, suggesting what I should see or do if I ever did go. Then he told me that he'd been hired by Nikolai Mateev to get custody of Gregory. He offered me a million dollars and I told him to get out of my home. He left, telling me that I'd be sorry." She paused.

"And then?"

"The next day Child Protective Services opened a case, claiming that I was an unfit mother." Viktoria glanced at Gregory. He still busily iced the cookies, but she wondered how much attention he'd paid to her story and more than that, how much he understood.

The sensation that she was trapped, locked in a cage with no hope of escape, made her begin to pace again. Back and forth in the tiny house. There wasn't enough room for her thoughts. Then it came to her. "His Russian name. We discussed that my name has a Russian spelling, but his given name is Pyotr—he uses Peter for business in America."

Cody shrugged. "It's better than nothing."

His fingers skipped on the keyboard and Viktoria moved back to his side and sat.

"Ready?" he said. The pointer hovered over the password field.

Viktoria exhaled. If this didn't work, she had nothing else to contribute and her future rested in the capricious hands of fate. "Ready," she said.

Cody clicked the mouse. The password field disappeared. Viktoria felt a smile pick up the corners mouth. They'd done it! They'd broken in to the file. The screen instantly turned white and then black. Her smile faltered and bile rose in the back of her throat.

A message appeared in the middle of the screen.

Password Error

Computer Lock Engaged

Then a timer began to count down from twelve hours. Eleven hours fifty-nine minutes and fifty-nine seconds. Eleven hours fifty-nine minutes and fifty-eight seconds...

Viktoria pressed her hands to her lips. "No," she murmured. "No. No. No." Then to Cody, "What happened?" She couldn't believe that they'd failed. She'd failed, really. It had been her guess that did it.

"I'm not giving up," said Cody. "We'll get into that computer."

"How?" Viktoria's throat burned. Her eyes stung. Her chest was constricted and she couldn't breathe. She was all too familiar with the feeling—despair.

Cody scratched his chin. "I might not be with the DEA anymore, but it doesn't mean that I don't have access to experts."

Viktoria drew in a shuddering breath and focused her thoughts. But each beat of her heart was like another tick of a countdown clock, beating out the seconds to losing Gregory.

Now Cody was on the phone. Viktoria struggled to focus on what he was saying and to stretch for that flimsy strand of hope. But a single word rose into her mind, resonating above all others. *Run*, it said. *Run, and never look back.*

Was that the answer? To fall off the grid? She'd done so successfully for several months already; certainly she could do it again. At the same time, she loathed the idea of living an isolated life again. On some level, though, she knew that her feelings didn't matter. She'd fought too long and hard to surrender now and let herself be arrested and to lose her son.

Cody set the phone on the table and hit a button. "Roman, you're on speaker phone. Viktoria Mateev is right beside me." He turned to her. "Roman De-Marco is a technical genius and can help us get into the computer."

At that, she pushed aside any hastily made plans. Maybe it would work out after all. "I hope you can help," said Viktoria.

"So do I," said Roman. "The first thing I want you to do is close down the computer and restart it. Let me know when that's done."

Cody's fingers danced over the keys and the screen went dark. He hit another button and the hardwood forest came into view again. "Done," said Cody.

Viktoria's frustration rose from the pit of her gut. Like lava from deep within the surface of the earth, her ire longed to break free. Shut down and restart? Even she could think of something as simple as that. But Roman then ordered Cody to hold down several keys at once.

"I'm in," said Cody. Another screen appeared, this one gray.

"Type exactly what I say."

Viktoria leaned forward and held her breath as Cody entered a series of numbers, letters and symbols. He typed line after line after line of code.

"Now hit colon," said Roman, "and enter."

Cody did as he was told. The screen went black. Viktoria's insides, fiery only moments before, cooled to icy. She began to tremble.

A series of electronic files appeared on the screen.

"Success," said Cody.

"Success," she repeated in a whisper.

Names began to appear beside each file. Or not names, rather another set of random numbers, symbols and letters—not unlike the code. Cody clicked on one file. It opened; the document was filled with the same gibberish as the title. "Damn," cursed Cody. "They're encrypted."

"All of them?"

Cody scrolled slowly through the list. "Every goddamn one of them." He cursed.

"Take out the hard drive," said Roman, "and bring it to the office as soon as the roads are open. I have programs there that can break the encryption, but nothing for you to do remotely."

"At least you got us in."

"One last thing—make a copy of the files. Even if they're encrypted, it won't hurt to have a backup."

"Thanks, man."

"I'm here if you need anything else."

Cody ended the call.

Viktoria stared at the screen until something caught her eye. It was Cyrillic, a language she both read and spoke, just as Belkin did. "That one." She touched the screen. "It's not encrypted—it's in Russian."

"Really?" Cody asked. "What does it say?"

"It's a name," said Viktoria. She hesitated. "It's your name. Cody Samuels."

For a second, Cody's ears rang.

"My name," he repeated. "What the hell?"

With his head buzzing, he opened the document to which Viktoria had pointed. His official DEA picture filled the screen. He scrolled down, glancing at the scrawl that filled the page, unable to make out a single word. "Can you read it?" he demanded.

Viktoria moved the computer so it faced her. She traced lines as she translated and read. "There's some biographical information about you. An address in Arvada, Colorado?"

"I rented a house there when I was with the DEA," Cody said, his words drowned out by the thrumming of his own pulse. How had his home address ended up on Belkin's computer?

"Who's Sarah Merrick?"

"Sarah?" Bile rose in the back of Cody's throat. "That's my sister."

"There's an address for her, too. Does she live in Montrose?"

He hadn't spoken to Sarah in almost year, not since their big fight in which she told him to get over being let go by the DEA and he'd accused her of being blind. She was right—*he* was the one who'd been blind. Not only had he allowed his anger to ruin their relationship, now he knew that his investigation into the Mateevs had put his sister at risk. In truth, Sarah was all he had.

"You need to warn your sister," said Viktoria. "Belkin might try to get to you by going after her."

Viktoria was right. He didn't know what to say. To Sarah. To Viktoria. To himself.

Viktoria must have sensed his hesitation and filled the silence: "I had to leave my parents without a word to save Gregory, and they're probably furious with me. But no matter what they think of me now, I couldn't know that they were in danger and not tell them. I'm just saying that family shouldn't be sacrificed lightly."

"Trust me—Sarah doesn't want to hear from me."

"She sent you a Christmas card. I think your sister is trying to make amends."

"I said some horrible things. She said some horrible things. Even if we make up now, who's to say that we won't argue again?"

"No one," said Viktoria. "In fact, you probably will. It's what happens. But even if you disagree, you can still apologize."

Cody shook his head. "I don't crawl. To anyone."

"Admitting you're wrong once doesn't mean you're always wrong. Just like one argument—even a big one—doesn't mean that a relationship needs to end."

The fact that she'd understood his worst fear left Cody claustrophobic in his own home, his own head. He'd call RMJ and have them put a protective detail on his sister and her kids. "Anything else?"

"Lots." Viktoria asked for paper and pen. He fetched her both. She scribbled a note and went back to reading the file silently. Cody's heart hammered. An eternity passed before Viktoria finally spoke. "It seems that you got wind of the Mateev family's involvement in a large heroin ring and they wanted you to stop." She paused. "Did you shoot and kill a confidential informant?"

Cody forced himself to feel nothing, his soul a barren wasteland. "Yes."

"Someone inside the DEA tipped Nikolai off about your investigation. Belkin was holding the guy's girlfriend and used her as leverage. The CI's gun was stolen in the melee that followed. You were set up by someone in the DEA, Cody."

He recalled the exact moment before the CI drew his gun. *I'm sorry, man*, he had said. *Peter Belkin has my girl.*

Had the signed affidavit been routed to the wrong person? "By who?" Cody asked.

"Belkin doesn't list a name, just refers to the person as *Kh*—that's *X* in Russian. But I think it was someone higher up. I can write out everything for you exactly if you'd like," she said.

Cody turned the computer to face him again. "Later," he said. He emailed the document to himself and then to Ian. Then he saved all the files to a flash drive. He handed it to Viktoria. "Keep this with you at all times. It's your protection from the Mateevs." He powered down the computer.

"I'm sorry," said Viktoria, squeezing his shoulder. He let her touch linger—but only for a minute—before gently shaking her off. It was her family who had orchestrated the ruin of his career, after all.

Placing blame on Viktoria wasn't fair, he knew. The Mateevs had done a number on her life, too. Maybe even more so than on his. Even from the beginning, Cody had known that Belkin was responsible for ending his career. And now he had proof. Proof that he'd done his job. Proof that he hadn't needlessly ended a life. Proof that he hadn't been wrong. He wondered why he didn't feel the warmth of pride or at the very least the cool relief of vindication.

Instead, Cody was left with the hot slap of shame. He'd unwittingly set a match to kindling, only to have the whole forest catch fire. Not only had he been burned, but he'd allowed the heat to char his relationship with his sister. Sure, he'd been right, but to have reacted so badly to Sarah's encouragement that he forget the whole Mateev incident now seemed...

Oh hell, he didn't know how he felt. Anxious energy filled him and he needed a release—on the slopes or in the boxing gym...or in Viktoria's arms, in the warmth of her flesh. But how could he think of her as a place to find comfort and solace?

Were they friends? Partners? Lovers? If they were, then Cody needed to trust that Viktoria wouldn't betray him. Yet, if Cody knew anything, it was that in the end, everyone was willing to deceive for their own purposes. Still, she looked so inviting—her arms, her lips, her thighs.

He needed air. He needed…clarity.

Cody walked to the door, his gaze drawn to Sarah's card.

"Where are you going?" Viktoria called as he stepped out into the storm.

"If I'm going to take out the hard drive, I need to get my tools," he said. "They're in the shed."

Freezing cold bit his face and hands. The chill was bracing and cleared his mind of every thought, save one—Belkin was not going to beat Cody. Not again.

Viktoria stared at the fire, as if the flames could portend her future—or at the very least guide her next move. Cody sat beside her and reattached the bottom of the laptop. He'd placed the slim hard drive into a Ziploc baggie that he'd hidden in the dryer, of all places. It seemed as if some of Cody's problems had been solved, but hers were far from over. Belkin was still out there. She wasn't sure if the evidence found on the laptop would be enough to put him away—despite Cody's assurances. After all, Belkin had gotten away with so much for so long, why should he be brought to justice now?

And Belkin just worked for the bad people.

Viktoria sat in silence as the snow continued to fall—the storm was both her salvation and damnation. She felt Cody's gaze burning her cheek. She turned and he regarded her with narrowed eyes.

"What?" she asked.

"Are you thinking of trying to hide again?"

Damn. He knew her too well. How had that happened in less than a day? "Maybe," she said.

"Why won't you listen to me? I told you I can keep you safe."

Viktoria believed that Cody believed in himself. But was she willing to place her future, her son's future and safety, in the hands of someone who, truthfully, she barely knew? "Don't," she said, "make promises you can't keep. Especially where Gregory is concerned."

"You can't keep running," said Cody. "It's not good for you. It's not good for your son."

"You don't think I know that? But how is having Gregory being raised by his mobster grandfather better?"

"Mommy?" called Gregory from the kitchen.

Double damn. What *had* her son heard?

"Yes, Captain Kiddo?"

"What's for dinner?"

"First, you need to wash your hands," Viktoria said as she rose from the sofa and opened the bathroom door. "Then we can talk about dinner."

While the water ran in the bathroom, Cody walked toward Viktoria. She eyed him warily. This man, who just hours ago had brought her body to such heights of passion, now made her feel…what?

Uneasy. After all, she reminded herself, she and her son were only a job. And now, he, too, was on the run from Belkin.

She wished she could feel his arms around her again and feel that safety and security. Believe that the rich and ruthless wouldn't win, and that she could have her life back—while also keeping her son. But she didn't want to go back to New York. The city was where she'd lived with Lucas, a man it seemed she didn't know at all. Viktoria wanted a new life for herself, for Gregory. A life very much like the day they'd just spent with Cody.

Too bad it looked like that would never happen.

By early evening the worst of the blizzard was over, bringing a leaden sky. Viktoria kept busy for the next hour making dinner—spaghetti and meat-balls along with a salad and garlic bread. It was far from a holiday feast, but the work kept her hands busy and her mind from wandering too far.

The snow had lessened and now only a few stray flakes fell from the sky. Cody had gone outside, taking Gregory with him. Together they had shov-eled a path from the front door to the nearby Range Rover, which they had swept clean. Too soon the roads would be cleared, and with that, the ability for someone to come for her and Gregory.

Run. The word came with each beat of her heart. *Run. Take your child and hide. Run, and never look back.* And yet, Viktoria remained rooted over a large pot full of boiling water and starchy pasta.

She set the table complete with two white can-dles she found in a drawer along with cloth napkins. The razor-sharp crease in the fabric made her guess they'd never been used. She thought of the things she'd lost in the fire in the cabin—a good amount of her cash included—and what she might need again to start life anew.

"Dinner smells great," said Cody as he and Gregory entered the small house. A gust of cold wind followed and swirled through the kitchen. Viktoria shivered, immediately understanding the inhospitableness of the outside world, and the safety and security offered in the little house—even if it was temporary.

Cody stood in the doorway and removed his hat. Then brushing it on his knee to dust off the snow, he said, "Spaghetti and sauce is my favorite."

"Yeah, Mom," Gregory repeated. "Dinner smells really good and spaghetti is my favorite, too." Gregory stood beside Cody. Her son wore a hat, coat and mittens—all borrowed from Cody. The clothes were much too large and with the rolled-up sleeves and drooping hat, Gregory looked even younger and smaller than his four years. Gregory had begun to copy everything Cody said and did. Now was no exception. Mimicking Cody, Gregory took off the hat and dusted it on his knee. Cody slipped out of his coat and a heartbeat later, so did the boy.

Viktoria owed her son a life of peace and safety. But, how could she best provide that? Stay and face the consequences for having left New York only to have him placed, at the very best, in protective custody? Or go on the run, armed with new knowledge of how easily a person can be found, but still give them a new home together, albeit one that was hidden away?

"Give me your wet things." Viktoria reached out for the damp and cold outerwear. "Dinner's ready." She hung everything up on the bathroom's shower door, then returned to the kitchen, where Cody knelt before the hearth, feeding logs into the flames. Gregory was already seated at the table with a fork in his hand. Cody stood as Viktoria entered the room, maneuvering in front of her and pulling out her chair as she approached the table.

"Thank you for making dinner," Cody said. He took his own seat. "I couldn't imagine a better way to spend Christmas Eve."

"We should eat this way every night," Gregory said.

A hard lump formed in Viktoria's throat and for a moment, she couldn't find her voice. In his innocence, Gregory had shared her exact wishes. Even when she'd fled New York, Viktoria had understood that she was breaking the law. But having Gregory with her, maintaining their family, was worth it. Now she feared that there might never again be a night like this one.

As Cody filled everyone's plates high with steaming pasta and savory-smelling sauce, Viktoria took a deep breath and exhaled slowly. *Run. Stay.* Each option could be disastrous.

As if he'd known she was struggling internally, Cody caught her eye. "It'll be okay."

"I hope you're right," she said.

"I was thinking," Cody said. "I can go to New York with you and tell them what happened here and that you were right to run. Then there's the fact that we have everything on Belkin's hard drive, plus the document about me. It'll only be a matter of time before this will be cleared up in a legal sense."

Viktoria took another bite of pasta. Could she rely on Cody? Were they really in this together?

Viktoria stood at the sink and washed dishes. Gregory, sprawled on the sofa, dozed as another Christmas cartoon played on the TV. Cody had just gone outside to collect more firewood. It was a very domestic scene, and anyone looking in from the outside would see a family enjoying the waning of another Christmas Eve.

Yet Viktoria's hands trembled in the soapy water and her stomach churned. She was torn with indecision. When Viktoria had left New York with Gregory, she'd done so calmly, methodically and without hesitation. Yet despite learning hours ago that she was still wanted by the authorities, she couldn't bring herself to pack up her son and leave.

And it was because of Cody.

Certainly, if she ran it would reflect badly on him and his job. She didn't want that. But the real reason was that Viktoria couldn't betray him—or their bond.

Through the window, she could see Cody's figure near the woodpile, unmistakable even in the night. The Range Rover sat near the door. The keys were in a dish on the counter.

Cody's back was to the house, his attention focused on gathering wood. How many minutes did she have before he came back? Three? Four? Even with ten minutes, Viktoria didn't have enough time to plan or think—only act. The snow had stopped hours earlier. Major roads would likely be cleared by now.

She knew what she had to do. True, she hated living off the grid—hiding from the world, not even able to call her friends or family. But did she hate that more than losing Gregory?

The answer was a simple *no*.

She stopped considering what running right now would mean to Cody or his job. Or even more important, what it would mean to their relationship. She knew that finding those answers would be far from easy. Grabbing the keys from the bowl, Viktoria called out, "Gregory, come with me. We have to go."

"But Mommy," he whined, "the show's not over."

"You can watch that later," she said, knowing that he would never have the chance. She held out her hand. "Come on," she said. Her pulse roared behind her ears and her voice held an uncustomary bite.

Gregory sighed and rolled up to sitting. His legs dangled off the edge of the sofa.

"I said, let's go."

Gregory stood, sensing the urgency in her voice. "Where are we going?" he asked.

"We need to leave," she said simply.

"What about Santa?" Tears clung to Gregory's lashes. "What about Cody?"

She tried to speak, but she couldn't find the words.

She looked at the sofa. Maybe it would be best to sit beside her son and hold him, just enjoy him for the next day and not wreak havoc on their lives again. But if they stayed, chaos would surely come to find them and there was no guarantee she'd be able to save him again, even with Cody's help. Not with the enemy they were up against.

She had no cash, no clothes, no plan beyond leaving. Still, she couldn't stay and let her son be taken from her.

"We just have to go, okay?" To lie to him that way upset her the moment it came out of her mouth. But what choice did she have? "I need you to listen to me, and to be a brave boy. Cody's going to be okay, I promise."

After a moment, Gregory placed his small hand in Viktoria's. As they walked to the door, she prayed that Gregory would quickly forget their momentary respite in Cody's home. She should pray to have that sort of amnesia herself, but she couldn't. Memories of Cody were all she could take with her. Those, and his sweats, which she still wore, and his Gore-Tex jacket that she had grabbed.

Oh, and the car she was stealing from him.

Viktoria held Gregory as they slipped from the warm and inviting house and into the frigid darkness. As the blizzard moved south, arctic air had followed in its wake and Viktoria imagined that tonight's low temperatures would plummet to well below zero. It was a horrible night to be out. Cody had retreated to the shed that sat on the far side of his lot and Viktoria knew this was her moment. She didn't have the strength of will to face Cody, not that he would willingly let her leave. Yet, she had to go and if he knew her at all, he'd understand why.

Using the fob, Viktoria remotely started the Range Rover's engine and unlocked its doors. She brushed snow from the windshield before opening the back door and lifting her son into the seat. "Sit in the middle," she said.

He did as she asked and dutifully slid across the bench. She struggled with the seat belt for a moment and after buckling her son in place, Viktoria climbed into the driver's seat. She checked the pocket of her sweats to make sure she still had the flash drive with Peter Belkin's encrypted computer files. She did.

"We're going to be okay," she said, adjusting the mirror.

"I know, Mommy," he said, his voice small but serious.

Thick frost covered the windows, and cocooned them in a separate world of white. Viktoria turned on the defroster, which cut a circle through the frozen condensation on the windshield. She eased down the driveway as more frost melted. Viktoria turned on the windshield wipers. They swept left and right, cleaning a wedge on the glass.

The car's headlights illuminated a swath of night. Viktoria gasped and slammed on the breaks. The Range Rover skidded and shuddered to a stop, its grill a hairbreadth away from Cody.

Chapter 13

Cody stood in the middle of the drive. The hood of the Range Rover almost touched his chest. Heat leaked from the engine and enveloped him, but it was the sense of betrayal he felt that burned him from within.

Viktoria blanched, her brows drawn together and her jaw tight. Then her countenance darkened. She revved the engine—an easily understood threat.

She was running again. He thought they worked together well, that they'd become a team. You never ran out on your teammate. He opened his mouth, furious and ready to tell her off, to order her to get out of the car.

Then he stopped.

Yes, she was running—leaving him. But wasn't

he at fault, too? In assuming she would remain at his house and wait to get arrested like a sitting duck, hadn't he abandoned his promise to keep her and her son safe, and preserve their family—the only family she had left?

Leaning forward, Cody placed both hands on the hood. "Run me over if you have to," he said, "but I'm not getting out of the way."

The driver's side window lowered with an electric whir. Heat escaped the car's interior in a wave. "I can't let them take Gregory," she said. "I will do anything to keep my child safe."

From the back seat, Gregory blanched and Cody hated that the kid would be traumatized again and again—with no way for Cody to keep him safe and feeling secure.

Yet, Viktoria's last words had been full of steel and resolve. Despite his pain, he was in awe of her. He didn't know where all that courage came from.

"You can't run forever. Eventually, you'll be found and the more miles you travel the worse you'll be viewed."

"Do you think I care what people think about me?"

"Viewed by the courts, law enforcement. Running implies guilt."

"Or that I'm being chased."

"And speaking of being chased—what do you think will happen when Belkin or Mateev finally catch you? You'll be murdered, just like they tried to do last night. And maybe there won't be someone around to help the next time."

"So, you're saying that I should just stay and wait for them to find me?"

Cody slammed his hand on the hood in frustration. "You can stay and let me help you."

"I know that you said you would. It's just…" her voice trailed off.

The silence gave Cody pause. "You don't trust me," he said.

The engine stilled. Through the windshield, he saw Viktoria lean into the headrest and place the heels of her hands over her eyes. She remained that way for a moment and Cody let his hands drop away from the car—as if he'd ever really had the power to stop her from leaving.

She opened the door and stepped out into the darkness. She wrapped her arms across her chest— to stay warm or to protect herself, Cody couldn't tell. The wind whipped around them and pulled Viktoria's hair across her face. Cody longed to run his fingers through the strands, to pull her to him, to feel her breath on his skin.

"Stay," he said.

"Because of your job?" she challenged.

"Are you really questioning my loyalty to you? After all we've been through?"

"I'm protecting my son. Don't you understand that I have to go?"

"Stay," he said again.

"Why?"

"Because." Cody swallowed. Because if she left, he would be alone. Because over the course of this single day, Cody had discovered what he wanted out of life. Because there was nothing he would not do for Viktoria. "Because," he said again, "I need you." The admission was a release—and yet, if she refused him, he knew it would cost him everything.

"Cody." Tears coursed down her cheeks. "I can't wait to be arrested for protecting my child from criminals, and then be treated like a criminal myself."

"No," said Cody, "you can't. But I'm not about to let you slip away like this," he said.

"I'm sorry. I wish it could be different."

"It can be," he said. "I'm going with you."

Belkin pulled out of the circular drive and headed the SUV down the mountain. His visit to Russia needed to be sped up, and perhaps extended. But first he had some loose ends to tie up.

And he couldn't get on that plane without Gregory Mateev.

He entered an address he found for Cody Samuels into the GPS, and started following the directions. The snow no longer fell, but the roads had yet to be plowed a final time and Belkin dared not drive too fast—lest he lose control of his vehicle.

In desperate need of some distraction, Peter Belkin turned on the radio. Carols blared from the speakers. Trees. Reindeer. Happy voices urging him to have a jolly Christmas. He'd come to hate them all.

He searched through the stations, finally finding one with a news-only format. He drove for over a quarter of an hour as banal stories of insignificant lives served as the backdrop to his own worries.

"And in local news," said the announcer, "the body of San Miguel County Sheriff Raymond Benjamin was discovered in his office early this morning, dead by a gunshot wound to the head."

Belkin stared at the radio, willing it to give him more information.

"In what appears to be an accident, Sheriff Benjamin was shot while cleaning his sidearm late on December the twenty-third. His body was found when the first shift of deputies arrived in the morning of the twenty-fourth."

That was a lie. Belkin could smell it, like fetid cheese. There was no way the shooting was accidental. Self-inflicted, certainly. Sheriff Benjamin knew exactly what he was doing and Peter Belkin knew why. At least one of his problems had been solved on its own.

The road descended a steep hill and the SUV picked up speed. Belkin came to a bend in the road. He began to ease his foot off the brake as a thought came to him, and he tensed, his mind absorbed by a new worry. Sheriff Benjamin had been troubled by taking the bribe and providing Belkin with the Mateev woman's location. He was beset with guilt—and guilty people often confessed. What if Sheriff Benjamin had called his wife before swallowing a bullet? Or worse yet, left a detailed note?

Belkin suddenly realized that the SUV was rocketing toward the bend at much too quick a speed. On one side was a steep cliff; the tops of trees at the bottom of the canyon were level with the road. On the other side rose a sheer mountainside. He let off the gas and swerved hard to avoid a fall over the cliff side and into the trees. The SUV's tires didn't respond and careened toward the abyss. Despite his better judgment, he slammed on the brakes. The SUV skidded and slammed into the mountainside, then bounced back, its engine still humming.

Peter Belkin gripped the steering wheel. His hands shook. With a shoulder, he wiped away the sweat trickling down his face and into his eyes. Belkin gingerly shifted the SUV into Reverse. To his amazement, the vehicle moved. Taking up both lanes, he kept his eyes trained on the car's rear bumper and the road beyond, careful not to veer too near to the edge.

The lights came quickly into his peripheral vision. He didn't have time to react, only to know that another car was barreling straight toward him.

Heart thumping, Viktoria braced her arms on the dashboard. Her foot slamming into the imaginary brake on the floor. "Cody!" she screamed. "Look out!"

At the same instant Cody cursed and jerked hard on the steering wheel. The grill of the Range Rover struck the rear bumper of another vehicle. Sparks flew as metal grated against metal. Viktoria held the dashboard as the Range Rover pitched backward with the impact.

The front driver's tire exploded and the Range Rover listed to the side. With the other three tires still turning, Cody's car swung around to the left and headed directly toward the drop-off.

Cody's leg furiously pumped as his foot continually slammed the brake pedal. Viktoria quickly unsnapped her seat belt, turned and pressed Gregory back into his seat. For a split second, Viktoria was weightless, suspended in midair. Then they crashed down; the airbag exploded into her back, shoving her hard into the seat. She lost her breath. The Range Rover bumped and jostled, falling farther and farther. It stopped with a jolt and Viktoria's head snapped back.

Wide-eyed she looked at Cody. He gripped the steering wheel. His foot was still firmly planted on the brake.

"Are you okay?" he asked.

Her neck hurt. "I'm fine," she said, breathless. She continued to press Gregory into the seat, where she had somehow kept him in place. His heartbeat raced under her palm. He whimpered and she shushed him with an "It's alright, Mommy's here."

"Avoid any sudden movements," said Cody.

Viktoria eased her hands off Gregory's chest and looked out the side window. The Range Rover sat at a downward angle. Thick trunks of pine trees lined her view.

"Can I turn around?" she asked.

"You can," said Cody, "but slowly."

Viktoria untwisted until she faced forward. The sight took her breath away.

The Range Rover's hood was crammed against the bases of several trees, wedged into an outcropping of the mountain. But the drop-off beyond was treacherous, as was the climb back out.

"Mommy," said Gregory, "I'm scared."

"I know, Captain Kiddo. That was pretty terrifying," Viktoria said to her son. Then lowering her voice, she said to Cody, "I've jeopardized all our safety. I'm sorry I got you into this."

"I'm not," he said. "I told you—I'm with you."

He reached for her hand.

They felt the slightest movement, and then the Range Rover rolled forward. One of the trees holding them in place cracked, its trunk bending at an ominous angle.

Cody refused to panic. He turned off the car and reached with his left hand and unlatched his seat belt. Next, he gently lifted the door handle and pushed. The door was stuck. Not to worry, he reminded himself, there were other doors to be opened, other ways to get out. He used the driver controls and tried to roll down the windows. They didn't budge.

He silently cursed.

To Viktoria he said, "Unbuckle Gregory." Then to the kid, he said, "Even after your mommy gets you out of the seat belt, I want you to stay put. That's real important, stay put. Got that, Gregory?"

The boy nodded, fear etched across his face.

Viktoria eased around and unbuckled her son. The boy listened and held himself with statue-like stillness. It would have been comical, if not for the deadly seriousness of their situation.

As long as they weren't pinned in the car, they could escape. Now they had to get out of the car.

From the back seat Gregory said, "Mommy, look. Fire."

A small tree next to their car, crushed and bent, was alight. The flames crackled and consumed the pine needles. It was only a matter of time before the fire reached the gas tank and caused an explosion. That was, if the smoke didn't overtake them first.

"Try your door," Cody said to Viktoria.

She jerked the handle several times. "It's stuck," she said, her voice high and filled with alarm.

Outside, he only saw the scarred and scratched trunk of the trees holding them in place. There wasn't enough room for Gregory to squeeze out, much less Viktoria or Cody. A quick glance told him that all the windows were covered. On one hand, it had helped to stop the Range Rover from careening down to the bottom of the canyon. It also held them steady in their downward pitch on the mountainside. On the other hand, they were truly trapped.

The Range Rover slid forward.

"Calm down," Cody said as he placed his arm on Viktoria's shoulder. Her muscles were tight and she trembled. "The worst thing we can do is panic," he said, keeping his voice even.

She bit her lip and nodded. "Okay."

"Don't think of what might happen, think of what needs to be done. Can you do that?"

She nodded again. "But if the windows are disabled and the doors are blocked, what can we do?"

There was only one possible way to escape. The rear hatch. "Stay where you are," Cody said as he slipped the key into his pocket. He eased out of the seat and backed up over the center console. He kept his movements light and minimal. The SUV remained steady. He stopped next to Gregory. Silent tears slid down the kid's cheeks. His fear lodged as a pain in Cody's chest. He gave the kid's cheek a quick pat as he passed. "We'll be okay, I promise."

Wide-eyed, Gregory nodded. Cody struggled to find something else reassuring to say, but didn't want to waste valuable time on sentiments.

Head bent and shoulders stooped, he climbed backward into the small cargo space.

Flames encircled the trees that had stopped their fall in a deadly embrace. Smoke was thicker at the rear of the vehicle and Cody's eyes began to water. He muffled a cough, lest his movements wrest the Range Rover loose from its precarious position.

He reached back. His hand danced blindly along the hatch until he found the handle. He pulled up and the rear gate opened. Cold air washed over Cody, then the updraft pulled a hot cloud of smoke and ash into the night.

He lifted the tailgate slowly. Slowly. Ever so slowly. The car remained still. Then the rear hatch stopped as metal grated against mountainside. He shoved the gate upward, trying to gain another inch. It didn't move. Cody didn't bother estimating the gap's width. It was too small for any of them to slip through.

Then he realized he had the key. If he could break the side window, he could break the rear one, as well. Shielding his eyes with one arm, he gripped the key fob and swung out as if he was delivering a cross punch. The car rocked as the tip of the key connected with a *crack*. The glass crumbled and rained down. Using his sleeve, Cody brushed away the remaining shards of glass then pulled the door closed.

Without another thought, he moved on to the next task: getting out.

"Viktoria," Cody urged. "Get Gregory and come back to me."

She crawled carefully out of her seat and leaned toward the middle bench. Viktoria lifted Gregory over the rear seat. Heat rushed over Cody as a loud pop shot through the night. Flames crept through the air-conditioning vents and began heating up the car. The dashboard smoldered and the instrumental panel started to bubble. The car shuddered and rolled forward again. The fire lit Viktoria from the back and her face was lost in the shadows. "Take Gregory and go," she said.

Cody reached for the boy and set him near the window where the air was cleanest and the flames were farthest away.

The Range Rover shuddered and rolled forward.

"Come on. Viktoria," urged Cody. "We're running out of time."

"Go," she said again, her tone more urgent. "Save my son."

"What are you talking about?" Cody reached for her, but his hand found nothing. "I'm not leaving without you."

Her voice came from the fiery abyss. "My foot's stuck. I can't move."

Belkin sat in the idling SUV and watched the home of Cody Samuels. He hadn't seen a single person on the ground floor. It could be, he reasoned, that they were all on the second story.

No, he decided, something wasn't right. He put the SUV into gear and moved to the far side of the house, where it was hidden from the road and not easily seen even from the front door.

Conscious of the noise, he carefully closed the door before trudging through the snow. By the time he reached the porch, his feet were wet and cold and balls of snow clung to his trousers.

He tried the doorknob. It turned and the door swung open. Belkin took in the room at a single glance. A fire smoldered in the hearth. A cartoon played on the TV. A plate of cookies with thick icing sat in the middle of the table. His own laptop sat on the counter.

As Belkin crossed the threshold, he withdrew the gun from the pocket of his coat and held it at the ready. The cartoon. The cookies. The computer.

They all told the same story—Viktoria and Gregory were here with Cody Samuels, and they were the ones who had made him a prisoner in his own home. But where, exactly, were they now?

Belkin climbed the staircase at the far side of the house. Upstairs he found two bedrooms and a half bath—all empty. Back downstairs he searched through another bathroom and a cluttered storage room. Without question, the house was unoccupied.

With the house awash with lights and a fire left untended, he guessed that Viktoria and Cody had not gone far nor for too long. Belkin opened his laptop and hit the power button. The screen and keyboard remained dark, obviously drained of power.

He rummaged through a drawer filled with odds and ends until he found a small screwdriver. Flipping over his laptop, he removed four screws and lifted off the back plate.

Gritting his teeth, he cursed. His hard drive was missing. He flung the laptop aside, visually taking in the room. Someone with Cody Samuels's level of knowledge wouldn't leave Belkin's hard drive lying around. He'd hide it—someplace safe.

But where? Then another thought came to Belkin and his chest began to burn. What if Samuels was delivering the hard drive to the FBI right now?

Belkin pulled open every drawer in the kitchen, dumping their contents on the floor.

Nothing.

He pulled the cushions from the furniture, tossing them aside.

Nothing.

Belkin began to sweat. He couldn't simply ransack the whole house. If the hard drive was still here, Samuels would have hidden it with care.

Surveying the destruction, Belkin thought of what he knew. Cody Samuels. Graduate of the University of Colorado. Former DEA agent.

While Belkin's knowledge of DEA agents wasn't exhaustive, his understanding of drug dealers was. They had a variety of creative places to hide their stash.

He opened the refrigerator and removed a tub of butter. Using a knife that he retrieved from the floor, Belkin plunged the blade into the container.

Nothing.

He examined the rest of the food before searching through the freezer. He opened the oven, careful to check behind the burners. When that search proved fruitless, Belkin checked the tanks of both toilets.

The possibility that Cody had taken Viktoria Mateev, her son and the hard drive to safety left Belkin ill. There was only one place left to look. He opened the washer and found it empty.

Then he opened the dryer. His knees went weak. Packaged in a Ziploc baggie was the computer's hard drive and every secret Belkin knew.

He exhaled with relief, a seed of confidence beginning to take root in his chest.

Belkin grabbed several cookies as he passed the table. After returning some cushions to the sofa, he settled down, determined to wait as long as needed for Cody and Viktoria to return with their most precious cargo, Gregory.

He chewed and wondered where they might have gone on a night like this one. The roads were unsafe. Hadn't Belkin just witnessed a family plummet to their deaths only moments before?

He stopped, midchew.

He tried to remember what he could of the other car. To him it had been nothing more than blinding headlights and screaming brakes. And yet, he might have caught a glimpse of the passenger. A woman… yes, it had been a woman. She had long blond hair, he recalled that much, as well.

Could it have been Viktoria Mateev? Well, if it was then she was dead and he'd never be implicated at all. He would have to deal with Nikolai Mateev and explain about his grandson, but Belkin had time to think of a story. He liked the idea of somehow implicating Dimitri—yes, it was Dimitri who took a bribe and double-crossed Belkin and Viktoria both. Taking another bite of cookie, Belkin propped his feet on the coffee table—all the better for the fire's warmth to dry his shoes as he waited for Samuels to return—and smiled. Perhaps this *would* be a very happy Christmas.

Blackness surrounded Viktoria. Heat dried her eyes. Her lungs felt hot and ragged. She coughed and coughed and yet she could not draw a single breath. Her foot. There was something about her foot. But, Gregory? In her mind, she saw a pair of crystalline blue eyes and knew that her son would be safe and cared for.

The searing heat became a welcoming warmth and Viktoria began to float on a cloud. She let her lids drift closed, yet then she saw a light. A form emerged, as if birthed from the brightness. It was Lucas she knew, although she didn't know how it could be.

She wanted to ask him so many questions, but she could not recall a single one. She also wanted to tell him that Gregory was safe. Lucas reached for her and called her name.

Cody knew two things: any movement toward the front of the vehicle to help Viktoria could cause the fiery Range Rover to careen down to the bottom of the ravine and kill them all. Also, he couldn't sacrifice the child to save the mother.

That made Cody's decision simple and at the same time, the hardest one ever. He turned and slipped Gregory through the shattered rear window, lowering him to the ground. The boy sank in snow that came up to his waist, but in all likelihood it was several feet deeper. The kid could easily sink and then the snow would collapse, entombing him. He dared not turn away and yet, he had to get Viktoria.

"Hold tight to the bumper," he said to Gregory.

Thick clouds of smoke rolled over the boy but he nodded and gripped the back of the Range Rover with hands that Cody found incredibly small for such an important job. Cody swallowed down any apprehension as he turned back to the interior of the Range Rover.

Heat pressed down like a hand, as flames of blue and orange stretched along the roof and reached for the open rear window. Smoke and ash blew into Cody's eyes, making it difficult to see. He cast the discomfort aside, along with the desperation that was forming a hard knot in his chest. He had one final task to accomplish and he refused to leave without Viktoria.

The Range Rover shuddered again. It rolled forward. From outside, Gregory screamed.

Goddamn it! He'd told the kid to hold on to the bumper. If the vehicle broke free, would he know enough to let go? Or worse yet, would he get pulled under the tires?

An explosion rocked the Range Rover as the front tire exploded. The car listed to the right and the rear end slipped around.

Cody called out Viktoria's name.

She didn't answer.

He tried again. "Viktoria," he said, "you need to answer me so I can find you."

"Cody," she said, her voice thin. And then, "Gregory."

Those words were all he needed to hear. Cody braced one hand on the floorboard and with the other he reached forward. He felt nothing, then his palm connected with fabric. His grip tightened and he pulled with all his might, dragging Viktoria over the rear seat. Soot covered her face and had turned her hair gray. Her eyes were red and watered. He'd never seen anyone more beautiful in his life.

The car rolled forward. He didn't have time to panic. With his hand still clutched tightly on her shirt, he dove out the rear window. Cody landed on his back and Viktoria on top of his chest. Only inches away, Gregory still held tight to the rear bumper. Tears streamed down his face. Cody reached for the kid and pulled him close.

The trees holding the Range Rover were fully alight. Thick black smoke billowed out of the rear window as flames danced on feet of destruction in and around the car. The total devastation gave him pause, and yet Cody was thankful they had all made it out of the inferno.

The trunk of a tree broke with a loud crack and the Range Rover began to roll downward. The fiery bumper was visible for only a minute before disappearing over the edge of a cliff.

Cody had promised to keep Viktoria and Gregory safe, and he had. But now there was one final challenge to be met: the steep and treacherous climb to the road.

Viktoria's chest burned. Her eyes watered. Her throat was raw. Her ankle throbbed where it had slipped and then stuck fast between the front seat and the console. Coughs racked her body with such vehemence that she thought she might retch. Yet, the discomfort and pain meant that she had made it out of the car alive.

They all huddled together on a small outcropping of an otherwise sheer cliff and waited as Viktoria caught her breath.

As if a band that had been constricting Viktoria's chest was loosened, she was finally able to draw breath and her coughs lessened. "I'm so sorry," she said, her first words a paltry substitution for the dark chasm of *what could have been*. "I put all three of us at risk." Another cough broke free from her chest. Cody drew her closer.

"We're okay," he said. "We made it out."

He looked over his shoulder and she followed his gaze. She knew what he was thinking, for she was thinking the same thing. They were far from safe and would have to scale the mountain wall before they became victims of exposure.

"Take a minute," he said. "With the trees on fire we've got heat, but fire's unpredictable and we don't want to be trapped as the flames spread."

"Let's get going then," Viktoria said. She kissed the top of Gregory's head. The scent of woodsmoke clung to his hair, and she realized he was wearing only the pajamas she'd put him in last night. In her haste to run she hadn't even grabbed a coat or jacket for Gregory, trusting the car's heater to keep him warm.

"We only have a hundred yards or so to the road," Cody said, "and it's climbable, but it'll be hard going."

"I was able to keep my boots on," she said, thankful for her shoes.

"Tighten your laces," Cody urged. He stood and removed his coat first and then his belt. He wound the belt through a loop at the small of his back and it resembled a tail. "I want you to hold on to this, Viktoria. It'll help you as you climb and keep us together."

Viktoria nodded and turned her attention to relacing her boots.

Kneeling again, Cody said, "Grab my neck, Gregory. You and I are going to race to the top of this mountain, okay?"

Gregory gave a solemn nod and looped his arms around Cody's neck.

"Viktoria," said Cody, "help me slip the coat over my back. It'll give Gregory a little more support, but mostly keep us both warm."

Cody was clever and skilled, and clearly thinking of ways to help them all survive. Why hadn't she believed in him before? Because she simply hadn't been willing to trust Gregory's welfare to anyone but herself. Viktoria knew it was time to reframe the way she looked at things—especially at Cody.

He wasn't just some random guy. Meeting Cody was the most important thing to happen to her in years. In her lifetime, really—second only to giving birth to Gregory.

"Grab the belt," said Cody. "Are you ready?"

She gave a light tug in response and they began their ascent. When Viktoria took her first step a bolt of pain shot around the front of her foot. She clenched her teeth and tried to ignore the ache. They were all together and her son didn't seem to be too troubled by their predicament. She put the other foot in front of the first. And again. And again.

Only her hands and face were exposed to the cold. She tucked her nose into the jacket's collar and used the sleeves as cover. *One hundred yards*, she said to herself. *The length of a football field. A track star can run the distance in under twelve seconds.* Surely, she could walk that far. True, most football fields weren't on the side of a mountain. Nor were many races run in several feet of snow. Viktoria refused to think of that and continued to climb. Instead she thought of Cody's home and a hot shower. She thought of having a nice cup of coffee along with an entire plate of Christmas cookies. She thought of the driver who'd been parked in the middle of the road and had hopefully called the authorities for help by now. Although it would bring the police into her life that much sooner, she also thought about Gregory being totally safe and cared for.

Then she thought about the driver of the other car again. A face flashed in her mind, seen for only a terror-fueled instant. Yet, what had she seen? A high forehead? Neatly trimmed hair? Could it have been Peter Belkin?

The car they'd struck was black and large, possibly an SUV, like the ones used during the raid on her cabin. But, the police weren't interested in speaking to Belkin, so he was still locked in the pantry. Unless...

No. She forced the possibility from her mind. It

could have been any one of thousands of people from the Telluride area. Thinking that she'd seen Peter Belkin was a trick of her mind—a byproduct of fatigue and stress.

To keep from worrying, she turned her mind back to the climb. They'd covered half the distance to the road so far. Gregory was still safely tucked underneath Cody's thick winter coat. Viktoria took a step and then another. Her thighs burned and a pain gripped her side. Cold wind bit her cheeks.

Onward they trudged. No one spoke. Viktoria knew that she didn't have enough breath to carry on a conversation anyhow. There were even things that made the treacherous ascent a little easier than it might have been. During the crash, the Range Rover had cut a neat path for them to follow, giving them broken branches and small stumps onto which they could hold. The tires and grill had packed down the snow and made walking possible. Upward. Upward. She kept moving.

"Here we are," said Cody.

A moment later, Viktoria stepped onto the roadway. She let go of the belt. Her legs throbbed. Her pulse raced at the base of her skull. Her throat and lungs still felt like they'd been scrubbed with sandpaper. Cody took off his coat and Gregory slid to the ground.

Her son ran to Viktoria and threw himself into her arms. Nothing hurt so badly that she couldn't scoop him up and hold him tight. "We made it," he said.

Viktoria squeezed Gregory tighter. "We did."

Cody placed a hand on her shoulder and Viktoria turned toward him, connecting the three of them with each other.

A gust of wind rushed down the mountainside, pushing forward a drift of snow. For a moment, they were lost in swirling ice. It stopped and Cody lifted Gregory into his arms.

"Come on," he said. "We don't want to be out here any longer than necessary. My place is only a few miles away."

A few miles. To Viktoria's sore body, that distance seemed one hundred times longer. Yet, she had no choice but to continue. "Lead the way," she said.

A set of headlights cut through the icy winter blackness as a vehicle edged over the rise. Viktoria saw that it was a bright red pickup truck. It slowed and pulled up next to where they all stood. The window eased down and a man leaned out.

"What the devil are you folks doing out on a night like this?" He looked at the path down the hill and the trees that still burned behind them. "Looks like you had a heap of trouble. I'm glad I came by when I did. Anyone else down there?"

The man's words were easy enough to understand, yet Viktoria blinked twice, not sure if she trusted her own eyes. He was a large man with a shock of white hair and yes, a white beard. He wore a flannel shirt of green, blue and red plaid. For a moment, she stood mute.

Then Gregory whispered, "Is that Santa?"

Even though she had just been thinking the same thing, Viktoria understood the impertinence of what her son had said. "Gregory," she chastised. "That's not polite."

"It's nothing I haven't heard before." The man laughed. "Especially this time of the year. What can I do to help?"

Cody stepped closer to the truck. "Our car went off the road and we'd really appreciate a ride. My place is back about three miles—right across from the entrance to the ski resort."

"Sure thing. Hop in."

Cody sat in the seat opposite the driver. Viktoria and Gregory sat in the two back jump seats. At one time she might have considered the space cramped, but not tonight. Her cold hands began to thaw and the soreness in her muscles lessened. Just being able to sit in someplace warm was a simple pleasure and one for which she was truly grateful.

"Is there anyone I can call for you?" the man offered as he began driving. "The highway patrol? Family?"

"We'll just make the calls when we get home," said Cody. "Although we're grateful that you're willing to help."

"It's no trouble at all," the man said. "I was just on my way to work. It'll be a busy night and I don't think I'll be home until morning."

"You have a lot of work to do on Christmas Eve?" asked Gregory. He gave his mother a sideways glance that she read as *I told you so.* She shook her head at him.

Her son ignored the chastisement and leaned forward. "What's your job?"

"I work for the Department of Transportation clearing the roads," said the driver. "This blizzard has shut everything down and it's going to take me all night to get it cleared." He laughed. "I suppose I am a little like Santa. I keep the roads clean and safe so that people can visit their loved ones."

"See?" Gregory mouthed.

From his seat in the front, Cody leaned forward. "That's my turnoff," he said.

The truck moved easily off the main road and cut through the snowdrifts that had shifted as the wind blew down from the mountains.

Cody continued, "My house is up ahead, on the right."

The truck pulled up in front of Cody's place. The man put the gearshift in Park and stepped out. He pulled his seat forward and offered a hand to Viktoria. With his help, she stepped out of the truck. While sitting in the warm cabin, her ankle had gotten stiff and she stumbled now as she tried to walk. A burst of pain exploded in her leg and she grabbed the hood of the truck. Cody was at her side in a moment, his strong arms supporting her as the driver helped Gregory down.

"Are you sure I can't call someone?" the driver asked.

"No," said Cody, "we're home safe now, which is the important thing. We'll call the highway patrol to report the wreck once we get inside."

"Thank you for everything," Viktoria said.

She looked longingly at Cody's house. Because she'd hoped to sneak away, everything was as they'd left it. The lights were still blazing along with the TV. Their warmth and comfort beckoned and she gingerly took slow steps. She stopped near the porch and turned to the man. He was already back in his truck. "You literally saved us," she said, "and we don't even know your name."

The man leaned his elbow on the window frame and raised his voice to be heard above the hum of the truck's engine. "You can call me Kris," the man said. With that, he gave a wave and backed out of Cody's drive.

"Kris," said Gregory, a little breathless. "Like Kris Kringle."

Cody smiled at Gregory. "Your mom was right. Santa can use his magic to get wherever he needs to be. And to help us make it home in time for Christmas morning." He turned the door handle and pushed it open.

As Gregory cheered his excitement for presents, all Viktoria could think about was *home*. That was all Viktoria wanted. A place to call her own, where she could raise her son in peace. Swallowing, she turned to walk through the open door, then stopped. Her blood froze. The cabin was in disarray. Cushions were strewn about.

Cutlery was scattered on the floor. But that wasn't the worst of it.

On the sofa sat Peter Belkin. Gun in hand, the barrel aimed at her chest.

Chapter 14

A wide smile spread across Belkin's face. He'd hit the trifecta with what had just walked through the door. Viktoria Mateev—a problem to be neutralized. Gregory Mateev—the precious cargo that needed to be delivered. Cody Samuels—the only other person who could implicate Belkin personally in any of the crimes.

"Merry Christmas," Belkin said, as he twitched the gun. "Come in from the cold," he continued, "and close the door. Do it."

Viktoria hesitated and reached for Gregory. Belkin made a deliberate show of resighting his gun and aiming it at the child.

"Come in," he repeated, "and no one gets hurt."

Huddled together, they all shuffled into the room.

Cody was the last through the door and he pulled it shut. Belkin noted that the latch did not catch—he imagined that Cody had purposefully left the door partially open—all the better for them to escape. A fine idea, except that Belkin didn't intend to let Viktoria or Cody leave the cabin alive.

"Sit at the table," he waved the gun to indicate where they should go. He needed them farther in the room, so he could be nearest to the exit. He stood and moved as the trio meekly did as they were told.

"I will be brief and speak plain," he said, not caring to waste any more time. "I found my hard drive and reinstalled it into my laptop. If you just hand over Gregory, I'll leave."

Cody Samuels stood, placing himself bodily between Belkin and Viktoria. "No way," he said.

"I have no time or patience to argue with you." Belkin sidestepped until once again he had Viktoria in his sights. Gregory was tucked into his mother's side.

He needed to get Gregory out of the cabin and decided to address the child directly. "Your grandfather hired me to bring you to him. I know you love your mother very much and will miss her terribly, but your grandfather is an important man in Russia. He wants you near him so you will be safe."

"No," said Gregory.

"Leave him alone, Belkin." Viktoria said.

"Gregory, I am speaking to you man-to-man. You must listen to me, your *Dyadya Pyotr*." Uncle Peter. "I am not leaving here without you. Your mother will try to keep you from going with me, and I will have to stop her. But, if you come with me peacefully no one needs to get hurt."

Belkin would have to kill both Viktoria and Cody Samuels but he wanted to keep Gregory as calm as possible. Nikolai was certain to question Gregory about his treatment and he knew that the child would have much to say already. For Belkin's sake, it would be better if Gregory thought that it was his idea to leave and that his mother was safe and alive.

The boy leaned back a little.

Belkin's shoulder began to ache—the one that Gregory had kicked and then had been filled with sedatives. He moved the gun from one hand to the next. "Come," he gestured to Gregory. "We need to leave and meet your grandfather."

"That," Viktoria muttered between clenched teeth, "will never happen."

Belkin was done with the Mateev woman. She needed to die right now. He grabbed her hair, pulling her to him. In that instant, Cody swooped down and grabbed a knife from the floor. He lunged at Belkin, the blade slicing though his wrist. Belkin jerked back, slamming into the door. His hold on Viktoria never lessened and they stumbled into the howling wind. Bits of ice and tiny snowflakes struck Belkin's cheeks and eyes, blinding him.

Viktoria pulled fiercely on Belkin's gun arm. He relented for a moment. She moved backward, drawn by the momentum of her body's weight. As her grip on him eased, he pulled away and kicked her in the middle. She stumbled backward. Without a hesitation, he lined up the Sig Sauer's sights with Viktoria's head and pulled the trigger.

Cody rushed to the doorway. The bullet, a flash of light and a sound that echoed off the mountains. Viktoria's head snapped, knocking her back into the bright white snow.

Every ounce of hope and joy which Viktoria had brought to him morphed into rage. Cody pushed off the floor and launched himself at Belkin, hitting the older man square in the chest. They landed hard with a satisfying crunch. Belkin wheezed like a broken bellows and Cody prayed he'd broken the man's ribs.

The gun skittered away. Cody didn't care. He wasn't going to shoot this pile of garbage; rather, he planned to tear him apart piece by miserable piece. Cody's fist landed on Belkin's face again and again.

As Belkin's appearance changed from smug to bloody, Cody eased up. And for the first time, he heard Gregory's piercing wail coming from inside the house. Grabbing Belkin by the collar, Cody hefted them both to their feet. Sweat dripped down Cody's back and his breath came in ragged gasps.

Belkin spat, turning the snow red. "What do you plan to do with me now?"

Cody wished he could kill him. A life for a life. But somehow, he knew that Viktoria wouldn't approve. "I'm going to call this in. Murder. Kidnapping. Attempted kidnapping. You'll go to jail for a long time."

Belkin snorted. "I think not," he said.

What if Belkin was right? What if the bad guys always won, and honor and justice were outdated ideals? A chasm of nothingness opened within him, turning the world gray.

A loud hiccupping cry came from inside. Cody pulled Belkin toward the house.

"Poor kid," Cody murmured.

What could he say to Gregory? Viktoria had been brave and loving and smart—and because of that she had given her own life to save her son's. Cody inhaled deeply and searched for the words he would need to explain the tragedy.

Belkin could tell that Cody was distracted, upset by the death of Viktoria Mateev and troubled by her son's grief. He shuffled along, playing the part of the beaten and beleaguered foe. All the while he scanned the area and his mind worked. Five feet to the left, granite-gray steel showed perfectly against the pristine whiteness of the snow. It was his gun with the single bullet. He tensed and waited for another screech from Gregory to tear open the night.

It came and drew Cody's attention.

Belkin threw his weight to the side and fell to the ground in a heap. He reached out. His fingers grazed the barrel of the gun. Cody quickly advanced toward him as Belkin swung the gun around. Cody lifted his foot, ready to kick Belkin in the side, incapacitating him once more. Belkin wrapped his fingers around the gun's grip. Cody's gaze landed on the gun and his eyes grew wide. He retreated, but not enough.

Belkin's finger found the trigger and he fired. The bullet slammed into Cody's shoulder, knocking him down. A bolt of white-hot pain shot through his arm as the air left his lungs in a single agonizing rush.

The gun's report echoed off the hills. His shoulder throbbed; a fierce ache rushed down his arm. Cody sat up and pushed to stand. His arm collapsed and he tumbled back down. In the distance, Gregory screamed.

Cody rolled to his knees, stood and staggered forward. Belkin rushed from the cabin. Tucked under one arm was the laptop. With the same hand, he held a squirming and crying Gregory. In Belkin's other hand was the automatic pistol. "Don't move," he said. He pulled the door of the SUV open with his gun hand and shoved Gregory into the car and threw the laptop in after him.

Cody didn't think, only reacted. He rushed forward. Then the gun was again leveled with his chest, stopping Cody short. Belkin pulled the trigger.

It was followed by a click.

Only two bullets. Damn. In the furor of the fight, Belkin had forgotten. Still, the Sig Sauer could prove useful, especially against one as injured as Cody Samuels. Belkin brought the butt down on Cody's temple with all the force he could muster. The larger man crumpled at the knees and fell forward.

Belkin lifted himself into the SUV and shifted into Drive. With snow spraying behind him, he raced down the road. Ignoring the crying Gregory, Belkin checked the time—9:15 p.m. If his security team had followed orders, they should be ready for takeoff as soon as he arrived at the airfield. Once airborne, nothing would stop Belkin from getting Gregory out of the country. Forty-five minutes to complete success.

Viktoria blinked at the glare. It dimmed from blinding light to darkness filled with swirling bits of white. She inhaled sharply. Icy air froze her nose. Snow blew past her face. Her hands were numb and her head throbbed with each beat of her heart.

It came back to her. Belkin. Gregory. Cody. The gun.

The pain in her head was now localized. She lifted a hand to gently touch her scalp. She found warmth and wetness and winced. She looked at her fingers stained red with her own blood. Slowly she rolled to her side. A wave of nausea crashed over her and Viktoria took slow, deep breaths. Her fuddled mind quickly brought back what had happened. She'd been shot, and it seemed that the bullet had grazed her scalp. It had knocked her down and left her unconscious.

She slowly pushed to sitting and once up, she scanned her surroundings. The door to Cody's house stood opened about three yards away. What had happened while she was out cold? Where were Gregory and Cody and Belkin?

She turned to look over her shoulder and saw him, nothing more than a lump in the snow.

Her heartbeat raced, an agonizing staccato pulsing through the side of her head. She stood. Faltered. Fell. On hands and knees, she scrambled forward. The hint of copper and a sickly sweetness filled the air. She reached for him. Her hands burned with cold. None of that mattered.

Cody's blue sweater was covered in blood—wet and black in the night. He had a gash on the side of his head. A thin line of blood trickled down his cheek and disappeared into his collar. She placed two fingers under his jaw and felt for a pulse. It was there, strong and steady.

Viktoria sobbed with relief.

Cody's eyes fluttered open. He reached up and touched the side of Viktoria's face. "How are you here?" he asked. "Or am I dead, too?"

She leaned in to his palm. "I'm here and you're alive. We both are."

"I knew heaven couldn't be this cold."

"Are you strong enough to sit? Can I help you?"

Cody pulled himself up. His face drained of all color, silver against the dark night and the swirling snow. He hung his head for a moment. Looking up, he reached for her. "I thought you were dead, Viktoria," he said, as she allowed him to envelop her in his strong arms. "Belkin shot you. I saw it."

"He did, but I don't think it's too bad." She turned to give him a view of the wound she had felt earlier.

He carefully lifted her hair. "Thank God the bullet barely touched you. We should get you to a doctor."

"Gregory?" she asked. Her own well-being was the last thing she cared about. "Where is he?"

He shook his head. "With Belkin," he said. "Gone."

Cody rose and pulled Viktoria to her feet. Viktoria's head felt light and warm and she teetered on unsteady legs. He wrapped an arm around her waist, keeping her stable. "I tried to stop them. He shot me in the shoulder. Thankfully he only had two rounds, because his next bullet would have been aimed better."

The detached feeling from before returned. "Gone?" she said; her voice faded within her own ears. "Gone, where?"

Cody gripped his shoulder, applying pressure. "Let's get back inside and figure out what to do next."

She knew there was more for them to do to stop Belkin. But what? If only she could focus. Viktoria leaned into Cody and he winced. "How badly are you hurt?"

"Not bad enough to keep me down."

They trudged to the cabin. The warmth from the fire in the fireplace was welcome. The glare of the electric lights overhead was not. Viktoria shielded her eyes while Cody turned off several of them, leaving only two table lamps lit.

"Sit," he gestured to a chair at the table. "Let me have a look at your head." He held one arm close to his body, and in the light Viktoria could see a blackened bullet hole both in the front of his shirt and the back.

"No way," she said, beginning to feel more like herself. "You have a seat. Your shoulder needs more attention than I do." She studied Cody and wondered how she could get his sweater off without making him lift his arm.

She scanned the utensil-covered kitchen floor and found a pair of scissors. "I hope this isn't your favorite shirt," she said, slipping the blade under the cuff at his wrist.

He shook his head grimly. "Cut away."

Viktoria slowly manipulated the scissors all the way up Cody's sleeve, then turned them around and cut down from the neck. The fabric fell open to reveal an angry red puncture wound that had punched its way straight through his shoulder, just missing the collarbone.

Only a small amount of blood seeped from the hole. "I think the cold and snow staunched some of your bleeding." Viktoria pieced the sweater, both front and back, together. No missing pieces of fabric in the wound to cause a nasty infection. "Do you have a first aid kit?"

"In the bathroom closet on the second shelf."

Viktoria walked across the room, relieved that her dizziness had abated. Better yet, the return of her physical facilities was coupled with the sharpening of her mental ones, too. Now that she could think, the obvious question was where Belkin might have taken Gregory.

At the bathroom sink, she took a moment to wash away some of the blood that had dried on her face and to daub antiseptic ointment on the furrow in her scalp. She also checked the front pocket of the sweatshirt for the flash drive. It was still there.

Having taken less than a minute on her own ministrations, she returned with the well-stocked first aid kit she'd found. Initially, she cleaned the wound on Cody's shoulder and then she wiped down the side of his face. A nasty purple bruise had risen on his temple.

Cody spoke as Viktoria applied an antiseptic ointment and a thick white bandage to both sides of the bullet wound. "Before we rush out of here to find Gregory, we need to figure out where Belkin has taken him this time."

"They won't go back to Belkin's house," Viktoria guessed, "even if they need more time. Didn't the goon on the walkie-talkie mention another safe house?"

"He also mentioned meeting at an airfield."

Viktoria wrapped a long piece of gauze around Cody's shoulder to secure the bandages in place. "What airfield would he be referring to?"

"There's Telluride Regional Airport."

"That sounds public. Would Belkin risk taking Gregory on a plane?"

"I agree that Belkin can't drag Gregory onto a commercial flight. What we heard definitely made it sound like he was planning to fly out on a private jet."

Her hands began to tremble and she willed them to stop. She'd been foolish to remain in Telluride at all, the weather and Cody Samuels be damned. And now she'd lost her son. Panicking, she knew, would not help her to find Gregory again. She breathed deeply and said the only rational thing that came to mind, "So he won't use Telluride Regional."

"Not necessarily. It also has a private terminal. Although, there is another private airstrip south of town."

"Two airports?" Viktoria feared she might retch. "Which means we have to pick one and hope we're right."

Cody finished the thought for her. "Because if we're wrong, Gregory's gone for good."

Chapter 15

Belkin edged the large SUV around a turn. The back wheels lost contact with the road and skidded sideways, spinning the vehicle like a lazy top.

He turned into the spin and cursed. *"Chert."* *Damn.* The SUV teetered to a stop. Belkin let out the long breath he had been holding and cast a glance at the dashboard clock—10:05 p.m. He was late but not concerned about his tardiness. The security team would wait for him no matter what. He was the one who signed their checks, and he had the goods that needed transport.

He moved the gearshift down a notch and into second gear. It'd put more pressure on the large engine, hopefully enough to propel the car up the hills to the waiting plane.

Using both feet, he simultaneously lifted one foot off the brake as he slowly depressed the accelerator. The SUV moved forward as Belkin felt the tires chew through the drift in front of him.

There was one good thing about the roads being so treacherous. It had stopped Gregory from bawling like a calf. The boy now sat in the passenger seat, holding the console that stood between the seats with one hand and his door with the other. His knuckles and face were white with anxiety.

"Do you like the snow?" he asked Gregory.

"I don't like *you*," Gregory said.

Even with the child's defiant words, Belkin recognized an undertone of acceptance of the situation.

"If you like snow, you will like Russia. We have snows that can bury a cabin for a month. A whole month! To survive in Russia you must be a strong boy. Are you a strong boy, Gregory Mateev?"

"I can run faster than anyone in my preschool class."

That was not Russian strength, but American weakness. Americans—always looking to better their friends. Never did they worry about outwitting their foes. And keeping that strategy in mind, Belkin said, *"Khorosho."* Then repeated, "Good. That means *good* in Russian." It was time his young listener started to learn his native language.

The in-car navigation chirped with a new set of directions. Belkin crept around the final turn and began the ascent to the isolated private airstrip. With all roads nearly impassable, he wondered about the state of the runway. The airport came into view. Lights on the tarmac cut through the ever-slowing snow to reveal a clean strip of black runway. A pickup truck with a snowplow attached to its grill drove back toward the metal hangar sitting in the shadow of an empty air traffic control tower.

A white Hawker 900 sat under the lights. The silver edging on the plane's upturned wings reflected the overhead beam. The door to the private jet sat open and the stairs were lowered. The heat signatures from the engines were visible, even from a distance.

Belkin had the child. The laptop. Viktoria Mateev, the only person who cared enough to pursue Belkin, was dead. And with any luck, Cody Samuels would perish as he lay unconscious in the cold.

He rounded the bend and entered through the airfield's open gates.

Viktoria had checked the clock on the back of the stove before leaving the cabin—10:15 p.m. They trekked the short distance through the snow to the garage, where Cody kept his pickup truck. The rush that had surged through her when she'd first found Cody was gone. Her determination to find Gregory was changing from an electric charge that spurred her ahead to a thick, gray slurry through which she had to wade. More than her injury, the pain in her skull came from her countless doubts that crashed together like an unrepentant sea on a rocky coast. Even if she found Belkin again, would she be able to save her son? Or was she too late this time?

Memories of Gregory came to her—a mewling newborn, pink and wrinkly, yet perfect all the same. A toddler, running through their apartment, giggling as he hit a pot with a spoon. Then, tonight, her son's eyes wide with terror, as he once again saw Peter Belkin.

Cody opened the door of the detached garage. He winced, even though he'd used his good arm to do it.

"I'll drive." Viktoria held out her hand for the keys.

"You've been shot. You could have a concussion."

"You've been shot, too. Besides, I can't sit in the passenger seat and wait to get Gregory back. I need to *do* something."

Cody paused. Nodding his head, he held out the car keys. "You drive, I'll navigate," he said.

Viktoria took the keys and slid behind the wheel as Cody climbed into the passenger seat. Viktoria turned the key, shifted to Drive and Cody opened the glove box. He retrieved a silver automatic pistol and clip full of ammunition. Sliding the magazine home, he pulled back the barrel and chambered a single round. With the gun loaded, he slipped it to the small of his back, presumably held in place by the waistband of his jeans.

"How far ahead of us is he, do you think?" Viktoria asked.

"No more than half an hour."

But not much less, Viktoria said to herself. She had been right to drive. It kept her mind off the hollowness in her chest and the tightness in her throat.

It also quieted the inner voice that screamed, *Gregory is gone. Forever.*

At the end of Cody's road, a distinct set of tire tracks turned to the left, toward Telluride. In her mind, Viktoria saw the map that Cody had spread across his kitchen table. The private airstrip was through town and on to the south. The regional airport would be west, nearer to the ski resort. Which way—left, and after the tire tracks, or right to the more likely place for Belkin to have a plane?

Viktoria gripped the steering wheel and stared into the night. She had no strong religious beliefs beyond those that dictated she live a moral and honorable life. Nor did she have any new age leanings. Yet as she sat there, she prayed and willed her soul to connect with that of Gregory's. He was flesh of her flesh. She had cared for and nurtured him his entire life. There had to be a connection more than the shared DNA. Maybe, somehow, he would feel her reaching out to him, and not feel so scared.

"Look," said Cody, pointing to the sky. "It's a plane," he said, "coming in low but definitely not heading to Telluride's regional airport. If that's Belkin's plane, it's going to the private airfield."

Viktoria let her shoulders drop. "At least we know where he's going."

"It is good that we have a better idea of which airport." Cody paused. In his silence, Viktoria heard the distinct *but*.

"What aren't you telling me?" Viktoria asked.

"It will take over a half an hour to get to the private airstrip. And judging by where that plane is now, Belkin will have plenty of time to escape."

Cold from the frozen tarmac seeped into Belkin's shoes. He shoved his hands deeper into his pockets and glared at Dimitri. "What do you mean?" Belkin asked. "The wings aren't frozen. There's no ice on them. I can see as much from here."

"The plane has been waiting since the night of the twenty-third. The metal is frozen solid. If we take off, the wings will rip from the aircraft. We tried turning on the engines, to warm things up, but it's too cold. We need a deicer, or foam," Dimitri continued. "That's something they don't have here because this facility is so small. Telluride Regional has the right equipment. No worries though. Another plane is en route and should arrive any minute."

Belkin could barely stand to have yet another problem blocking his way, but he clearly had no other choice but to wait. "Is this plane's galley stocked? What about a sedative for the kid?" Or if anything else went wrong, Belkin would need something strong for his nerves, as well.

"No sedatives, but there's plenty of food for the trip to British Columbia. It will only take us a few minutes to move everything to the new plane. And after we land in Canada, we'll only need to refuel and can be in Moscow by dinnertime tomorrow."

"Call whoever you need. I want something at the airport when we land to keep the kid quiet," said Belkin. He turned his back on the other man and opened the door of the warm SUV. No need for them both to stand outside in the freezing cold. An idea struck him and he pivoted. "Get something for the kid to eat—a cookie, maybe. And bring me a vodka."

"Do you want anything in the drink?"

After having endured the past few days, Belkin would happily greet his old friend—the numbness that followed a stiff drink—with enthusiasm. "Just vodka," he said, "with more vodka on top."

Viktoria leaned forward in her seat and concentrated on the road ahead. The wind had picked up, buffeting the truck with the occasional gust. A huge drift blew past and created near-whiteout conditions, then dissipated. The truck's headlights cut through, revealing a long stretch of clean pavement, thanks to the blowing wind.

"That's lucky," said Cody. Pointing with his good hand at the newly cleaned road.

It was. She nodded grimly and flicked her eyes to the dashboard clock—10:30 p.m. Ninety minutes since they had been ambushed by Belkin. Fifteen minutes since Cody and she had left his house. It was an eternity. Viktoria pressed down on the accelerator and the pickup shot forward.

The farther she drove, the more certain she became that they were going in the right direction. She felt it in her bones. Gregory was close. The invisible tether that linked mother to child was leading her in the right direction. She took the final turn and slowed. Mother Nature hadn't cleared the road leading up to the private airstrip and once again a wall of snow blocked her way.

She stopped and let the engine idle. Peering into the distance, she saw only darkness. There were no more lights in the sky, or even lights on the hilltop to show that the airfield was open.

Was she mistaken? Had she imagined the pull of Gregory's soul upon hers? Was the plane they followed headed to another airport? She refused to consider that the plane they saw might not have been coming in for a landing, but rather Belkin's flight taking off from Telluride Regional.

Cody brushed his finger over Viktoria's cheek. "We've come too far for you to second-guess yourself. Now, go! We won't save Gregory sitting here and wondering."

Viktoria licked her lips. Nodded.

She put the pickup in second gear, revved the engine and pushed the car into the snow.

Belkin sat in the warm SUV, a drink in his hand and his knee bouncing. The anesthetized sensation that he sought eluded him. Instead the alcohol jumped on his nerves, making him twitchy and irritable. The new plane, an older model and much less comfortable Cessna King Air with dual prop engines, had just landed. The pilot had taxied to the hangar where he was refueling the aircraft.

A sharp rap of knuckles on glass came at the window. Belkin started. Vodka sloshed over the side of his glass and soaked the cuff of his cashmere sweater. He cursed and licked his exposed wrist. After passing the drink from one hand to the other, he lowered the window.

"Fifteen more minutes," said Dimitri. His angular nose was red and dripping. Wind blew his short dark hair until it stood upright. He shoved his gloved hands into his coat pockets and shifted on the balls of his feet. "Thirty minutes, at the outside."

"Which is it?" snapped Belkin. "Fifteen minutes or a half hour?"

"The pilot needs to check the wind speed. With a headwind like this, we'd be going backward." He gave a feeble laugh at his attempt at a joke.

"Fifteen minutes," said Belkin. He hit the window button and it whirred as it lifted. *"Pridurok,"* Belkin added. Jerk.

"I think that man doesn't like you and thinks that you are the *pridurok*," said Gregory from the passenger seat. A chocolate crumb was stuck to the side of his face.

"Do you even know what *pridurok* means?"

"I know it's not nice," said Gregory.

Belkin shrugged. "What would you do if the people working for you were so..." he rolled his hand and searched for another word. *"Nekompetentnyy."*

"What does that mean?"

Belkin sipped his drink and watched the Cessna as it exited the hangar. "Incompetent," he said. "Unable to do their jobs."

Gregory shifted in his seat. "I would be nicer to them. Don't you need them to do stuff for you?

Why would they help if you are mean to them all the time?"

Belkin turned to level a gaze at the kid. Gregory scratched his nose.

"That is not the way of the world," said Belkin. Those with money, power and influence create the rules. The rest of the sheep making up the mass of humanity just follow along, bleating their sad bleat. How very much like an American to think that all men had some value. Belkin sipped his drink and settled back in his seat. "You will learn, child. You will learn."

The pickup crested a hill. In the distance, Viktoria saw a golden glow rising from the darkened horizon.

"That's the airfield," said Cody. He leaned forward, the seat belt tight across his chest. "Over there, see those lights?"

Across a field sat a single-runway airport. A chain-link fence surrounded the perimeter. The tarmac was cleared. Two planes passed as they were being wheeled across the ground. One was returning to a domed metal hangar and the other was taxiing to the end of the runway. Nearby sat a black SUV.

"Belkin," she said.

"Follow the road. It goes around to the right and the entrance is on the other side of the hangar."

"I'm not waiting that long to get Gregory. And I'm done playing by the rules."

"Okay," said Cody. He gestured to the road. "The entrance is up ahead. Just go!"

"That's their entrance. Ours is straight ahead."

Backing up, Viktoria turned the steering wheel and pointed the hood of their pickup right at Belkin's SUV. The only thing separating her from her boy was a chain-link fence—that and an armed gunman, a plane, ready for takeoff—and Peter Belkin himself. She gunned the engine and they launched across the snow-covered field.

Belkin stared out into the night. The first plane was being tucked away into the hangar, awaiting a new crew to return it to Newark, New Jersey, where his law firm kept their fleet. He sipped from his glass and let the vodka turn his tongue numb.

Boxes of food were being loaded onto the second plane. Belkin gritted his teeth to keep from screaming. The Cessna King Air could cover a little more than 300 miles every hour. That made the trip to Victoria, British Columbia, about four hours and twenty minutes. How much food did they think they needed? He belted back another swallow.

Gregory stared out the window, his eyes wide. Following the child's gaze, Belkin's skin grew damp and clammy. He leaned forward and stared unbelieving into the night.

A battered pickup was driving full-speed across the field, headed straight for the plane.

Quickly, Belkin picked up the laptop from the floor near Gregory's feet. His drink tumbled from his hand, wetting his pants and filling the SUV with an antiseptic stench.

"Come with me." He gripped Gregory's arm hard. Felt his fingers bite into the tender flesh.

"Oww," Gregory howled.

Belkin kicked the door open and tried to pull Gregory over the console. The kid went rigid. It was like pulling out a fifty-pound log. Icy wind whipped around the SUV, burning Belkin's cheeks. The more he pulled, the tighter Gregory wedged himself into the car. It was no use. He had to go to the other door.

"Prepare for takeoff," he yelled toward the security team that surrounded the plane.

The wind stole his words and carried them over the mountaintops.

"You," he yelled at Dimitri, as he waved wildly. "Come here."

The wind slammed the door shut, barely missing Belkin's flailing arm.

Dimitri turned to Belkin and held a finger up to his ear. The *pridurok* couldn't hear? Typical. He couldn't think or follow orders, either. Belkin pointed to the field on the other side of the chain-link fence. Twin headlights cut through the night as a vehicle raced toward them. Finally seeming to understand, Dimitri nodded furiously and ran toward the waiting plane.

Belkin rounded the SUV and pulled on the passenger side door handle. It was stuck fast. He pulled again. Harder.

Gregory Mateev pressed his face to the cold glass. "It's locked," he said. "Who is the *pridurok* now?"

* * *

Cody pressed his cell phone to his ear. He could scarcely hear his own voice over the roar of the pickup's engine and the noise as the vehicle's undercarriage cut through the snow-covered field.

"The private airfield outside of Telluride," he yelled into the phone. "Peter Belkin has the child, Gregory Mateev, and is attempting to take him from the country. He's armed and dangerous. Send backup."

Cody listened for a reply. None came. He checked the phone and found he had no service. The last sentence was all that mattered and he prayed that Ian had heard enough. If not, they were completely on their own.

A narrow road surrounded the airfield. On the other side was a steep ditch. The pickup bucked and heaved as it came onto the asphalt. The tires skidded on the pavement and the truck turned a tight 360 degrees.

Viktoria didn't follow the road. He didn't think she would. With a shock-collapsing, teeth-breaking rev to the engine, she pushed forward and dropped into the ravine.

The pickup truck kept coming, despite a ditch that surrounded the entire airstrip. Nose up, it crested the ridge and then down again, as it plunged into the snowdrift. In that split second, Belkin had the perfect view of the vehicle's interior.

Viktoria Mateev drove. Her eyes were coal black

and intense. Could the woman never stay dead? At her side was Cody Samuels. Belkin's insides froze.

Belkin frantically pulled at the door handle, and when it wouldn't budge he slammed his open palm against the window. "Open this door now!"

Gregory stuck out his tongue, then turned his impassive gaze away.

Belkin quickly flipped through his possible options. The single set of keys sat on the console between the seats, so unlocking the door was out. There were plenty of items in the hangar he could use to break the window, but the hangar was a hundred yards away. Running for a wrench would take more time than he had.

Belkin had nothing on him except his laptop. The futuristic metal case had rounded edges, but it was hard, solid. Maybe a little thermodynamics would help. The extreme cold outside versus the warm interior could create instability in the window's pane of glass.

Behind him, the dual propellers of the King Air spun to life.

Gripping the computer two-handed, Belkin brought it down on the passenger window like an ax to a tree.

The pickup hit the ditch at fifty miles per hour. The front wheels slammed into the earth and the back of the vehicle hung in the air for an instant, before coming back down hard. Cody braced himself on the dashboard with his good arm as all four tires still spun, connected and dug through the snow.

Holy crap. Viktoria could drive. He stole a glance at her. Sweat streamed down her cheeks and dampened her hair. She gunned the engine and the truck rocketed forward.

An eight-foot-high chain-link fence surrounded the entire airstrip. Every ten feet a metal pole stood sentry and held up the sheet of fencing. "Aim there," Cody said to Viktoria. He pointed to a spot between two posts, where the fence would be weakest.

She turned the truck, instinctively aiming toward the SUV, Belkin and her son.

"Drive toward the plane," said Cody as he withdrew his weapon.

"Not a chance. I'm getting Gregory."

Cody rolled down the window and braced on the doorframe. "That's exactly what we're doing, but first we have to get him away from Belkin."

For Belkin, two things happened at once. The SUV's window shattered and the pickup truck mowed down the fence that surrounded the airstrip. Small balls of safety glass covered Gregory, who had moved from the passenger seat to the driver's side. The fence, ripped from its mooring, covered the pickup's hood for an instant before being thrown off by the force of the impact and was dragged several yards. With sparks flying, the truck looked like a chariot of the damned. Belkin understood how wrong he had been to underestimate Viktoria Mateev and

Cody Samuels, because they most certainly would drag him to hell.

Belkin had just stuck his arm through the shattered window glass, unlocked the door and gripped Gregory by the arm when he heard the crack of a bullet being fired. The report thundered off the surrounding hills. He ducked behind the door. But the pickup wasn't coming for him, nor was the gun aimed in his direction. Rather, they were going toward the plane. For a moment, Belkin sagged with relief. But as he watched the men from his security team scramble on board, he came to realize that he truly was the ultimate target.

Viktoria saw Belkin crouch behind the door of his rented SUV. He held onto Gregory's arm as he pulled her son from the car. All her motherly instincts drew her to that vehicle. Gregory was there. He was the reason she had jeopardized her freedom, endured isolation, even risked death. And if she needed to do it all over again, she would.

No. She gripped the steering wheel tighter, keeping her original trajectory. This was going to end tonight. One way or the other, she was done running.

The pickup swerved and jostled as the snowy terrain became blacktop. Cody lined up his sights and his finger moved to the trigger. The plan was simple: get the plane to leave without Belkin and Gregory.

Viktoria had done as Cody told her and maneuvered between Belkin's SUV and the plane, while still giving the aircraft enough room on the runway for takeoff. Her golden hair streamed down her shoulders and her jaw was tense, set in determination.

Cody focused on his target—the plane—and fired just shy of the nose. A man dressed in black—probably one of the thugs from the cabin who had kidnapped Gregory—jumped as the bullet hit close to where he stood. He dodged and ran for cover inside the waiting plane.

Two men in white shirts with gold epaulets ran for the aircraft. One of them ducked beneath the wings and pulled the triangular rubber blocks from the wheels. An instant later, the faces of both men, pilot and copilot, filled the cockpit. As Cody had predicted, the dual prop plane began to maneuver away from the hangar and toward the end of the runway.

Cody fired again.

He used the side-view mirror to glance at Belkin, who held a very squirmy Gregory by the arm. Belkin was trying to run to the plane, but to reach his destination, he'd have to get past the pickup first, which meant he'd have to get past Cody.

Gregory went limp in Belkin's grasp. The weight of the child pulled them both over. Belkin stood and threw Gregory over his shoulder. Despite being kicked and punched by the boy, Belkin started to run toward the plane.

If Cody had anything to do with it, Belkin would never make his flight.

* * *

Belkin held tight to the only two things that mattered. His computer and the kid. The laptop was no trouble. Gregory Mateev on the other hand...

The child squirmed, kicked and even bit Belkin on the back hard enough to leave a painful small-toothed bruise. The pickup squealed to a stop twenty feet in front of him. Both the driver's and passenger's doors flung open simultaneously and Cody and Viktoria rushed from the truck.

Cody Samuels kept his back to Belkin. His left arm outstretched, he advanced on the plane. One-handed, he fired. Belkin's heartbeat slowed to a sluggish pace as the plane's door snapped shut and the propeller's rotations increased to a blur. The aircraft gained momentum as it sped to the end of the runway and lifted off the ground.

Belkin had no time to worry about his failed escape plan. Gregory had kept up his kicking, biting and pulling away. Cody rounded the side of the plane, his firearm aimed at Belkin's head. Viktoria, the woman who would not die, sprinted toward Belkin. Like a football player, she leapt out and caught Belkin around the middle. Belkin, Gregory, the laptop and Viktoria fell to the ground in a heap. Before Belkin could roll to his side, Gregory ran to Cody Samuels.

A thin line of blood trickled down Viktoria's cheek. He'd shot her, he knew. But he now understood that his bullet had not been fatal, as he'd hoped, that he'd only given her a flesh wound. She wiped the blood away with the side of her hand. A red smear remained.

She got to her feet and walked backward to Cody. Belkin remained sprawled on the ground. The former DEA agent held out a firearm. This time, it was Belkin who faced the barrel of a gun.

The wail of faraway sirens swirled around Viktoria, carried on an icy gust of wind. She relaxed into Cody's embrace. "It's over," she said. "Gregory's safe and more than that, we have Peter Belkin."

Gregory nestled closer into her chest. The three of them together felt right. It had only been a little more than a day, but this was a family. She could feel it.

"Get up," Cody ordered Belkin. "And keep your hands where I can see them."

Belkin rose to his knees with his palms lifted. A sneer twisted his lips. "I do not know what you think you have won, but this is far from over. Your American justice system is blind, and easily manipulated. And I'll take great pleasure in doing just that." He stood. "The men who just flew away were rogue paramilitary. I was, as were you, trying to find the child."

"We have evidence that says otherwise," Viktoria began.

Belkin interrupted. "What, *your* testimony? A mother who is wanted on kidnapping charges and a disgraced DEA agent? Who would believe either of you over an upstanding lawyer such as myself?"

"We can prove you set me up while I was at the

DEA," said Cody. Viktoria couldn't help but feel proud of Cody. It wasn't often that a person was given a chance to completely clear his name. "You forgot to encrypt one of your files."

Belkin's fingers trembled. "And why you personally care so much for your American justice is a mystery to me. In Russia, we never could have framed someone like you, a *chestnyy chelovek*." He paused and translated, "Honest man. Truly, this system favors the criminals and because of that, I will go free and moreover, remain unscathed."

"Justice might be blind," said Cody. "But, she's not stupid. Neither am I. I sent the file you kept on me to Rocky Mountain Justice. By now it's made the rounds in the FBI and DEA."

"Then there are the encrypted files we saved to this." Viktoria took the flash drive from her pocket and held it up.

Belkin went pale. *"Вруth."* Liar.

"Give up," said Cody, "and turn yourself in. Prison is the least of your worries. Nikolai Mateev won't let you live long enough to have those files opened. The only way you'll survive will be in protective custody."

As if to prove his point, three large sedans with Colorado State Patrol emblazoned on their sides sped onto the tarmac. The cars formed a semicircle. Their headlights shone on the tableau of Cody, Viktoria and Gregory, a safe unit tight together, and Belkin—a lone actor—trapped by his own reprehensible schemes. Six armed officers exited the vehicles.

"Hands up," the officers called. "All of you."

Viktoria set Gregory on the ground and lifted both her hands. Cody lifted his left arm. His gun was hooked around the trigger guard of his automatic pistol. Belkin remained as he was, his hands already lifted.

"You," one of the officers called out. "I need to see both hands in the air."

"I can't," said Cody. "I've been shot."

"Are you Samuels, from Rocky Mountain Justice?"

"I am. My identification is in my jacket. I am going to lay down my sidearm and reach into my pocket."

"Keep your hands where I can see them," said the officer.

Cody followed the order.

A patrol officer in a dusty blue parka and khaki slacks approached. He took Cody's gun first and then reached into the coat's interior pocket. After retrieving a slim black billfold, he checked the identification. "It's him, Sarge," the officer said.

"It appears that we have a lot to sort through," said the sergeant. "I need names and statements from everyone. Call Child Protective Services for the minor and an ambulance for everyone else."

Belkin stepped forward.

"Excuse, please, Sergeant," said Belkin. "My name is Peter Belkin and I need to speak to a representative from the United States Attorney's office."

"About what?" the sergeant asked.

"I have information regarding a drug trafficking ring that operates over a four-state radius and is run by Russian organized crime. Until I am in contact with the United States Attorney's office and have guarantees about my personal safety, I have no further comment to make."

"Tom," called out the sergeant. "Get on the horn to Denver. I need someone from the US A down here, pronto. Until then, take Peter Belkin into custody."

"I have a hard drive with encrypted information that will corroborate everything Belkin is saying. It came from his laptop," Cody added.

A pair of handcuffs were slipped around Peter Belkin's wrists, pinning both arms behind his back.

"Those are tight," Belkin complained as the officer led him away.

"Well, they're new and should stretch out the longer you wear them." The officer's sarcasm cut through the night.

As Belkin was placed in the back seat of a highway patrol cruiser, tears of gratitude stung Viktoria's eyes. Was her nightmare actually over?

"I'll need statements from you all," said the sergeant, "and I want you examined by the emergency medical services when they arrive. Until then, you folks can wait in your car."

Cody picked up Gregory and led Viktoria back to the car. Once the door was open, her son climbed into the back seat, where he immediately lay down.

"Is it over, Mommy?" he asked. "Is that bad man really gone?"

She glanced at Cody. He nodded. "He sure is, Captain Kiddo."

"The bad man is going to jail for a long time, Gregory," said Cody. "You have my word on that."

Finally safe, Viktoria snuggled into the seat. Yet, she could no longer ignore the final question that continued to plague her. A single tear escaped from the corner of her eye and snaked down her cheek, following the curvature to her lips. She licked it away and turned to Cody. "Do you think the Mateevs will ever leave Gregory and me alone?"

"I think that Peter Belkin will never bother you again."

"What about Nikolai?"

"He's going to be very busy as an international fugitive," Cody said.

It wasn't the answer she wanted, but at least it was honest. She nodded. A set of red lights cast their rotating shadows in the distance, and the plaintive wail of the ambulance's siren followed. The muscles in Viktoria's shoulders relaxed for what seemed like the first time in months.

"Eleven o'clock," Cody said, referring to the time on the dashboard. "I bet Santa's close. Maybe he's in Kansas. Or do you think he comes in from the north, and through Wyoming, Gregory?"

There was no answer. Viktoria turned to look at her son in the back seat. His eyes were closed, his head cradled on his arm, his breaths deep and rhythmic. He was fast asleep.

"Poor little guy. He's been through a lot," said Viktoria.

"I know I've said this before, but he's a heck of a kid," said Cody.

Viktoria's eyes were also beginning to feel heavy. "I can listen to you say that all day long."

Cody turned on the radio. The low tones of "Silent Night" came out of the speakers. He reached for her hand. Her palm fitted perfectly in his.

"We make a heck of a team, too."

Viktoria gazed at Cody. She stroked the side of his face. The stubble on his cheek tickled her fingertips. "You have the most amazing eyes," she said. "You know that, right?"

"Yeah, but I can listen to you say that all day long." He leaned forward. His lips brushed hers.

His kiss felt right.

"Merry Christmas, Viktoria," he said.

"Merry Christmas, Cody."

And from the back seat came the very sleepy voice of Gregory. "This has been the best Christmas ever."

Chapter 16

As far as Viktoria was concerned, Christmas morning was perfect. Gregory's plate with a half-eaten pancake sat on the kitchen table. The strong, nutty aroma of coffee filled the room. She wore a cozy set of sweats on loan from Cody. Her son knelt in front of the tree with a pile of small colorful blocks scattered about him. She had just spent a tearful half an hour on the phone with her parents. The call ended when her father booked a flight, online, to Telluride. By noon tomorrow, Viktoria would be reunited with her parents.

On the floor, Cody leaned on his left elbow and a

sling held his right arm in place. "When I was a boy," he said, picking up a building block, "we didn't have directions for these things. We just used our imagination and built. Since I have an older sister, it was usually something for a doll."

"That's funny," said Gregory. "I wish I had a sister."

"You do? I think you'd be a terrific big brother," Cody said.

Was there something wistful in the way he said that to Gregory? Viktoria stirred another spoonful of sugar into her coffee and sipped. It was sweet and light, just the way she liked it. She came to sit on the sofa, tucking her legs beneath her.

"It looks like you two are having fun," said Viktoria.

"Did you see everything that Santa brought me, Mommy? When I woke up this morning and came down to the tree I saw that he had left me three big sets of building blocks!" His head lolled back, like the memory had bowled him over. "Maybe the ride that he gave us back here in his truck was my favorite present, though."

"Santa really spoiled you this year! More than being a great guy, he's generous," she said. Catching Cody's eye, she added, "Maybe too generous."

"Nonsense," said Cody. He sat up and moved to rest his back on the sofa's base, right by Viktoria. He grabbed her toe and wiggled it. "Santa can never be too generous."

Paramedics had treated Viktoria and Gregory for

their minor injuries at the airstrip the night before. Cody was taken to the local hospital for his gunshot wound, treated and released. Viktoria was offered a room at a posh local hotel. She had refused, and without any questions and very little discussion, Viktoria and Gregory had returned home with Cody. They shared a room as before, but waking in Cody's house had been a true Christmas blessing. She smiled, and stroked the nape of Cody's neck.

"Hey, Gregory." Cody pointed to the tree. "I think I see another gift. There, in the corner."

Gregory scooted around and dove toward the tree's base. He came out with another box, this one wrapped in bright red paper. "It says it's for you, Mommy. From Santa."

"It does, does it?" Viktoria accepted the gift with a smile. "I wonder how Santa knew I'd be here."

She unwrapped the paper and pulled out a red cashmere sweater.

"He has a sister who's about your size," said Cody.

"It's very beautiful, but won't Santa's sister be upset that her gift was given to someone else?"

"Hey, Cody. Santa has a sister, just like you!" said Gregory.

"You know, you're right." Cody gave Viktoria a conspiratorial wink.

"How come Santa didn't leave you anything, Cody?" asked Gregory. "You have to be on his nice list."

"He did, Gregory. He brought you and your mom to spend Christmas with me. Remember how sad my house was without you? Now we're all together and happy."

From across the room, the cell phone sounded. As Cody rose to answer it, Gregory grabbed several figures from his building set and ran up the stairs, making flying noises as if they were all propelled by a jet engine. Cody returned and set the phone on the coffee table. He hit the speaker button as he sat next to her on the sofa. "Viktoria's right here, Ian. You can give us both an update."

"Well, happy Christmas to you both" came his deep upper-class British voice. "I am very pleased to hear that you have all recovered from the excitement of the past few days."

"Merry Christmas to you," said Viktoria. She tucked a strand of hair behind her ear, suddenly nervous to be talking to Cody's boss. "Cody deserves a medal. He's a true hero." She touched the back of Cody's hand. "And a good man."

"He is that," said Ian before continuing. "I have the great fortune to inform you that Peter Belkin began speaking with the authorities last night. The state of New York has dropped all charges against you, Mrs. Mateev."

Viktoria pressed a hand to her mouth. "That *is* good news."

Ian concluded, "I'm sure I'll have more to report in time. But for now, happy Christmas, again. Cody, heal well, and I expect to see you in Denver right after the New Year."

"Thanks. And merry Christmas." Cody clicked off.

Viktoria checked the time and thought about the other call she had made secretly that morning. She wondered what Cody's reaction would be to her Christmas surprise. Perhaps she shouldn't have interfered in another family squabble. It hadn't gone well for the Mateevs last time. But she truly thought that this situation was different. Before she got a chance to confess to him, there was a knock at the door.

"Who in the world?" Cody mumbled as he slowly rose to his feet.

Viktoria wanted to say something, to warn him. But her mouth went dry and she merely followed him to the door, anxious to see his reaction.

Cody stood on the threshold, impervious to the cold, and stared with unblinking eyes. After a minute, he realized that his mouth hung open. He snapped his jaw shut and then swallowed. "Sarah," he said. He could hardly believe that his sister stood on his stoop.

His pigtailed niece and his nephew, who had grown inches since Cody last had seen him, rushed forward. "Uncle Cody!" they cried in unison as they grabbed his middle.

"I… I don't know what to say."

"How about *Come on in, Sarah!*"

Cody stepped back from the door. "Yeah, of course. Come in. Get out of the cold."

The kids ran in and his brother-in-law, Paul, offered his hand as he passed. "Merry Christmas, buddy," he said.

They shook hands. "Same to you."

He overheard Viktoria calling to Gregory, to come downstairs and meet some new friends.

Then it was just Cody and Sarah. His mouth felt as if it suddenly had filled with marbles.

"I got a phone call this morning from one of Santa's helpers," she said.

"Viktoria, obviously."

"She said we'd be welcome. I hope she was right."

"The last time we talked…" said Cody. He stopped. He needed to do more, say more. He began again. "I shouldn't have cut you out of my life like I did, Sarah. At the time, I felt because you didn't support me, you were against me."

"You're my little brother—I'm always on your side. But it is possible to love someone and tell them things they don't want to hear."

"I understand…" Cody moved from one foot to the other. "I'm no good at apologizing, Sarah. I'm worse at forgiveness, especially asking for it."

"You don't have to say anything, Cody. I know what's in your heart."

She was wrong, again. He did have to apologize. Otherwise, he'd never get the chance to reshape his life. He swallowed. "Forgive me?"

"Only if you forgive me."

"I did a long time ago."

Wind whipped around the house and swirled at their feet. Yet, the last block of ice in Cody's heart melted.

Viktoria helped Sarah in the kitchen as they prepared Christmas dinner. The two worked in companionable silence as the men played in the snow with the kids. The resemblance between brother and sister—dark hair and complexion, mixed with light blue eyes—was unmistakable and Viktoria felt completely at ease.

It also helped that Gregory was enjoying himself—throwing snow, laughing and enjoying a game that could only be called Try to Knock Cody Over. Occasionally, Cody would feign teetering, only to lift a child in each arm and run.

"My brother's usually pretty intense," Sarah said at length.

Viktoria gave a laugh. "I noticed."

"He's lightened up a lot since we last spoke."

"He's lightened up in the past two days," said Viktoria.

"Then it is you. You're the one who helped my brother heal."

Viktoria's face flushed and it wasn't from steam rising from various pots on the stove. "I'm not sure about that..."

The door burst open and five snow-covered figures filed in, laughing. "Wet things off, so I can hang them up," Viktoria ordered. She stopped and said to Sarah, "Sorry, I shouldn't be taking charge in your brother's house. Must be my bossy New Yorker roots showing."

Sarah waved away the apology as she gestured to the quintet stripping out of their snow-covered coats and gloves. "They're listening to you. Looks like you're the lady of the house."

Again, Viktoria's face flushed. Sarah rounded up the group and herded them all toward the upstairs bedrooms, where they could change into dry clothes. Cody stayed behind. His coat was open and a fleece cap was pulled back on his head. A sprinkling of stubble covered his cheeks and chin. Viktoria longed to touch him. But should she? Could she? Sure, they'd endured more over the past two days than most couples had in a lifetime, but the intensity of their relationship stemmed from the need to defeat a common foe. Which brought up the real question—now that Belkin was in custody, what did Viktoria mean to Cody?

"I hope you aren't mad that I called Sarah, who is great, by the way," she said.

At the same moment, he spoke, "You and my sister seem to be getting along well."

They laughed. "You go," they said in tandem.

Cody lifted Viktoria's hand to his lips and kissed her knuckles. "I'm not angry," he said, his words a breath on her skin.

"It was presumptuous of me to call her."

"It *was* bold, but I was being pigheaded by not apologizing to my sister. Maybe I was ashamed. I don't know. I'm not good at analyzing my feelings."

"You seem to be doing alright now."

"Then I'll keep going." Cody wrapped his arms around Viktoria's waist. She melted into his warm and solid frame. "I care about you, Viktoria."

"I care about you, too."

Cody placed his lips on hers. He kissed her softly, oh-so softly. It stole her breath. He pressed his forehead into hers.

"It's crazy to think that it was less than two days ago when this all started, because I can't remember what my life was like without you."

She snuggled tighter into his embrace. "Neither can I."

"It was bleak, I know that. In fact, I remember how broken I felt in those few moments before Belkin showed up at your cabin. Like there were pieces of me missing that I'd never find."

"We've hashed this out before, but I am glad you were there. You saved Gregory and me."

"That's where you're wrong, Viktoria. It's you and Gregory who've been my salvation. Is it too early to say that I love you?"

"No, because, Cody, I love you, too."

Cody cupped Viktoria's face in his hands. "You make me so happy," he said.

Viktoria went up on tiptoe, placing her lips on his. "Likewise, Cody Samuels."

"We don't know everything about each other, but we do know what's important," he said. "You, me and Gregory."

"And I cannot wait to figure out the rest," she finished for him.

Cody kissed her again and she sighed. This was not the end, not by a long shot. Viktoria broke away from their kiss and pulled Cody's hat from his head. She tossed it on the counter and raked her fingers through his hair. "Merry Christmas to you," she said, "my Rocky Mountain Santa."

Epilogue

New Year's Eve

Peter Belkin found the interview room in the federal detention center almost as bland as his cell in the county jail. A wooden laminate table sat in the middle of the room. Grimy beige tile that at one time might have been white covered the floor. Long tubes of fluorescent lights hung from the ceiling and buzzed softly. One wall was filled with a reflective window and a video camera—its record light glowing green—stood in the corner.

Two men in crisply ironed white shirts and dark suits sat side by side on uncomfortable molded plastic chairs and stared at Peter Belkin as he wrote. Belkin was envious of the men and their business attire. He wore a shapeless orange jumpsuit with the letters CDOC, standing for Colorado Department of Corrections, stenciled on the back. It was one of two, and along with two pairs of dull white socks, a set of shower shoes and industrial underwear, the jumpsuits were the only things that Peter Belkin now possessed.

One of the men, an FBI agent, twirled a pen through his fingers and back again. The other, another special agent with the Bureau, leaned back in the chair and sighed heavily. These men didn't like being at the federal detention center any more than Belkin did. It was, after all, New Year's Eve. There were wives at home becoming anxious about arriving late to parties, and plastic platters of soggy shrimp waiting to be eaten between toasts to the New Year.

Belkin, however, would not be going home. Not now. Not ever.

But if he cooperated, he could still have a life outside a cell, or so he was told. It was all part of his plea bargain that eventually would get him out of jail, and ensure that all charges against him would be dropped. But jail was only one of his worries. To remain alive, he needed protection. To that end, he continued to write, giving every detail he could recall, which were many and varied. He flipped to the next page in the yellow legal pad.

Names. Dates. Businesses. Plans. Bank accounts— none of his own. Peter Belkin knew everything about Nikolai Mateev. Belkin's fingers cramped from writing for so long, but finally, he had come to the end. He threw the pen on the table and pushed the pad toward the agents before shaking feeling back into his hand.

"This it?" asked the first special agent.

"It is," said Belkin.

The older agent took the legal pad and flipped through the pages. He folded all but the final sheet back and set the tablet in front of Belkin again. "Sign it and date it," he said, pointing to a spot at the bottom of the page.

So, this man was the one in charge. It mattered little to Belkin who had the title of supervisory special agent or not. He would soon be handed off to other people who would change his identity, his looks, his life.

Belkin once again picked up the pen, signed his name and added the date. "There," he said, shoving both across the table once more.

"The US Attorney has to look at this and approve your plea. But if everything goes as planned you'll be transferred to Witness Protection after the beginning of the year," said the agent in charge.

"Everything will go as planned," Belkin said, although in truth nothing had worked out since he'd agreed to take Gregory Mateev away from his mother. Who knew that a stay-at-home mom would be the catalyst of his downfall. It was almost funny. Almost, but not really.

"Well then," said the agent in charge as he stood, "I'll be in touch next week."

The junior agent stood, as well. He opened the door and both men slipped out. From his vantage point in the chair, Peter Belkin could see into the corridor. He saw a man, a face he remembered but could not place. Perhaps they had never met—just seen his photo. Before Belkin could decide who it was, the door slammed shut.

Sir Ian Wallace stood in the corridor alongside representatives of the Drug Enforcement Administration, the Colorado Bureau of Investigation and the United States Marshals Service. In truth, he had no jurisdictional reason to be a part of the group, but had been included because it was his employee who had delivered Peter Belkin to the authorities.

The two FBI agents tasked with debriefing Belkin exited the room. The senior agent, Marcus Jones, held a legal pad that he slapped on his open palm. "I think this guy just gave me my Christmas present late," he said. "Walk with me, gentlemen. There's a conference room up ahead."

The group followed SA Jones to a room with frosted windows, maroon carpeting and the FBI's seal on the wall. The seal was flanked by flags from both the United States of America and the state of Colorado. Everyone took a seat around an oblong wood table as Marcus stood at the head.

"According to this statement." He tapped the legal pad. "We now know how Mateev launders his money. He runs the cash through a seedy bar in Boulder called The Prow."

The junior agent spoke up. "It's owned by the son

of a Russian immigrant. A kid named Oleg Zavalov. The guy likes to party but has no priors."

"More than that," Jones, the senior guy, continued, "Nikolai's great nephew is an employee. Now that Gregory is out of his reach we should assume that Nikolai will contact his next closest male heir."

"Do we have a name?" a representative from CBI asked.

The junior federal agent answered. "Belkin didn't know."

"What we need is intel, someone on the inside," said a man from the DEA.

"That takes a lot of court orders, subpoenas, basic red tape up the wazoo," the man from CBI said.

"If I may," said Ian. He ran a hand through his dark blond hair, a habit he'd picked up at university and had never managed to break. "I might have a solution."

All eyes turned to him. He continued, "As private contractors, Rocky Mountain Justice is in a unique position. We can't bring charges against a person nor can we arrest them, but we can provide information."

The men around the table looked at each other then back to Ian.

"It's worth exploring," said Special Agent Jones.

Ian rapped his knuckles on the table. "Good," he said, "because I have the perfect man for the job."

* * * * *

Don't miss
HER ROCKY MOUNTAIN DEFENDER
the next thrilling installment of
ROCKY MOUNTAIN JUSTICE
Jennifer D. Bokal's new miniseries for
Harlequin Romantic Suspense
Coming in April 2018
Available wherever Harlequin books
and ebooks are sold!

She was a quick learner and from the couch, Scrabble gave a soft woof.

"Thanks, sweetie," Marie said to the dog, breaking the lesson to go rub Scrabble's ears.

He stared at the two of them. "Choke hold."

Marie's eyebrows arched high as she gave him her attention. "Really?"

He caught her hands and put them on his throat, immediately regretting the contact. There was a warmth in her touch that left him craving her hands on other parts of his body. To save his sanity, he made her grip stronger. "Hold on. First, keep your head."

"All right." Her eyes locked on his mouth and she licked her lips.

A bolt of desire shot through his system. "Raise your arms overhead and clasp your hands." He demonstrated and her gaze drifted up his arms to his hands and back down to his biceps.

This was a bad idea. "Now sweep down and twist to one side." Gently, in slow motion, he showed her how to escape the hold.

"And run," she said for him when he was free of her.

"Your turn." He moved in front of her. "Ready?"

She gave an uncertain nod.

He wrapped his hands lightly around her throat, the blood in her veins fluttering under his hands. "This is practice," he reminded her as her eyes went wide and distant. Her hair was soft as silk against his knuckles. "Marie." He flexed his fingers, just enough to get her attention. "Keep your head."

He struggled to heed his own advice since everything inside him clamored to pull her into a much different embrace and discover if her lips were as soft as they looked.

"Uh-huh." Her arms came up, her hands clasped and she executed the motion perfectly, breaking his hold and dancing out of his reach.

"Well-done." He straightened his shirt and tucked it back into place.

"Thank you, Emiliano." She perched on the couch next to his dog. "That helps me feel better already."

Good news for one of them. Edgier than ever, he needed an escape. "I'll be in the study." He glanced at Scrabble, but she didn't budge from her place by Marie.

He left the room without another word. Her determination to be prepared and take care of herself made him want to lower his defenses and care for her. He couldn't afford that kind of mistake. His team was counting on him to do his part for the investigation and he would not let them down.

*Don't miss "Special Agent Cowboy"
by Regan Black in KILLER COLTON CHRISTMAS,
available December 2017 wherever
Harlequin® Romantic Suspense books and ebooks are sold.*

www.Harlequin.com

HRSEXP1117

Get 2 Free Books,
<u>Plus</u> 2 Free Gifts—
just for trying the
Reader Service!

⬥ HARLEQUIN
ROMANTIC suspense

YES! Please send me 2 FREE Harlequin® Romantic Suspense novels and my 2 FREE gifts (gifts are worth about $10 retail). After receiving them, if I don't wish to receive any more books, I can return the shipping statement marked "cancel." If I don't cancel, I will receive 4 brand-new novels every month and be billed just $4.99 per book in the U.S. or $5.74 per book in Canada. That's a savings of at least 12% off the cover price! It's quite a bargain! Shipping and handling is just 50¢ per book in the U.S. and 75¢ per book in Canada.* I understand that accepting the 2 free books and gifts places me under no obligation to buy anything. I can always return a shipment and cancel at any time. The free books and gifts are mine to keep no matter what I decide.

240/340 HDN GLWQ

Name _____ (PLEASE PRINT)

Address _____ Apt. #

City _____ State/Prov. _____ Zip/Postal Code

Signature (if under 18, a parent or guardian must sign)

Mail to the **Reader Service:**
IN U.S.A.: P.O. Box 1341, Buffalo, NY 14240-8531
IN CANADA: P.O. Box 603, Fort Erie, Ontario L2A 5X3

Want to try two free books from another line?
Call 1-800-873-8635 or visit www.ReaderService.com.

*Terms and prices subject to change without notice. Prices do not include applicable taxes. Sales tax applicable in N.Y. Canadian residents will be charged applicable taxes. Offer not valid in Quebec. This offer is limited to one order per household. Books received may not be as shown. Not valid for current subscribers to Harlequin Romantic Suspense books. All orders subject to approval. Credit or debit balances in a customer's account(s) may be offset by any other outstanding balance owed by or to the customer. Please allow 4 to 6 weeks for delivery. Offer available while quantities last.

Your Privacy—The Reader Service is committed to protecting your privacy. Our Privacy Policy is available online at www.ReaderService.com or upon request from the Reader Service.

We make a portion of our mailing list available to reputable third parties that offer products we believe may interest you. If you prefer that we not exchange your name with third parties, or if you wish to clarify or modify your communication preferences, please visit us at www.ReaderService.com/consumerchoice or write to us at Reader Service Preference Service, P.O. Box 9062, Buffalo, NY 14240-9062. Include your complete name and address.

HRSI7R2